FATHER BROWN
OF THE CHURCH OF ROME

G. K. CHESTERTON

FATHER BROWN OF THE CHURCH OF ROME

Selected Mystery Stories

Edited and with an Introduction by

John Peterson

IGNATIUS PRESS   SAN FRANCISCO

Cover design by Roxanne Mei Lum

© 1996 Ignatius Press, San Francisco
All rights reserved
ISBN 0–89870–590–8 (HB)
ISBN 0–89870–953–9 (PB)
Library of Congress catalogue number 96–83638
Printed in the United States of America ⬯

CONTENTS

INTRODUCTION

THE TITLE of this collection of short stories is not meant to be an affront to non-Catholics, and it would be a very poor strategy indeed if the title of a book were offensive to half the readers who were supposed to be attracted to it. The stories were written by Chesterton to entertain, and everyone is welcome to read them, with only (as the great man once said of his own Distributist League) the possible exception of Devil Worshippers. But our title does reflect a key point that figured in the selection of the stories: they are all rather more overtly and aggressively Roman Catholic than we might expect or remember about Chesterton's tales of Father Brown. Anti-Catholic bigots, whether in or outside of the Church, will not be pleased with these stories and are forewarned.

Saying that something Chesterton wrote is "Catholic" does not seem much of a claim, for of course everything he wrote was Catholic. He was Catholic down to his bones. Every utterance of his adult life revealed a Catholic view of things—an unfailing awareness of the Incarnation and of the sacramental presence of the Transcendent God in every person, place, and thing in the material cosmos. All of his life, and long before he was received into the Church at the age of forty-eight, he was devoted to our Lady, which is the sure and unmistakable sign of a Catholic mind. And his Catholic leanings are obvious in the Father Brown mysteries, all of them, because their central character is a "popish priest", one who is always Catholic and orthodox whenever matters of faith and morals are mentioned.

The ten stories selected here, however, are even more Catholic, and not in subtle ways, either. One of the stories concludes with Father Brown's thoughts at Benediction, as he prays and meditates before the Blessed Sacrament. In another, Father Brown swings into action to stop a newspaper campaign designed to slander the Church. In another, our priest-sleuth clears the name of a member of his parish on the grounds that the man was a saint and therefore could not possibly have been stealing the necklaces. In yet another, Father Brown refuses to sympathize with the victim of a theft because he is living amid stolen goods himself—his great mansion is a converted abbey, one stolen from the Church during the Catholic Suppression of 1536 under King Henry VIII.

These, and the other stories collected here, are simply the ones from among all the Father Brown titles that most overtly and plainly exhibit the Roman Catholic affiliation of Chesterton's detective and, at least for those stories written after his conversion in 1922, of the author himself. They are very good stories, excellent short detective yarns in the classic British tradition of Sherlock Holmes—puzzling concoctions of mysterious crimes, dubious suspects, and ambiguous clues. They are among the very best of the Father Brown stories; however, they are not among the best known. The attention of editors and compilers of anthologies has thus far been focused elsewhere, apparently dominated by such standard favorites as "The Blue Cross", "The Invisible Man", and "The Queer Feet", each of which has been reprinted dozens of times.

"The Chief Mourner of Marne" is a good case in point. It is perhaps the best of all the Father Brown stories. That it is at least one of the best is unarguable. Yet in the countless editorial decisions that have determined the makeup of hundreds of anthologies and collections of detective stories, "The Chief Mourner of Marne" has been chosen exactly once. It was included in the 1949 anthology *Stories of Our Century by Catholic Authors*.

All of this is not by way of expressing a grievance. An editor whose interest is detective fiction and not religion, someone who might be vaguely anti-Catholic or amiably secularist in his personal beliefs, can hardly be expected to appreciate or to promote a story with, in his mind, gratuitous and meaningless intrusions of popish nonsense. There are respected critics who say this quite forthrightly. For whatever the reasons, it is a fact that anyone's list of both the very good and the "very Catholic" Father Brown stories will be a list of titles largely ignored by editors and anthologists. Indeed, that is why the stories for this present collection were selected. They are all very good stories, all very Catholic, and none has been reprinted as often as might be expected, given their high level of quality as stories.

Reading them as a group will provide a special pleasure for those who are weary of the sort of belligerent and condescending bigotry that is considered fashionable when it is directed against the Church. Father Brown is wonderfully subversive when he confronts the kind of crank whose conversation so often runs something like this:

> "The priests got hold of him, they say," grumbled the old general. "I know he gave thousands to found a monastery, and he lives himself rather like a monk—or, at any rate, a hermit. Can't understand what good they think that will do."
>
> "Goddarned superstition," snorted Cockspur; "that sort of thing ought to be shown up. Here's a man that might have been useful to the Empire and the world, and these vampires

get hold of him and suck him dry. I bet with their unnatural notions they haven't even let him marry."

It would not be proper to reveal here the text of Father Brown's response to unsavory reflections such as these. That is a pleasure reserved for readers of the conclusion to "The Chief Mourner of Marne". But the effect of the story will not be harmed in revealing something of the flavor of the priest's answer. He begins:

> "You must forgive me if I was not altogether crushed by your contempt for my uncharitableness today; or by the lectures you read me about pardon for every sinner. For it seems to me that you only pardon the sins that you don't really think sinful. . . ."

The rest of it will have you cheering or throwing your hat in the air. Or weeping for joy.

What has all this to do with murder mysteries? Murder mysteries are, after all, about the discovery of the truth. Readers will note that the hoax perpetrated in "The Curse of the Golden Cross" would never have succeeded had the victims not been woefully ignorant of medieval history. "What a lot of Latin words!" says an irritated Lady Diana to Father Brown. The priest points out to her that she would know the history if it had to do with the ancient Egyptians or Babylonians.

"But," he says,

> "the men who built your own parish churches, and gave the names to your own towns and trades and the very roads you walk on—it has never occurred to you to know anything about them."

The truth of the stories, and much of the fun in them, is tied up in the anti-Catholic prejudices of the supporting cast of characters. The puzzle of "The Secret Garden" turns on the fanatical anticlericalism of the police inspector. "The Miracle of Moon Crescent" would not be a story at all without the blast of contempt for "Father Brown's saints and angels" with which the mystery begins and without the laughable declaration of apology and support with which it ends. And without the prejudices of Mr. Snaith of Kansas City, to whom Father Brown is "a pompous old High Priest of Mumbo-Jumbo", there could be no conspiracy for the priest to thwart in "The Resurrection of Father Brown".

Aside from this theological fencing, entertaining as it is, there really are many more good Catholic touches of a less combative sort to be discovered and enjoyed throughout these stories: Father Brown quoting St. Anthony of Padua in "The Curse of the Golden Cross" ("It is only fishes who survive the deluge"), using St. Luke to defend a thief in "The Man with Two Beards" ("This night thou shalt be with Me in Paradise"), or being startled out of a rather benign complacency by the sight of a mutilated missal in "The Honour of Israel Gow".

Ruby Adams, in "The Flying Stars", cannot remember the word *Socialist* and resorts to using the phrase "what's-his-name".

> "You know what I mean. What do you call a man who wants to embrace the chimney-sweep?"
> "A saint," said Father Brown.

Enough. That Chesterton chose to write the Father Brown stories is a great good fortune for those who cherish his other writings, for he never found a literary form more agreeable to his genius. It is also a great good fortune for devoted readers of murder mysteries, for such stories have never been presented with anything approaching his complexity and depth.

And, as this introduction has attempted to suggest, these ten stories offer an added bonus for those whose contempt for bigotry is broad enough to include even bigotry toward Roman Catholics.

So, on behalf of beleaguered Catholics who suffer from the one form of prejudice still acceptable in our culture of enforced sensitivity and tolerance, we can do no better than echo the agitated Father Brown, who in "The Insoluble Problem" was heard to mutter, "Holy Mary, Mother of God, pray for us sinners." We cannot say better than that.

The Chief Mourner of Marne

A BLAZE of lightning blanched the grey woods, tracing all the wrinkled foliage down to the last curled leaf, as if every detail were drawn in silver-point or graven in silver. The same strange trick of lightning by which it seems to record millions of minute things in an instant of time, picked out everything, from the elegant litter of the picnic spread under the spreading tree to the pale lengths of winding road, at the end of which a white car was waiting. In the distance a melancholy mansion with four towers like a castle, which in the grey evening had been but a dim and distant huddle of walls like a crumbling cloud, seemed to spring into the foreground, and stood up with all its embattled roofs and blank and staring windows. And in this, at least, the light had something in it of revelation. For to some of those grouped under the tree that castle was, indeed, a thing faded and almost forgotten, which was to prove its power to spring up again in the foreground of their lives.

The light also clothed for an instant, in the same silver splendour, at least one human figure that stood up as motion-

"The Chief Mourner of Marne" first appeared in the United States in the May 1925 issue of *Harper's* magazine; its first British publication was in the July 1925 issue of *Cassell's* magazine.

13

less as one of the towers. It was that of a tall man standing on a rise of ground above the rest, who were mostly sitting on the grass or stooping to gather up the hamper and crockery. He wore a picturesque short cloak or cape clasped with a silver clasp and chain, which blazed like a star when the flash touched it; and something metallic in his motionless figure was emphasized by the fact that his closely curled hair was of the burnished yellow that can be really called gold; and had the look of being younger than his face, which was handsome in a hard aquiline fashion, but looked, under the strong light, a little wrinkled and withered. Possibly it had suffered from wearing a mask of make-up, for Hugo Romaine was the greatest actor of his day. For that instant of illumination the golden curls and ivory mask and silver ornament made his figure gleam like that of a man in armour; the next instant his figure was a dark and even black silhouette against the sickly grey of the rainy evening sky.

But there was something about its stillness, like that of a statue, that distinguished it from the group at his feet. All the other figures around him had made the ordinary involuntary movement at the unexpected shock of light; for though the skies were rainy it was the first flash of the storm. The only lady present, whose air of carrying grey hair gracefully, as if she were really proud of it, marked her a matron of the United States, unaffectedly shut her eyes and uttered a sharp cry. Her English husband, General Outram, a very stolid Anglo-Indian with a bald head and black moustache and whiskers of antiquated pattern, looked up with one stiff movement and then resumed his occupation of tidying up. A young man of the name of Mallow, very big and shy, with brown eyes like a dog's, dropped a cup and apologized awkwardly. A third man, much more dressy, with a resolute head, like an inquisitive terrier's, and grey hair brushed stiffly back, was no other than the great newspaper proprietor, Sir John Cockspur; he cursed freely, but not in an English idiom or accent, for he came from Toronto.[1] But the tall man in the short cloak stood up literally like a statue in the twilight; his eagle face under the full glare had been like the bust of a Roman Emperor, and the carved eyelids had not moved.

A moment after, the dark dome cracked across with thunder, and the statue seemed to come to life. He turned his head over his shoulder and said casually:

"About a minute and half between the flash and the bang, but I think the storm's coming nearer. A tree is not supposed to be a good umbrella for the lightning, but we shall want it soon for the rain. I think it will be a deluge."

The young man glanced at the lady a little anxiously and said: "Can't we get shelter anywhere? There seems to be a house over there."

"There is a house over there," remarked the general, rather grimly; "but not quite what you'd call a hospitable hotel."

"It's curious," said his wife sadly, "that we should be caught in a storm with no house near but that one, of all others."

Something in her tone seemed to check the younger man, who was both sensitive and comprehending; but nothing of that sort daunted the man from Toronto.

"Why, what's the matter with it?" he asked. "Looks rather like a ruin."

"That place," said the general dryly, "belongs to the Marquis of Marne."

"Gee!" said Sir John Cockspur. "I've heard all about that bird, anyhow; and a queer bird, too. Ran him as a front-page

[1] Chesterton's English audience of 1925 would have instantly recognized that the Canadian-born newspaper magnate William Aitken, Lord Beaverbrook (1879-1964), was the model for Sir John Cockspur.

mystery in the *Comet* last year. 'The Nobleman Nobody Knows.'"

"Yes, I've heard of him, too," said young Mallow in a low voice. "There seem to be all sorts of weird stories about why he hides himself like that. I've heard that he wears a mask because he's a leper. But somebody else told me quite seriously that there's a curse on the family; a child born with some frightful deformity that's kept in a dark room."

"The Marquis of Marne has three heads," remarked Romaine gravely. "Once in every three hundred years a three-headed nobleman adorns the family tree. No human being dares approach the accursed house except a silent procession of hatters, sent to provide an abnormal number of hats. But"—and his voice took one of those deep and terrible turns, that could cause such a thrill in the theatre—"my friends, *those hats are of no human shape.*"[2]

The American lady looked at him with a frown and a slight air of distrust, as if that trick of voice had moved her in spite of herself.

"I don't like your ghoulish jokes," she said; "and I'd rather you didn't joke about this, anyhow."

"I hear and obey," replied the actor; "but am I, like the Light Brigade, forbidden even to reason why?"[3]

"The reason," she replied, "is that he isn't the Nobleman Nobody Knows. I know him myself, or, at least, I knew him very well when he was an attaché at Washington thirty years

[2] Romaine is having fun with traditional legends of an aristocratic "family curse" (such as that surrounding Scotland's Glamis Castle, with its rumored monster-child locked in a secret chamber) and with Edgar Allan Poe's "The Murders in the Rue Morgue" (1841), in which the narrator exclaims, "this is no *human* hair" and "this is the mark of no human hand."

[3] Romaine echoes the words "Ours not to reason why" from "The Charge of the Light Brigade" (1855), by the English poet Alfred Lord Tennyson.

ago, when we were all young. And he didn't wear a mask, at least, he didn't wear it with me. He wasn't a leper, though he may be almost as lonely. And he had only one head and only one heart, and that was broken."

"Unfortunate love affair, of course," said Cockspur. "I should like that for the *Comet*."

"I suppose it's a compliment to us," she replied thoughtfully, "that you always assume a man's heart is broken by a woman. But there are other kinds of love and bereavement. Have you never read 'In Memoriam'? Have you never heard of David and Jonathan?[4] What broke poor Marne up was the death of his brother; at least, he was really a first cousin, but had been brought up with him like a brother, and was much nearer than most brothers. James Mair, as the marquis was called when I knew him, was the elder of the two, but he always played the part of worshipper, with Maurice Mair as a god. And, by his account, Maurice Mair was certainly a wonder. James was no fool, and very good at his own political job; but it seems that Maurice could do that and everything else; that he was a brilliant artist and amateur actor and musician, and all the rest of it. James was very good-looking himself, long and strong and strenuous, with a high-bridged nose; though I suppose the young people would think he looked very quaint with his beard divided into two bushy whiskers in the fashion of those Victorian times. But Maurice was clean-shaven, and, by the portraits shown to me, certainly quite beautiful; though he looked a little more like a tenor than a gentleman ought to look. James was always asking me again and again whether his friend was not a marvel, whether any

---

[4] Mrs. Outram recalls two notable expressions of the grief of brothers or, rather, brothers-in-law: the first, Tennyson's elegiac poem "In Memoriam A.A.H." (1850), and the second, King David's lament for Jonathan in 2 Samuel 1:19–27.

woman wouldn't fall in love with him, and so on, until it became rather a bore, except that it turned so suddenly into a tragedy. His whole life seemed to be in that idolatry; and one day the idol tumbled down, and was broken like any china doll. A chill caught at the seaside, and it was all over."

"And after that," asked the young man, "did he shut himself up like this?"

"He went abroad at first," she answered; "away to Asia and the Cannibal Islands[5] and Lord knows where. These deadly strokes take different people in different ways. It took him in the way of an utter sundering or severance from everything, even from tradition and as far as possible from memory. He could not bear a reference to the old tie; a portrait or an anecdote or even an association. He couldn't bear the business of a great public funeral. He longed to get away. He stayed away for ten years. I heard some rumour that he had begun to revive a little at the end of the exile; but when he came back to his own home he relapsed completely. He settled down into religious melancholia, and that's practically madness."

"The priests got hold of him, they say," grumbled the old general. "I know he gave thousands to found a monastery, and lives himself rather like a monk—or, at any rate, a hermit. Can't understand what good they think that will do."

"Goddarned superstition," snorted Cockspur; "that sort of thing ought to be shown up. Here's a man that might have been useful to the Empire and the world, and these vampires get hold of him and suck him dry. I bet with their unnatural notions they haven't even let him marry."

"No, he has never married," said the lady. "He was engaged when I knew him, as a matter of fact, but I don't think

[5] For a time, Fiji was popularly known as "the Cannibal Islands".

it ever came first with him, and I think it went with the rest when everything else went. Like Hamlet and Ophelia—he lost hold of love because he lost hold of life.[6] But I knew the girl; indeed, I know her still. Between ourselves, it was Viola Grayson, daughter of the old admiral. She's never married, either."

"It's infamous! It's infernal!" cried Sir John, bounding up. "It's not only a tragedy, but a crime. I've got a duty to the public, and I mean to see all this nonsensical nightmare . . . in the twentieth century—"

He was almost choked with his own protest, and then, after a silence, the old soldier said:

"Well, I don't profess to know much about those things, but I think these religious people need to study a text which says, 'Let the dead bury their dead.' "[7]

"Only, unfortunately, that's just what it looks like," said his wife with a sigh. "It's just like some creepy story of a dead man burying another dead man, over and over again for ever."

"The storm has passed over us," said Romaine, with a rather inscrutable smile. "You will not have to visit the inhospitable house after all."

She suddenly shuddered.

"Oh, I'll never do that again!" she exclaimed.

Mallow was staring at her.

"Again! Have you tried it before?" he cried.

"Well, I did once," she said, with a lightness not without a touch of pride; "but we needn't go back on all that. It's not raining now, but I think we'd better be moving back to the car."

---

[6] Mrs. Outram refers to events in Shakespeare's play and the preoccupation of Ophelia's suitor, Hamlet, with death and revenge—leading first to her suicide and then to his own death.

[7] General Outram is quoting Matthew 8:22.

As they moved off in procession, Mallow and the general brought up the rear; and the latter said abruptly, lowering his voice:

"I don't want that little cad Cockspur to hear, but as you've asked you'd better know. It's the one thing I can't forgive Marne; but I suppose these monks have drilled him that way. My wife, who had been the best friend he ever had in America, actually came to that house when he was walking in the garden. He was looking at the ground like a monk, and hidden in a black hood that was really as ridiculous as any mask. She had sent her card in, and stood there in his very path. And he walked past her without a word or a glance, as if she had been a stone. He wasn't human; he was like some horrible automaton. She may well call him a dead man."

"It's all very strange," said the young man rather vaguely. "It isn't like—like what I should have expected."

Young Mr. Mallow, when he left that rather dismal picnic, took himself thoughtfully in search of a friend. He did not know any monks, but he knew one priest, whom he was very much concerned to confront with the curious revelations he had heard that afternoon. He felt he would very much like to know the truth about the cruel superstition that hung over the house of Marne, like the black thundercloud he had seen hovering over it.

After being referred from one place to another, he finally ran his friend Father Brown to earth in the house of another friend, a Roman Catholic friend with a large family. He entered somewhat abruptly to find Father Brown sitting on the floor with a serious expression, and attempting to pin the somewhat florid hat belonging to a wax doll on to the head of a Teddy bear.

Mallow felt a faint sense of incongruity; but he was far too full of his problem to put off the conversation if he could help it. He was staggering from a sort of set-back in a subconscious process that had been going on for some time. He poured out the whole tragedy of the house of Marne as he had heard it from the general's wife, along with most of the comments of the general and the newspaper proprietor. A new atmosphere of attention seemed to be created with the mention of the newspaper proprietor.

Father Brown neither knew nor cared that his attitudes were comic or commonplace. He continued to sit on the floor, where his large head and short legs made him look very like a baby playing with toys. But there came into his great grey eyes a certain expression that has been seen in the eyes of many men in many centuries through the story of nineteen hundred years; only the men were not generally sitting on floors, but at council tables, or on the seats of chapters, or the thrones of bishops and cardinals; a far-off, watchful look, heavy with the humility of a charge too great for men. Something of that anxious and far-reaching look is found in the eyes of sailors and of those who have steered through so many storms the ship of St. Peter.[8]

"It's very good of you to tell me this," he said. "I'm really awfully grateful, for we may have to do something about it. If it were only people like you and the general, it might be only a private matter; but if Sir John Cockspur is going to spread some sort of scare in his papers—well, he's a Toronto Orangeman,[9] and we can hardly keep out of it."

---

[8] For Chesterton's view of the Catholic Church as "the ship of St. Peter", weathering the storms of nineteen hundred years, see *The Collected Works*, vol. II, for the concluding chapters of *The Everlasting Man*, which were written at about the same time as was this story, in 1925.

[9] Father Brown identifies Cockspur with the Ulster secret society named for William of Orange and founded in 1795 to promote Irish Protestantism.

"But what will you say about it?" asked Mallow anxiously.

"The first thing I should say about it," said Father Brown, "is that, as you tell it, it doesn't sound like life. Suppose, for the sake of argument, that we are all pessimistic vampires blighting all human happiness. Suppose I'm a pessimistic vampire." He scratched his nose with the Teddy bear, became faintly conscious of the incongruity, and put it down. "Suppose we do destroy all human and family ties. Why should we entangle a man again in an old family tie just when he showed signs of getting loose from it? Surely it's a little unfair to charge us both with crushing such affection and encouraging such infatuation. I don't see why even a religious maniac should be that particular sort of monomaniac, or how religion could increase that mania, except by brightening it with a little hope."

Then he said, after a pause: "I should like to talk to that general of yours."

"It was his wife who told me," said Mallow.

"Yes," replied the other; "but I'm more interested in what he didn't tell you than in what she did."

"You think he knows more than she does?"

"I think he knows more than she says," answered Father Brown. "You tell me he used a phrase about forgiving everything except the rudeness to his wife. After all, what else was there to forgive?"

Father Brown had risen and shaken his shapeless clothes, and stood looking at the young man with screwed up eyes and a slightly quizzical expression. The next moment he had turned, and picking up his equally shapeless umbrella and large shabby hat, went stumping down the street.

He plodded through a variety of wide streets and squares till he came to a handsome old-fashioned house in the West End, where he asked the servant if he could see General Outram. After some little palaver he was shown into a study, fitted out less with books than with maps and globes, where the bald-headed, black-whiskered Anglo-Indian sat smoking a long, thin, black cigar and playing with pins on a chart.

"I am sorry to intrude," said the priest, "and all the more because I can't help the intrusion looking like interference. I want to speak to you about a private matter, but only in the hope of keeping it private. Unfortunately some people are likely to make it public. I think, general, that you know Sir John Cockspur."

The mass of black moustache and whisker served as a sort of mask for the lower half of the old general's face; it was always hard to see whether he smiled, but his brown eyes often had a certain twinkle.

"Everybody knows him, I suppose," he said. "I don't know him very well."

"Well, you know everybody knows whatever he knows," said Father Brown, smiling, "when he thinks it convenient to print it. And I understand from my friend Mr. Mallow, whom, I think, you know, that Sir John is going to print some scorching anti-clerical articles founded on what he would call the Marne Mystery. 'Monks Drive Marquis Mad,' etc."

"If he is," replied the general, "I don't see why you should come to me about it. I ought to tell you I'm a strong Protestant."

"I'm very fond of strong Protestants," said Father Brown. "I came to you because I was sure you would tell the truth. I hope it is not uncharitable to feel less sure of Sir John Cockspur."

The brown eyes twinkled again, but the general said nothing.

"General," said Father Brown, "suppose Cockspur or his sort were going to make the world ring with tales against your country and your flag. Suppose he said your regiment ran away in battle, or your staff were in the pay of the enemy. Would you let anything stand between you and the facts that would refute him? Wouldn't you get on the track of the truth at all costs to anybody? Well, I have a regiment, and I belong to an army. It is being discredited by what I am certain is a fictitious story; but I don't know the true story. Can you blame me for trying to find it out?"

The soldier was silent, and the priest continued:

"I have heard the story Mallow was told yesterday, about Marne retiring with a broken heart through the death of his more than brother. I am sure there was more in it than that. I came to ask you if you know any more."

"No," said the general shortly; "I cannot tell you any more."

"General," said Father Brown with a broad grin, "you would have called me a Jesuit if I had used that equivocation."[10]

The soldier laughed gruffly, and then growled with much greater hostility.

"Well, I won't tell you, then," he said. "What do you say to that?"

"I only say," said the priest mildly, "that in that case I shall have to tell you."

The brown eyes stared at him; but there was no twinkle in them now. He went on:

"You compel me to state, less sympathetically perhaps than you could, why it is obvious that there is more behind. I am quite sure the marquis has better cause for his brooding and secretiveness than merely having lost an old friend. I doubt whether priests have anything to do with it; I don't even know if he's a convert or merely a man comforting his con-

---

[10] For Chesterton's own view of the controversy surrounding mental reservation, see *The Collected Works*, vol. III, pp. 90 and 208.

science with charities; but I'm sure he's something more than a chief mourner. Since you insist, I will tell you one or two of the things that made me think so.

"First, it was stated that James Mair was engaged to be married, but somehow became unattached again after the death of Maurice Mair. Why should an honourable man break off his engagement merely because he was depressed by the death of a third party? He's much more likely to have turned for consolation to it; but, anyhow, he was bound in decency to go through with it."

The general was biting his black moustache, and his brown eyes had become very watchful and even anxious; but he did not answer.

"A second point," said Father Brown, frowning at the table. "James Mair was always asking his lady friend whether his cousin Maurice was not very fascinating, and whether women would not admire him. I don't know if it occurred to the lady that there might be another meaning to that inquiry."

The general got to his feet and began to walk or stamp about the room.

"Oh, damn it all," he said, but without any air of animosity.

"The third point," went on Father Brown, "is James Mair's curious manner of mourning—destroying all relics, veiling all portraits, and so on. It does sometimes happen, I admit; it might mean mere affectionate bereavement. But it might mean something else."

"Confound you," said the other, "how long are you going on piling this up?"

"The fourth and fifth points are pretty conclusive," said the priest calmly, "especially if you take them together. The first is that Maurice Mair seems to have had no funeral in particular, considering he was a cadet of a great family. He must have been buried hurriedly; perhaps secretly. And the last point is, that James Mair instantly disappeared to foreign parts; fled, in fact, to the ends of the earth.

"And so," he went on, still in the same soft voice, "when you would blacken my religion to brighten the story of the pure and perfect affection of two brothers, it seems—"

"Stop!" cried Outram in a tone like a pistol shot. "I must tell you more, or you will fancy worse. Let me tell you one thing to start with. It was a fair fight."

"Ah," said Father Brown, and seemed to exhale a huge breath.

"It was a duel," said the other. "It was probably the last duel fought in England, and it is long ago now."

"That's better," said Father Brown. "Thank God; that's a great deal better."

"Better than the ugly things you thought of, I suppose?" said the general gruffly. "Well, it's all very well for you to sneer at the pure and perfect affection; but it was true for all that. James Mair really was devoted to his cousin, who'd grown up with him like a younger brother. Elder brothers and sisters do sometimes devote themselves to a child like that, especially when he's a sort of infant phenomenon. But James Mair was the sort of simple character in whom even hate is in a sense unselfish. I mean that even when his tenderness turns to rage it is still objective, directed outwards to its object; he isn't conscious of himself. Now poor Maurice Mair was just the opposite. He was far more friendly and popular; but his success had made him live in a house of mirrors. He was first in every sort of sport and art and accomplishment; he nearly always won and took his winning amiably. But if ever, by any chance, he lost, there was just a glimpse of something not so amiable; he was a little jealous. I needn't tell you the whole miserable story of how he was a little jealous of his cousin's engagement; how he couldn't keep his restless vanity from interfering. It's enough to say that one of the few things in which James Mair was admittedly ahead of him was marksmanship with a pistol; and with that the tragedy ended."

"You mean the tragedy began," replied the priest. "The tragedy of the survivor. I thought he did not need any monkish vampires to make him miserable."

"To my mind he's more miserable than he need be," said the general. "After all, as I say, it was a ghastly tragedy, but it was a fair fight. And Jim had great provocation."

"How do you know all this?" asked the priest.

"I know it because I saw it," answered Outram stolidly. "I was James Mair's second, and I saw Maurice Mair shot dead on the sands before my very eyes."

"I wish you would tell me more about it," said Father Brown reflectively. "Who was Maurice Mair's second?"

"He had a more distinguished backing," replied the general grimly. "Hugo Romaine was his second; the great actor, you know. Maurice was mad on acting and had taken up Romaine (who was then a rising but still a struggling man), and financed the fellow and his ventures in return for taking lessons from the professional in his own hobby of amateur acting. But Romaine was then, I suppose, practically dependent on his rich friend; though he's richer now than any aristocrat. So his serving as second proves very little about what he thought of the quarrel. They fought in the English fashion, with only one second apiece; I wanted at least to have a surgeon, but Maurice boisterously refused it, saying the fewer people who knew, the better, and at the worst we could immediately get help. 'There's a doctor in the village not half a mile away,' he said; 'I know him and he's got the fastest horse in the country. He could be brought here in no time; but there's no need to bring him here till we know.' Well, we all knew that Maurice ran most risk, as the pistol was not his weapon; so when he refused aid nobody liked to ask for it. The duel was fought on a flat stretch of sand on the east coast of Scotland; and both the sight and sound of it were masked from the hamlets inland by a long rampart of sandhills patched with rank grass; probably part of the links, though in those days no Englishman had heard of golf. There was one deep, crooked cranny in the sandhills through which we came out on the sands. I can see them now; first a wide strip of dead yellow, and beyond a narrower strip of dark red; a dark red that seemed already like the long shadow of a deed of blood.

"The thing itself seemed to happen with horrible speed; as if a whirlwind had struck the sand. With the very crack of sound Maurice Mair seemed to spin like a teetotum and pitch upon his face like a ninepin. And queerly enough, while I'd been worrying about him up to that moment, the instant he was dead all my pity was for the man who killed him; as it is to this day and hour. I knew that with that, the whole huge terrible pendulum of my friend's lifelong love would swing back; and that whatever cause others might find to pardon him, he would never pardon himself for ever and ever. And so, somehow, the really vivid thing, the picture that burns in my memory so that I can't forget it, is not that of the catastrophe, the smoke and the flash and the falling figure. That seemed to be all over, like the noise that wakes a man up. What I saw, what I shall always see, is poor Jim hurrying across towards his fallen friend and foe; his brown beard looking black against the ghastly pallor of his face, with its high features cut out against the sea; and the frantic gestures with which he waved me to run for the surgeon in the hamlet behind the sandhills. He had dropped his pistol as he ran; he had a glove in one hand and the loose and fluttering fingers of it seemed to elongate and emphasize his wild pantomime of pointing or hailing for help. That is the picture that really remains with me; and there is nothing else in that picture, except the striped background of sands and sea and the dark, dead body lying still as a stone and the dark figure of the dead man's second standing grim and motionless against the horizon."

"Did Romaine stand motionless?" asked the priest. "I should have thought he would have run even quicker towards the corpse."

"Perhaps he did when I had left," replied the general. "I took in that undying picture in an instant and the next instant I had dived among the sandhills, and was far out of sight of the others. Well, poor Maurice had made a good choice in the matter of doctors; though the doctor came too late, he came quicker than I should have thought possible. This village surgeon was a very remarkable man, red-haired, irascible, but extraordinarily strong in promptitude and presence of mind. I saw him but for a flash as he leapt on his horse and went thundering away to the scene of death, leaving me far behind. But in that flash I had so strong a sense of his personality that I wished to God he had really been called in before the duel began; for I believe on my soul he would have prevented it somehow. As it was, he cleaned up the mess with marvellous swiftness; long before I could trail back to the sea-shore on my two feet his impetuous practicality had managed everything; the corpse was temporarily buried in the sandhills and the unhappy homicide had been persuaded to do the only thing he could do—to flee for his life. He slipped along the coast till he came to a port and managed to get out of the country. You know the rest; poor Jim remained abroad for many years; later, when the whole thing had been hushed up or forgotten, he returned to his dismal castle and automatically inherited the title. I have never seen him from that day to this, and yet I know what is written in red letters in the inmost darkness of his brain."

"I understand," said Father Brown, "that some of you have made efforts to see him?"

"My wife never relaxed her efforts," said the general. "She refuses to admit that such a crime ought to cut a man off for ever; and I confess I am inclined to agree with her. Eighty years before it would have been thought quite normal; and really it was manslaughter rather than murder. My wife is a great friend of the unfortunate lady who was the occasion of the quarrel; and she has an idea that if Jim would consent to see Viola Grayson once again, and receive her assurance that old quarrels are buried, it might restore his sanity. My wife is calling a sort of council of old friends to-morrow, I believe. She is very energetic."

Father Brown was playing with the pins that lay beside the general's map; he seemed to listen rather absent-mindedly. He had the sort of mind that sees things in pictures; and the picture which had coloured even the prosaic mind of the practical soldier took on tints yet more significant and sinister in the more mystical mind of the priest. He saw the dark red desolation of sand, the very hue of Aceldama,[11] and the dead man lying in a dark heap, and the slayer, stooping as he ran, gesticulating with a glove in demented remorse, and always his imagination came back to the third thing that he could not yet fit into any human picture: the second of the slain man standing motionless and mysterious, like a dark statue on the edge of the sea. It might seem to some a detail; but for him it

[11] *Aceldama*, or *hakeldama*, is Aramaic for "Field of Blood" and refers to the potter's field in the Hinnon Valley near Jerusalem bought with blood money earned by Judas, the betrayer of Jesus, according to Acts 1:18–19 and Matthew 27:5–7.

was that stiff figure that stood up like a standing note of interrogation.

Why had not Romaine moved instantly? It was the natural thing for a second to do, in common humanity, let alone friendship. Even if there were some double dealing or darker motive not yet understood, one would think it would be done for the sake of appearances. Anyhow, when the thing was all over, it would be natural for the second to stir long before the other second had vanished beyond the sandcliffs.

"Does this man Romaine move very slowly?" he asked.

"It's queer you should ask that," answered Outram, with a sharp glance. "No, as a matter of fact he moves very quickly when he moves at all. But, curiously enough, I was just thinking that only this afternoon I saw him stand exactly like that, during the thunderstorm. He stood in that silver-clasped cape of his, and with one hand on his hip, exactly in every line as he stood on those bloody sands long ago. The lightning blinded us all, but he did not blink. When it was dark again he was standing there still."

"I suppose he isn't standing there now?" inquired Father Brown. "I mean, I suppose he moved sometime?"

"No, he moved quite sharply when the thunder came," replied the other. "He seemed to have been waiting for it, for he told us the exact time of the interval . . . is anything the matter?"

"I've pricked myself with one of your pins," said Father Brown. "I hope I haven't damaged it." But his eyes had snapped and his mouth abruptly shut.

"Are you ill?" inquired the general, staring at him.

"No," answered the priest; "I'm only not quite so stoical as your friend Romaine. I can't help blinking when I see light."

He turned to gather up his hat and umbrella; but when he had got to the door he seemed to remember something and turned back. Coming up close to Outram, he gazed up into his face with a rather helpless expression, as of a dying fish, and made a motion as if to hold him by the waistcoat.

"General," he almost whispered, "for God's sake don't let your wife and that other woman insist on seeing Marne again. Let sleeping dogs lie, or you'll unleash all the hounds of hell."

The general was left alone with a look of bewilderment in his brown eyes, as he sat down again to play with his pins.

Even greater, however, was the bewilderment which attended the successive stages of the benevolent conspiracy of the general's wife, who had assembled her little group of sympathizers to storm the castle of the misanthrope. The first surprise she encountered was the unexplained absence of one of the actors in the ancient tragedy. When they assembled by agreement at a quiet hotel quite near the castle, there was no sign of Hugo Romaine, until a belated telegram from a lawyer told them that the great actor had suddenly left the country. The second surprise, when they began the bombardment by sending up word to the castle with an urgent request for an interview, was the figure which came forth from those gloomy gates to receive the deputation in the name of the noble owner. It was no such figure as they would have conceived suitable to those sombre avenues or those almost feudal formalities. It was not some stately steward or major-domo, nor even a dignified butler or tall and ornamental footman. The only figure that came out of the cavernous castle doorway was the short and shabby figure of Father Brown.

"Look here," he said, in his simple, bothered fashion. "I told you you'd much better leave him alone. He knows what he's doing and it'll only make everybody unhappy."

Lady Outram, who was accompanied by a tall and quietly dressed lady, still very handsome, presumably the original Miss Grayson, looked at the little priest with cold contempt.

"Really, sir," she said, "this is a very private occasion, and I don't understand what you have to do with it."

"Trust a priest to have to do with a private occasion," snarled Sir John Cockspur. "Don't you know they live behind the scenes like rats behind a wainscot burrowing their way into everybody's private rooms. See how he's already in possession of poor Marne." Sir John was slightly sulky, as his aristocratic friends had persuaded him to give up the great scoop of publicity in return for the privilege of being really inside a society secret. It never occurred to him to ask himself whether *he* was at all like a rat in a wainscot.

"Oh, that's all right," said Father Brown, with the impatience of anxiety. "I've talked it over with the marquis and the only priest he's ever had anything to do with; his clerical tastes have been much exaggerated. I tell you he knows what he's about; and I do implore you all to leave him alone."

"You mean to leave him to this living death of moping and going mad in a ruin!" cried Lady Outram, in a voice that shook a little. "And all because he had the bad luck to shoot a man in a duel more than a quarter of a century ago. Is that what you call Christian charity?"

"Yes," answered the priest stolidly; "that is what I call Christian charity."

"It's about all the Christian charity you'll ever get out of these priests," cried Cockspur bitterly. "That's their only idea of pardoning a poor fellow for a piece of folly; to wall him up alive and starve him to death with fasts and penances and pictures of hell-fire. And all because a bullet went wrong."

"Really, Father Brown," said General Outram, "do you honestly think he deserves this? Is that your Christianity?"

"Surely the true Christianity," pleaded his wife more gently, "is that which knows all and pardons all; the love that can remember—and forget."

"Father Brown," said young Mallow, very earnestly, "I generally agree with what you say; but I'm hanged if I can follow you here. A shot in a duel, followed instantly by remorse, is not such an awful offence."

"I admit," said Father Brown dully, "that I take a more serious view of his offence."

"God soften your hard heart," said the strange lady, speaking for the first time. "I am going to speak to my old friend."

Almost as if her voice had raised a ghost in that great grey house, something stirred within and a figure stood in the dark doorway at the top of the great stone flight of steps. It was clad in dead black, but there was something wild about the blanched hair and something in the pale features that was like the wreck of a marble statue.

Viola Grayson began calmly to move up the great flight of steps; and Outram muttered in his thick black moustache: "He won't cut her dead as he did my wife, I fancy."

Father Brown, who seemed in a collapse of resignation, looked up at him for a moment.

"Poor Marne has enough on his conscience," he said. "Let us acquit him of what we can. At least he never cut your wife."

"What do you mean by that?"

"He never knew her," said Father Brown.

As they spoke the tall lady proudly mounted the last step and came face to face with the Marquis of Marne. His lips moved, but something happened before he could speak.

A scream rang across the open space and went wailing away in echoes along those hollow walls. By the abruptness and agony with which it broke from the woman's lips it might have been a mere inarticulate cry. But it was an articulated word; and they all heard it with a horrible distinctness.

"Maurice!"

"What is it, dear?" cried Lady Outram, and began to run up the steps; for the other woman was swaying as if she might fall down the whole stone flight. Then she faced about and began to descend, all bowed and shrunken and shuddering. "Oh, my God," she was saying. "Oh, my God . . . it isn't Jim at all . . . it's Maurice!"

"I think, Lady Outram," said the priest gravely, "you had better go with your friend."

As they turned, a voice fell on them like a stone from the top of the stone stair, a voice that might have come out of an open grave. It was hoarse and unnatural, like the voices of men who are left alone with wild birds on desert islands. It was the voice of the Marquis of Marne, and it said: "Stop!"

"Father Brown," he said, "before your friends disperse I authorize you to tell them all I have told you. Whatever follows, I will hide from it no longer."

"You are right," said the priest, "and it shall be counted to you."

"Yes," said Father Brown quietly to the questioning company afterwards. "He has given me the right to speak; but I will not tell it as he told me, but as I found it out for myself. Well, I knew from the first that the blighting monkish influence was all nonsense out of novels. Our people might possibly in certain cases encourage a man to go regularly into a monastery, but certainly not to hang about in a mediaeval castle. In the same way, they certainly wouldn't want him to dress up as a monk when he wasn't a monk. But it struck me that he might himself want to wear a monk's hood or even a mask. I had heard of him as a mourner, and then as a murderer; but already I had hazy suspicions that his reason for hiding might not only be concerned with what he was, but with who he was.

"Then came the general's vivid description of the duel; and the most vivid thing in it to me was the figure of Mr. Romaine in the background; it was vivid because it was in the background. Why did the general leave behind him on the sand a dead man, whose friend stood yards away from him like a stock or a stone? Then I heard something, a mere trifle, about a trick habit that Romaine has of standing quite still when he is waiting for something to happen; as he waited for the thunder to follow the lightning. Well, that automatic trick in this case betrayed everything. Hugo Romaine, on that old occasion, also was waiting for something."

"But it was all over," said the general. "What could he have been waiting for?"

"He was waiting for the duel," said Father Brown.

"But I tell you I saw the duel!" cried the general.

"And I tell you you didn't see the duel," said the priest.

"Are you mad?" demanded the other. "Or why should you think I am blind?"

"Because you were blinded—that you might not see," said the priest. "Because you are a good man and God had mercy on your innocence, and he turned your face away from that unnatural strife. He set a wall of sand and silence between you and what really happened on that horrible red shore, abandoned to the raging spirits of Judas and of Cain."

"Tell us what happened!" gasped the lady impatiently.

"I will tell it as I found it," proceeded the priest. "The next thing I found was that Romaine, the actor, had been training Maurice Mair in all the tricks of the trade of acting. I once had a friend who went in for acting. He gave me a very amusing account of how his first week's training consisted entirely of falling down; of learning how to fall flat without a stagger, as if he were stone dead."

"God have mercy on us!" cried the general, and gripped the arms of his chair as if to rise.

"Amen," said Father Brown. "You told me how quickly it seemed to come; in fact, Maurice fell before the bullet flew and lay perfectly still, waiting. And his wicked friend and teacher stood also in the background, waiting."

"We are waiting," said Cockspur, "and I feel as if I couldn't wait."

"James Mair, already broken with remorse, rushed across to the fallen man and bent over to lift him up. He had thrown away his pistol like an unclean thing; but Maurice's pistol still lay under his hand and it was undischarged. Then as the elder man bent over the younger, the younger lifted himself on his left arm and shot the elder through the body. He knew he was not so good a shot, but there was no question of missing the heart at that distance."

The rest of the company had risen and stood staring down at the narrator with pale faces. "Are you sure of this?" asked Sir John at last, in a thick voice.

"I am sure of it," said Father Brown, "and now I leave Maurice Mair, the present Marquis of Marne, to your Christian charity. You have told me something to-day about Christian charity. You seemed to me to give it almost too large a place; but how fortunate it is for poor sinners like this man that you err so much on the side of mercy, and are ready to be reconciled to all mankind."

"Hang it all," exploded the general; "if you think I'm going to be reconciled to a filthy viper like that, I tell you I wouldn't say a word to save him from hell. I said I could pardon a regular decent duel, but of all the treacherous assassins—"

"He ought to be lynched," cried Cockspur excitedly. "He ought to burn alive like a nigger in the States. And if there is such a thing as burning for ever, he jolly well—"

"I wouldn't touch him with a barge pole myself," said Mallow.

"There is a limit to human charity," said Lady Outram, trembling all over.

"There is," said Father Brown dryly; "and that is the real difference between human charity and Christian charity. You must forgive me if I was not altogether crushed by your contempt for my uncharitableness to-day; or by the lectures you read me about pardon for every sinner. For it seems to me that you only pardon the sins that you don't really think sinful. You only forgive criminals when they commit what you don't regard as crimes, but rather as conventions. So you tolerate a conventional duel, just as you tolerate a conventional divorce. You forgive because there isn't anything to be forgiven."

"But, hang it all," cried Mallow, "you don't expect us to be able to pardon a vile thing like this?"

"No," said the priest; "but *we* have to be able to pardon it."

He stood up abruptly and looked round at them.

"We have to touch such men, not with a barge pole, but with a benediction," he said. "We have to say the word that will save them from hell. We alone are left to deliver them from despair when your human charity deserts them. Go on your own primrose path pardoning all your favourite vices and being generous to your fashionable crimes;[12] and leave us in the darkness, vampires of the night, to console those who

---

[12] Father Brown echoes Shakespeare, as in Ophelia's words to her brother Laertes in *Hamlet* 1:3:50:

> Do not, as some ungracious pastors do,
> Show me the steep and thorny way to heaven,

really need consolation; who do things really indefensible, things that neither the world nor they themselves can defend; and none but a priest will pardon. Leave us with the men who commit the mean and revolting and real crimes; mean as St. Peter when the cock crew, and yet the dawn came."

"The dawn," repeated Mallow doubtfully. "You mean hope—for *him*?"

"Yes," replied the other. "Let me ask you one question. You are great ladies and men of honour and secure of yourselves; you would never, you can tell yourselves, stoop to such squalid treason as that. But tell me this. If any of you had so stooped, which of you, years afterwards, when you were old and rich and safe, would have been driven by conscience or confessor to tell such a story of yourself? You say you could not commit so base a crime. Could you confess so base a crime?"

The others gathered their possessions together and drifted by twos and threes out of the room in silence. And Father Brown, also in silence, went back to the melancholy castle of Marne.

Whiles, like a puffed and reckless libertine,
Himself the primrose path of dalliance treads. . . .
and Macbeth's porter's, "professions that go the primrose way to the everlasting bonfire" (2:3:22).

The Red Moon of Meru

EVERYONE agreed that the bazaar at Mallowood Abbey (by kind permission of Lady Mounteagle) was a great success; there were roundabouts and swings and side-shows, which the people greatly enjoyed; I would also mention the Charity, which was the excellent object of the proceedings, if any of them could tell me what it was.

However, it is only with a few of them that we are here concerned; and especially with three of them, a lady and two gentlemen, who passed between two of the principal tents or pavilions, their voices high in argument. On their right was the tent of the Master of the Mountain, that world-famous fortune-teller by crystals and chiromancy; a rich purple tent, all over which were traced, in black and gold, the sprawling outlines of Asiatic gods waving any number of arms like octopods. Perhaps they symbolized the readiness of divine help to be had within; perhaps they merely implied that the ideal being of a pious palmist would have as many hands as possible. On the other side stood the plainer tent of Phroso the Phrenologist; more austerely decorated with diagrams of the heads

"The Red Moon of Meru" first appeared in the March 1927 issue of *Harper's* magazine in the United States; its first British appearance was in the April 1927 issue of *Storyteller* magazine.

of Socrates and Shakespeare, which were apparently of a lumpy sort. But these were presented merely in black and white, with numbers and notes, as became the rigid dignity of a purely rationalistic science. The purple tent had an opening like a black cavern, and all was fittingly silent within. But Phroso the Phrenologist, a lean, shabby, sunburnt person, with an almost improbably fierce black moustache and whiskers, was standing outside his own temple, and talking, at the top of his voice, to nobody in particular, explaining that the head of any passer-by would doubtless prove, on examination, to be every bit as knobby as Shakespeare's. Indeed, the moment the lady appeared between the tents, the vigilant Phroso leapt on her and offered, with a pantomime of old-world courtesy, to feel her bumps.

She refused with civility that was rather like rudeness; but she must be excused, because she was in the middle of an argument. She also had to be excused, or at any rate was excused, because she was Lady Mounteagle. She was not a nonentity, however, in any sense; she was at once handsome and haggard, with a hungry look in her deep, dark eyes and something eager and almost fierce about her smile. Her dress was bizarre for the period; for it was before the Great War had left us in our present mood of gravity and recollection. Indeed, the dress was rather like the purple tent; being of a semi-oriental sort, covered with exotic and esoteric emblems. But everyone knew that the Mounteagles were mad; which was the popular way of saying that she and her husband were interested in the creeds and culture of the East.

The eccentricity of the lady was a great contrast to the conventionality of the two gentlemen, who were braced and buttoned up in all the stiffer fashion of that far-off day, from the tips of their gloves to their bright top hats. Yet even here there was a difference; for James Hardcastle managed at once to look correct and distinguished, while Tommy Hunter only looked correct and commonplace. Hardcastle was a promising politician; who seemed in society to be interested in everything except politics. It may be answered gloomily that every politician is emphatically a promising politician. But to do him justice, he had often exhibited himself as a performing politician. No purple tent in the bazaar, however, had been provided for him to perform in.

"For my part," he said, screwing in the monocle that was the only gleam in his hard, legal face, "I think we must exhaust the possibilities of mesmerism before we talk about magic. Remarkable psychological powers undoubtedly exist, even in apparently backward peoples. Marvelous things have been done by fakirs."

"Did you say done by fakers?" asked the other young man, with doubtful innocence.

"Tommy, you are simply silly," said the lady. "Why will you keep barging in on things you don't understand? You're like a schoolboy screaming out that he knows how a conjuring trick is done. It's all so Early Victorian—that schoolboy scepticism. As for mesmerism, I doubt whether you can stretch it to—"

At this point Lady Mounteagle seemed to catch sight of somebody she wanted; a black stumpy figure standing at a booth where children were throwing hoops at hideous table ornaments. She darted across and cried:

"Father Brown, I've been looking for you. I want to ask you something. Do you believe in fortune-telling?"

The person addressed looked rather helplessly at the little hoop in his hand and said at last:

"I wonder in which sense you are using the word 'believe.' Of course, if it's all a fraud—"

"Oh, but the Master of the Mountain isn't a bit of a

fraud," she cried. "He isn't a common conjurer or a fortune-teller at all. It's really a great honour for him to condescend to tell fortunes at my parties; for he's a great religious leader in his own country; a Prophet and a Seer. And even his fortune-telling isn't vulgar stuff about coming into a fortune. He tells you great spiritual truths about yourself, about your ideals."

"Quite so," said Father Brown. "That's what I object to. I was just going to say that if it's all a fraud, I don't mind it so much.[1] It can't be much more of a fraud than most things at fancy bazaars; and there, in a way, it's a sort of practical joke. But if it's a religion and reveals spiritual truths—then it's all as false as hell and I wouldn't touch it with a barge pole."

"That is something of a paradox," said Hardcastle, with a smile.

"I wonder what a paradox is," remarked the priest in a ruminant manner. "It seems to me obvious enough. I suppose it wouldn't do very much harm if somebody dressed up as a German spy, and pretended to have told all sorts of lies to the Germans. But if a man is trading in the *truth* with the Germans—well! So I think if a fortune-teller is trading in *truth* like that—"

"You really think," began Hardcastle grimly.

"Yes," said the other; "I think he is trading with the Enemy."

---

[1] Father Brown's paradox is Chesterton's own, as expressed, for example, in his *Illustrated London News* column for October 6, 1906, "Superstition and Modern Justice", *Collected Works*, vol. XXVII, pp. 295-300: "It is a peculiarity of the case of witchcraft that if you have convicted a human being of the fraud, you have acquitted him of the crime. He is pardonable if he is false; he is only detestable if he is sincere"; or February 7, 1925, "The Paradox of Spiritualism", *Collected Works*, vol. XXXIII, pp. 495–99: "If spiritualism were a fraud I should think it a good thing that men should study it."

Tommy Hunter broke into a chuckle. "Well," he said, "if Father Brown thinks they're good so long as they're frauds, I should think he'd consider this copper-coloured prophet a sort of saint."

"My cousin Tom is incorrigible," said Lady Mounteagle. "He's always going about showing up adepts, as he calls it. He only came down here in a hurry when he heard the Master was to be here, I believe. He'd have tried to show up Buddha or Moses."

"Thought you wanted looking after a bit," said the young man, with a grin on his round face. "So I toddled down. Don't like this brown monkey crawling about."

"There you go again!" said Lady Mounteagle. "Years ago, when I was in India, I suppose we all had that sort of prejudice against brown people. But now I know something about their wonderful spiritual powers, I'm glad to say I know better."

"Our prejudices seem to cut opposite ways," said Father Brown. "You excuse his being brown because he is brahminical; and I excuse his being brahminical because he is brown.[2] Frankly, I don't care for spiritual powers much myself. I've got much more sympathy with spiritual weaknesses. But I can't see why anybody should dislike him merely because he is the same beautiful colour as copper, or coffee, or nut-brown ale, or those jolly peat-streams in the North. But then," he added, looking across at the lady and screwing up his eyes, "I suppose I'm prejudiced in favour of anything that's called brown."

"There now!" cried Lady Mounteagle with a sort of triumph. "I knew you were only talking nonsense!"

[2] Father Brown's reference is to the Brahmins and their priests—Hindus of the highest caste who worship the absolute and impersonal deity, Brahma.

"Well," grumbled the aggrieved youth with the round face. "When anybody talks sense you call it schoolboy scepticism. When's the crystal-gazing going to begin?"

"Any time you like, I believe," replied the lady. "It isn't crystal-gazing, as a matter of fact, but palmistry; I suppose you would say it was all the same sort of nonsense."

"I think there is a *via media*[3] between sense and nonsense," said Hardcastle, smiling. "There are explanations that are natural and not at all nonsensical; and yet the results are very amazing. Are you coming in to be operated on? I confess I am full of curiosity."

"Oh, I've no patience with such nonsense," spluttered the sceptic, whose round face had become rather a red face with the heat of his contempt and incredulity. "I'll let you waste your time on your mahogany mountebank; I'd rather go and throw at coconuts."

The Phrenologist, still hovering near, darted at the opening.

"Heads, my dear sir," he said, "human skulls are of a contour far more subtle than that of coconuts. No coconut can compare with your own most—"

Hardcastle had already dived into the dark entry of the purple tent; and they heard a low murmur of voices within. As Tom Hunter turned on the Phrenologist with an impatient answer, in which he showed a regrettable indifference to the line between natural and preternatural sciences, the lady was just about to continue her little argument with the little priest, when she stopped in some surprise.

James Hardcastle had come out of the tent again, and in his

---

[3] Latin for "middle way". Hardcastle's use of the phrase recalls the Elizabethan church settlement that established the Church of England as the *via media*, or compromise between Protestant doctrine and Catholic ceremony.

grim face and glaring monocle, surprise was even more vividly depicted.

"He's not there," remarked the politician abruptly. "He's gone. Some aged nigger, who seems to constitute his suite,[4] jabbered something to me to the effect that the Master had gone forth rather than sell sacred secrets for gold."

Lady Mounteagle turned radiantly to the rest. "There now," she cried. "I told you he was a cut above anything you fancied! He hates being here in a crowd; he's gone back to his solitude."

"I am sorry," said Father Brown gravely. "I may have done him an injustice. Do you know where he has gone?"

"I think so," said his hostess equally gravely. "When he wants to be alone, he always goes to the cloisters, just at the end of the left wing, beyond my husband's study and private museum, you know. Perhaps you know this house was once an abbey."

"I have heard something about it," answered the priest, with a faint smile.[5]

"We'll go there, if you like," said the lady, briskly. "You really ought to see my husband's collection; or the Red Moon at any rate. Haven't you ever heard of the Red Moon of Meru? Yes, it's a ruby."

"I should be delighted to see the collection," said Hardcastle quietly, "including the Master of the Mountain, if that prophet is one exhibit in the museum." And they all turned towards the path leading to the house.

"All the same," muttered the sceptical Thomas, as he

---

[4] French for "retinue"; "attendants".

[5] Father Brown is well aware of Henry VIII and the Suppression of 1536–40 in which hundreds of Catholic abbeys were looted and razed, while some were converted into Anglican churches or sold to laymen as mansions for their private use.

brought up the rear, "I should very much like to know what the brown beast *did* come here for, if he didn't come to tell fortunes."

As he disappeared, the indomitable Phroso made one more dart after him, almost snatching at his coat-tails.

"The bump—" he began.

"No bump," said the youth, "only a hump. Hump I always have when I come down to see Mounteagle." And he took to his heels to escape the embrace of the man of science.

On their way to the cloisters the visitors had to pass through the long room that was devoted by Lord Mounteagle to his remarkable private museum of Asiatic charms and mascots. Through one open door, in the length of the wall opposite, they could see the Gothic arches and the glimmer of daylight between them, marking the square open space, round the roofed border of which the monks had walked in older days. But they had to pass something that seemed at first sight rather more extraordinary than the ghost of a monk.

It was an elderly gentleman, robed from head to foot in white, with a pale green turban, but a very pink and white English complexion and the smooth white moustaches of some amiable Anglo-Indian colonel. This was Lord Mounteagle, who had taken his Oriental pleasures more sadly, or at least more seriously, than his wife. He could talk of nothing, whatever, except Oriental religion and philosophy; and had thought it necessary even to dress in the manner of an Oriental hermit. While he was delighted to show his treasures, he seemed to treasure them much more for the truths supposed to be symbolized in them than for their value in collections, let alone cash. Even when he brought out the great ruby, perhaps the only thing of great value in the museum, in a merely monetary sense, he seemed to be much more interested in its name than in its size, let alone its price.

The others were all staring at what seemed a stupendously large red stone, burning like a bonfire seen through a rain of blood. But Lord Mounteagle rolled it loosely in his palm without looking at it; and staring at the ceiling, told them a long tale about the legendary character of Mount Meru, and how in the Gnostic mythology it had been the place of the wrestling of nameless primeval powers.

Towards the end of the lecture on the Demiurge of the Gnostics (not forgetting its connexion with the parallel concept of Manichaeus),[6] even the tactful Mr. Hardcastle thought it time to create a diversion. He asked to be allowed to look at the stone; and as evening was closing in, and the long room with its single door was steadily darkening, he stepped out in the cloister beyond, to examine the jewel by a better light. It was then that they first became conscious, slowly and almost creepily conscious, of the living presence of the Master of the Mountain.

The cloister was on the usual plan, as regards its original structure; but the line of Gothic pillars and pointed arches that formed the inner square was linked together all along by a low wall, about waist high, turning the Gothic doors into Gothic windows and giving each a sort of flat window-sill of stone. This alteration was probably of ancient date; but there were other alterations of a quainter sort, which witnessed to the rather unusual individual ideas of Lord and Lady Mounteagle. Between the pillars hung thin curtains, or rather veils, made of beads or light canes, in a continental or southern manner; and on these again could be traced the lines and colours of Asiatic dragons or idols, that contrasted with the grey Gothic framework in which they were suspended. But

---

[6] The Gnosticism and Manichaeism of Mounteagle's lecture were early Christian heresies of a dual creation: Spirit was created by a good god, and Matter was created by an evil god, the "Demiurge".

this, while it further troubled the dying light of the place, was the least of the incongruities of which the company, with very varying feelings, became aware.

In the open space surrounded by the cloisters there ran, like a circle in a square, a circular path paved with pale stones and edged with some sort of green enamel like an imitation lawn. Inside that, in the very centre, rose the basin of a dark green fountain, or raised pond, in which water-lilies floated and goldfish flashed to and fro; and high above these, its outline dark against the dying light, was a great green image. Its back was turned to them and its face so completely invisible in the hunched posture that the statue might almost have been headless. But in that mere dark outline, in the dim twilight, some of them could see instantly that it was the shape of no Christian thing.

A few yards away, on the circular path, and looking towards the great green god, stood the man called the Master of the Mountain. His pointed and finely finished features seemed moulded by some skilful craftsman as a mask of copper. In contrast with this, his dark grey beard looked almost blue like indigo; it began in a narrow tuft on his chin, and then spread outwards like a great fan or the tail of a bird. He was robed in peacock green and wore on his bald head a high cap of un-common outline; a head-dress none of them had ever seen before; but it looked rather Egyptian than Indian. The man was standing with staring eyes; wide open, fish-shaped eyes, so motionless that they looked like the eyes painted on a mummy-case. But though the figure of the Master of the Mountain was singular enough, some of the company, in-cluding Father Brown, did not look at him; they still looked at the dark-green idol at which he himself was looking.

"This seems a queer thing," said Hardcastle, frowning a little, "to set up in the middle of an old Abbey cloister."

"Now, don't tell me you're going to be silly," said Lady Mounteagle. "That's just what we meant; to link up the great religions of East and West; Buddha and Christ. Surely you must understand that all religions are really the same."

"If they are," said Father Brown mildly, "it seems rather unnecessary to go into the middle of Asia to get one."

"Lady Mounteagle means that they are different aspects or facets, as there are of this stone," began Hardcastle; and becoming interested in the new topic, laid the great ruby down on the stone sill or ledge under the Gothic arch. "But it does not follow that we can mix the aspects in one artistic style. You may mix Christianity and Islam, but you can't mix Gothic and Saracenic, let alone real Indian."[7]

As he spoke the Master of the Mountain seemed to come to life like a cataleptic, and moved gravely round another quarter segment of the circle, and took up his position outside their own row of arches, standing with his back to them and looking now towards the idol's back. It was obvious that he was moving by stages round the whole circle, like a hand round a clock; but pausing for prayer or contemplation.

"What *is* his religion?" asked Hardcastle, with a faint touch of impatience.

"He says," replied Lord Mounteagle, reverently, "that it is older than Brahminism and purer than Buddhism."

"Oh," said Hardcastle, and continued to stare through his single eyeglass, standing with both his hands in his pockets.

"They say," observed the nobleman in his gentle but didac-

---

[7] Hardcastle's view is that each religion has its characteristic architectural style: the Gothic (Christian), the Saracen (Moslem), and the Indian (Buddhist or Hindu). Chesterton said much the same and at greater length in his *Illustrated London News* essay for February 7, 1925, "The Message of Architecture" (*Collected Works*, vol. XXXIII, pp. 369–72).

tic voice, "that the deity called the God of Gods is carved in a colossal form in the cavern of Mount Meru—"

Even his lordship's lecturing serenity was broken abruptly by the voice that came over his shoulder. It came out of the darkness of the museum they had just left, when they stepped out into the cloister. At the sound of it the two younger men looked first incredulous, then furious, and then almost collapsed into laughter.

"I hope I do not intrude," said the urbane and seductive voice of Professor Phroso, that unconquerable wrestler for the truth, "but it occurred to me that some of you might spare a little time for that much despised science of Bumps, which—"

"Look here," cried the impetuous Tommy Hunter, "I haven't got any bumps; but you'll jolly well have some soon, you—"

Hardcastle mildly restrained him as he plunged back through the door; and for the moment all the group had turned again and were looking back into the inner room.

It was at that moment that the thing happened. It was the impetuous Tommy, once more, who was the first to move, and this time to better effect. Before anyone else had seen anything, when Hardcastle had barely remembered with a jump that he had left the gem on the stone sill, Tommy was across the cloister with the leap of a cat and, leaning with his head and shoulders out of the aperture between two columns, had cried out in a voice that rang down all the arches: "I've got him!"

In that instant of time, just after they turned, and just before they heard his triumphant cry, they had all seen it happen. Round the corner of one of the two columns, there had darted in and out again a brown or rather bronze-coloured hand, the colour of dead gold; such as they had seen elsewhere. The hand had struck as straight as a striking snake; as instantaneous as the flick of the long tongue of an ant-eater. But it had licked up the jewel. The stone slab of the window-sill shone bare in the pale and fading light.

"I've got him," gasped Tommy Hunter; "but he's wriggling pretty hard. You fellows run round him in front—he can't have got rid of it, anyhow."

The others obeyed, some racing down the corridor and some leaping over the low wall, with the result that a little crowd, consisting of Hardcastle, Lord Mounteagle, Father Brown, and even the undetachable Mr. Phroso of the bumps, had soon surrounded the captive Master of the Mountain, whom Hunter was hanging on to desperately by the collar with one hand, and shaking every now and then in a manner highly insensible to the dignity of Prophets as a class.

"Now we've got him, anyhow," said Hunter, letting go with a sigh. "We've only got to search him. The thing must be here."

Three-quarters of an hour later, Hunter and Hardcastle, their top-hats, ties, gloves, slips and spats somewhat the worse for their recent activities, came face to face in the cloister and gazed at each other.

"Well," asked Hardcastle with restraint, "have you any views on the mystery?"

"Hang it all," replied Hunter; "you can't call it a mystery. Why, we all saw him take it ourselves."

"Yes," replied the other, "but we didn't all see him lose it ourselves. And the mystery is, where has he lost it so that we can't find it?"

"It must be somewhere," said Hunter. "Have you searched the fountain and all round that rotten old god there?"

"I haven't dissected the little fishes," said Hardcastle, lifting his eyeglass and surveying the other. "Are you thinking of the ring of Polycrates?"[8]

Apparently the survey, through the eyeglass, of the round face before him, convinced him that it covered no such meditation on Greek legend.

"It's not on him, I admit," repeated Hunter, suddenly, "unless he's swallowed it."

"Are we to dissect the Prophet, too?" asked the other smiling. "But here comes our host."

"This is a most distressing matter," said Lord Mounteagle, twisting his white moustache with a nervous and even tremulous hand. "Horrible thing to have a theft in one's house, let alone connecting it with a man like the Master. But, I confess, I can't quite make head or tail of the way in which he is talking about it. I wish you'd come inside and see what you think."

They went in together, Hunter falling behind and dropping into conversation with Father Brown, who was kicking his heels round the cloister.

"You must be very strong," said the priest pleasantly. "You held him with one hand; and he seemed pretty vigorous, even when we had eight hands to hold him, like one of those Indian gods."

They took a turn or two round the cloister, talking; and then they also went into the inner room, where the Master of the Mountain was seated on a bench, in the capacity of a captive, but with more of the air of a king.

It was true, as Lord Mounteagle said, that his air and tone were not very easy to understand. He spoke with a serene, and yet secretive sense of power. He seemed rather amused at

[8] Hardcastle alludes to the luck of Polycrates of ancient Samos who, according to Herodotus, threw a ring into the sea only to find it later inside a fish (*The Persian Wars*, III:40–42).

their suggestions about trivial hiding-places for the gem; and certainly he showed no resentment whatever. He seemed to be laughing, in a still unfathomable fashion, at their efforts to trace what they had all seen him take.

"You are learning a little," he said, with insolent benevolence, "of the laws of time and space; about which your latest science is a thousand years behind our oldest religion. You do not even know what is really meant by hiding a thing. Nay, my poor little friends, you do not even know what is meant by *seeing* a thing; or perhaps you would see this as plainly as I do."

"Do you mean it is here?" demanded Hardcastle harshly.

"Here is a word of many meanings, also," replied the mystic. "But I did not say it was here. I only said I could see it."

There was an irritated silence, and he went on sleepily.

"If you were to be utterly, unfathomably, silent, do you think you might hear a cry from the other end of the world? The cry of a worshipper alone in those mountains, where the original image sits, itself like a mountain. Some say that even Jews and Moslems might worship that image; because it was never made by man. Hark! Do you hear the cry with which he lifts his head and sees in that socket of stone, that has been hollow for ages, the one red and angry moon that is the eye of the mountain?"

"Do you really mean," cried Lord Mounteagle, a little shaken, "that you could make it pass from here to Mount Meru? I used to believe you had great spiritual powers, but—"

"Perhaps," said the Master, "I have more than you will ever believe."

Hardcastle rose impatiently and began to pace the room with his hands in his pockets.

"I never believed so much as you did; but I admit that powers of a certain type may... Good God!"

His high, hard voice had been cut off in mid-air, and he stopped staring; the eyeglass fell out of his eye. They all turned their faces in the same direction; and on every face there seemed to be the same suspended animation.

The Red Moon of Meru lay on the stone window-sill, exactly as they had last seen it. It might have been a red spark blown there from a bonfire, or a red rose petal tossed from a broken rose; but it had fallen in precisely the same spot where Hardcastle had thoughtlessly laid it down.

This time Hardcastle did not attempt to pick it up again; but his demeanour was somewhat notable. He turned slowly and began to stride about the room again; but there was in his movements something masterful, where before it had been only restless. Finally, he brought himself to a standstill in front of the seated Master, and bowed with a somewhat sardonic smile.

"Master," he said, "we all owe you an apology; and, what is more important, you have taught us all a lesson. Believe me, it will serve as a lesson as well as a joke. I shall always remember the very remarkable powers you really possess, and how harmlessly you use them. Lady Mounteagle," he went on, turning towards her, "you will forgive me for having addressed the Master first; but it was to you I had the honour of offering this explanation some time ago. I may say that I explained it before it had happened. I told you that most of these things could be interpreted by some kind of hypnotism. Many believe that this is the explanation of all those Indian stories about the mango plant and the boy who climbs a rope thrown into the air. It does not really happen; but the spectators are mesmerized into imagining that it happened. So we were all mesmerized into imagining this theft had happened. That brown hand coming in at the window, and whisking away the gem, was a momentary delusion; a hand in a dream. Only, having seen the stone vanish, we never looked for it where it was before. We plunged into the pond and turned every leaf of the water lilies; we were almost giving emetics to the goldfish. But the ruby has been here all the time."

And he glanced across at the opalescent eyes and smiling bearded mouth of the Master, and saw that the smile was just a shade broader. There was something in it that made the others jump to their feet with an air of sudden relaxation and general, gasping relief.

"This is a very fortunate escape for us all," said Lord Mounteagle, smiling rather nervously. "There cannot be the least doubt it is as you say. It has been a most painful episode and I really don't know what apologies—"

"I have no complaints," said the Master of the Mountain, still smiling. "You have never touched Me at all."

While the rest went off rejoicing, with Hardcastle for the hero of the hour, the little Phrenologist with the whiskers sauntered back towards his preposterous tent. Looking over his shoulder he was surprised to find Father Brown following him.

"Can I feel your bumps?" asked the expert, in his mildly sarcastic tone.

"I don't think you want to feel any more, do you?" said the priest good-humouredly. "You're a detective, aren't you?"

"Yep," replied the other. "Lady Mounteagle asked me to keep an eye on the Master, being no fool, for all her mysticism; and when he left his tent, I could only follow by behaving like a nuisance and a monomaniac. If anybody had come into my tent, I'd have had to look up Bumps in an encyclopaedia."

"Bumps, What Ho She; see Folk-Lore," observed Father

Brown, dreamily.[9] "Well, you were quite in the part in pestering people—at a bazaar."

"Rum case, wasn't it?" remarked the fallacious Phrenologist. "Queer to think the thing was there all the time."

"Very queer," said the priest.

Something in his voice made the other man stop and stare.

"Look here!" he cried. "What's the matter with you? What are you looking like that for? Don't you *believe* that it was there all the time?"

Father Brown blinked rather as if he had received a buffet; then he said slowly and with hesitation, "No . . . the fact is . . . I can't—I can't quite bring myself to believe it."

"You're not the sort of chap," said the other shrewdly, "who'd say that without reason. Why don't you think the ruby had been there all the time?"

"Only because I put it back myself!" said Father Brown. The other man stood rooted to the spot, like one whose hair was standing on end. He opened his mouth without speech.

"Or rather," went on the priest, "I persuaded the thief to let me put it back. I told him what I'd guessed and showed him there was still time for repentance. I don't mind telling you in professional confidence; besides, I don't think the Mounteagles would prosecute, now they've got the thing back, especially considering who stole it."

"Do you mean the Master?" asked the late Phroso.

"No," said Father Brown, "the Master didn't steal it."

"But I don't understand," objected the other. "Nobody was outside the window except the Master; and a hand certainly came from outside."

[9] Father Brown recalls the derisive cry "What ho, she bumps!" in vogue in 1899 among English boat-racers, and the popular song from 1900, by Mills and Castling, with the phrase for its title.

"The hand came from outside, but the thief came from the inside," said Father Brown.

"We seem to be back among the mystics again. Look here, I'm a practical man: I only wanted to know if it is all right with her ruby—"

"I knew it was all wrong," said Father Brown, "before I even knew there was a ruby."

After a pause he went on thoughtfully. "Right away back in that argument of theirs, by the tents, I knew things were going wrong. People will tell you that theories don't matter and that logic and philosophy aren't practical. Don't you believe them. Reason is from God, and when things are unreasonable there is something the matter. Now, that quite abstract argument ended with something funny. Consider what the theories were. Hardcastle was a trifle superior and said that all things were perfectly possible; but they were mostly done merely by mesmerism, or clairvoyance; scientific names for philosophical puzzles, in the usual style. But Hunter thought it all sheer fraud and wanted to show it up. By Lady Mounteagle's testimony, he not only went about showing up fortune-tellers and such like, but he had actually come down specially to confront this one. He didn't often come; he didn't get on with Mounteagle, from whom, being a spendthrift, he always tried to borrow; but when he heard the Master was coming, he came hurrying down. Very well. In spite of that, it was Hardcastle who went to consult the wizard and Hunter who refused. He said he'd waste no time on such nonsense; having apparently wasted a lot of his life on proving it to be nonsense. That seems inconsistent. He thought in this case it was crystal-gazing; but he found it was palmistry."

"Do you mean he made that an excuse?" asked his companion, puzzled.

"I thought so at first," replied the priest; "but I know now it was not an excuse, but a reason. He really was put off by finding it was a palmist, because—"

"Well," demanded the other impatiently.

"Because he didn't want to take his glove off," said Father Brown.

"Take his glove off?" repeated the inquirer.

"If he had," said Father Brown mildly, "we should all have seen that his hand was painted pale brown already. . . . Oh, yes, he did come down specially because the Master was here. He came down very fully prepared."

"You mean," cried Phroso, "that it was Hunter's hand, painted brown, that came in at the window? Why, he was with us all the time!"

"Go and try it on the spot and you'll find it's quite possible," said the priest. "Hunter leapt forward and leaned out of the window; in a flash he could tear off his glove, tuck up his sleeve, and thrust his hand back round the other side of the pillar, while he gripped the Indian with the other hand and hallooed out that he'd caught the thief. I remarked at the time that he held the thief with one hand, where any sane man would have used two. But the other hand was slipping the jewel into his trouser pocket."

There was a long pause and then the ex-Phrenologist said slowly, "Well, that's a staggerer. But the thing stumps me still. For one thing, it doesn't explain the queer behaviour of the old magician himself. If he was entirely innocent, why the devil didn't he say so? Why wasn't he indignant at being accused and searched? Why did he only sit smiling and hinting in a sly way what wild and wonderful things he could do?"

"Ah!" cried Father Brown, with a sharp note in his voice, "there you come up against it! Against everything these people don't and won't understand. All religions are the same, says Lady Mounteagle. Are they, by George! I tell you some of

them are so different that the best man of one creed will be
callous, where the worst man of another will be sensitive. I
told you I didn't like spiritual power, because the accent is on
the word power. I don't say the Master would steal a ruby;
very likely he wouldn't; very likely he wouldn't think it
worth stealing. It wouldn't be specially his temptation to take
jewels; but it would be his temptation to take credit for
miracles that didn't belong to him any more than the jewels.
It was to *that* sort of temptation, to *that* sort of stealing that he
yielded today. He liked us to think that he had marvellous
mental powers that could make a material object fly through
space; and even when he hadn't done it, he allowed us to
think he had. The point about private property wouldn't occur primarily to him at all. The question wouldn't present
itself in the form, 'Shall I *steal* this pebble?' but only in the
form: 'Could I make a pebble vanish and reappear on a distant
mountain?' The question of *whose* pebble would strike him as
irrelevant. That is what I mean by religions being different.
He is very proud of having what he calls spiritual powers. But
what he calls spiritual doesn't mean what we call moral. It
means rather mental; the power of the mind over matter; the
magician controlling the elements. Now we are not like that,
even when we are no better; even when we are worse. We,
whose fathers at least were Christians, who have grown up
under those mediaeval arches even if we bedizen them with
all the demons in Asia—we have the very opposite ambition
and the very opposite shame. We should all be anxious that
nobody should think we had done it. He was actually anxious
that everybody should think he had—even when he hadn't.
He actually stole the credit of stealing. While we were all
casting the crime from us like a snake, he was actually luring
it to him like a snake-charmer. But snakes are not pets in this
country! Here the traditions of Christendom tell at once

under a test like this. Look at old Mounteagle himself, for instance! Ah, you may be as Eastern and esoteric as you like, and wear a turban and a long robe and live on messages from Mahatmas; but if a bit of stone is stolen in your house, and your friends are suspected, you will jolly soon find out that you're an ordinary English gentleman in a fuss. The man who really did it would never want us to think he did it, for he also was an English gentleman. He was also something very much better; he was a Christian thief. I hope and believe he was a penitent thief."

"By your account," said his companion laughing, "the Christian thief and the heathen fraud went by contraries. One was sorry he'd done it and the other was sorry he hadn't."

"We mustn't be too hard on either of them," said Father Brown. "Other English gentlemen have stolen before now, and been covered by legal and political protection; and the West also has its own way of covering theft with sophistry. After all, the ruby is not the only kind of valuable stone in the world that has changed owners; it is true of other precious stones; often carved like cameos and coloured like flowers."

The other looked at him inquiringly; and the priest's finger was pointed to the Gothic outline of the great Abbey.

"A great graven stone," he said, "and that was also stolen."

The Miracle of Moon Crescent

MOON CRESCENT was meant in a sense to be as romantic as its name; and the things that happened there were romantic enough in their way. At least it had been an expression of that genuine element of sentiment—historic and almost heroic—which manages to remain side by side with commercialism in the elder cities on the eastern coast of America. It was originally a curve of classical architecture really recalling that eighteenth-century atmosphere in which men like Washington and Jefferson had seemed to be all the more republicans for being aristocrats. Travellers faced with the recurrent query of what they thought of our city were understood to be specially answerable for what they thought of our Moon Crescent. The very contrasts that confuse its original harmony were characteristic of its survival. At one extremity or horn of the crescent its last windows looked over an enclosure like a strip of a gentleman's park, with trees and hedges as formal as a Queen Anne garden.[1] But

"The Miracle of Moon Crescent" first appeared in the May 1924 issue of *Nash's* magazine.

[1] Queen Anne of Great Britain (1665–1714) created a vogue in spacious and elaborately ornate gardens when she introduced the English aristocracy to the concept of landscape architecture.

immediately round the corner, the other windows, even of the same rooms, or rather "apartments," looked out on the blank, unsightly wall of a huge warehouse attached to some ugly industry. The apartments of Moon Crescent itself were at that end remodelled on the monotonous pattern of an American hotel, and rose to a height, which, though lower than the colossal warehouse, would have been called a sky-scraper in London. But the colonnade that ran round the whole frontage upon the street had a grey and weather-stained stateliness suggesting that the ghosts of the Fathers of the Republic might still be walking to and fro in it. The in-sides of the rooms, however, were as neat and new as the last New York fittings could make them, especially at the north-ern end between the neat garden and the blank warehouse wall. They were a system of very small flats, as we should say in England, each consisting of a sitting-room, bedroom, and bathroom, as identical as the hundred cells of a hive. In one of these the celebrated Warren Wynd sat at his desk sorting letters and scattering orders with wonderful rapidity and ex-actitude. He could only be compared to a tidy whirlwind.

Warren Wynd was a very little man with loose grey hair and a pointed beard, seemingly frail but fierily active. He had very wonderful eyes, brighter than stars and stronger than magnets, which nobody who had ever seen them could easily forget. And indeed in his work as a reformer and regulator of many good works he had shown at least that he had a pair of eyes in his head. All sorts of stories and even legends were told of the miraculous rapidity with which he could form a sound judgment, especially of human charac-ter. It was said that he selected the wife who worked with him so long in so charitable a fashion, by picking her out of a whole regiment of women in uniform marching past at some official celebration, some said of the Girl Guides and some of the Women Police.[2] Another story was told of how three tramps, indistinguishable from each other in their community of filth and rags, had presented themselves before him asking for charity. Without a moment's hesitation he had sent one of them to a particular hospital devoted to a certain nervous disorder, had recommended the second to an inebriates' home, and had engaged the third at a handsome salary as his own private servant, a position which he filled successfully for years afterwards. There were, of course, the inevitable anecdotes of his prompt criticisms and curt repartees when brought in contact with Roosevelt, with Henry Ford, and with Mrs. Asquith and all other persons with whom an American public man ought to have a historic interview, if only in the newspapers.[3] Certainly he was not likely to be overawed by such personages; and at the moment here in question he continued very calmly his centrifugal whirl of papers, though the man confronting him was a personage of almost equal importance.

Silas T. Vandam, the millionaire and oil magnate, was a lean man with a long, yellow face and blue-black hair, colours which were the less conspicuous yet somehow the more sinister because his face and figure showed dark against the window and the white warehouse wall outside it; he was buttoned up tight in an elegant overcoat with strips of astrachan. The eager face and brilliant eyes of Wynd, on the other hand, were in the full light from the other window overlooking the little garden, for his chair and desk stood facing it; and though the face was preoccupied, it did not seem unduly

[2] The "Girl Guide" in Chesterton's England was the original of the American Girl Scout.

[3] U.S. President Theodore Roosevelt (1858–1919), industrialist Henry Ford (1863–1947), and English socialite-author Margaret Tennant Asquith (1864–1945), whom the American press had lionized as a lecturer.

preoccupied about the millionaire. Wynd's valet or personal servant, a big, powerful man with flat fair hair, was standing behind his master's desk holding a sheaf of letters; and Wynd's private secretary, a neat, red-haired youth with a sharp face, had his hand already on the door handle, as if guessing some purpose or obeying some gesture of his employer. The room was not only neat but austere to the point of emptiness; for Wynd, with characteristic thoroughness, had rented the whole floor above, and turned it into a loft or storeroom, where all his other papers and possessions were stacked in boxes and corded bales.

"Give these to the floor-clerk, Wilson," said Wynd to the servant holding the letters, "and then get me the pamphlet on the Minneapolis Night Clubs; you'll find it in the bundle marked G. I shall want it in half an hour, but don't disturb me till then. Well, Mr. Vandam, I think your proposition sounds very promising; but I can't give a final answer till I've seen the report. It ought to reach me to-morrow afternoon, and I'll 'phone you at once. I'm sorry I can't say anything more definite just now."

Mr. Vandam seemed to feel that this was something like a polite dismissal; and his sallow, saturnine face suggested that he found a certain irony in the fact.

"Well, I suppose I must be going," he said.

"Very good of you to call, Mr. Vandam," said Wynd, politely; "you will excuse my not coming out, as I've something here I must fix at once. Fenner," he added to the secretary, "show Mr. Vandam to his car, and don't come back again for half an hour. I've something here I want to work out by myself; after that I shall want you."

The three men went out into the hallway together, closing the door behind them. The big servant, Wilson, was turning down the hallway in the direction of the floor-clerk and the other two moving in the opposite direction towards the lift; for Wynd's apartment was high up on the fourteenth floor. They had hardly gone a yard from the closed door when they became conscious that the corridor was filled with a marching and even magnificent figure. The man was very tall and broad-shouldered, his bulk being the more conspicuous for being clad in white or a light grey that looked like it, with a very wide white panama hat and an almost equally wide fringe or halo of almost equally white hair. Set in this aureole his face was strong and handsome, like that of a Roman emperor, save that there was something more than boyish, something a little childish, about the brightness of his eyes and the beatitude of his smile.

"Mr. Warren Wynd in?" he asked, in hearty tones.

"Mr. Warren Wynd is engaged," said Fenner; "he must not be disturbed on any account. I may say I am his secretary and can take any message."

"Mr. Warren Wynd is not at home to the Pope or the Crowned Heads," said Vandam, the oil magnate, with sour satire. "Mr. Warren Wynd is mighty particular. I went in there to hand him over a trifle of twenty thousand dollars on certain conditions, and he told me to call again like as if I was a call-boy."

"It's a fine thing to be a boy," said the stranger, "and a finer to have a call; and I've got a call he's just got to listen to. It's a call out of the great good country out West where the real American is being made while you're all snoring. Just tell him that Art Alboin of Oklahoma City has come to convert him."

"I tell you nobody can see him," said the red-haired secretary sharply. "He has given orders that he is not to be disturbed for half an hour."

"You folks down East are all against being disturbed," said

the breezy Mr. Alboin, "but I calculate there's a big breeze getting up in the West that will have to disturb you. He's been figuring out how much money must go to this and that stuffy old religion; but I tell you any scheme that leaves out the new Great Spirit movement in Texas and Oklahoma, is leaving out the religion of the future."

"Oh, I've sized up those religions of the future," said the millionaire, contemptuously. "I've been through them with a tooth-comb; and they're as mangy as yellow dogs. There was that woman called herself Sophia; ought to have called herself Sapphira, I reckon. Just a plum fraud. Strings tied to all the tables and tambourines. Then there were the Invisible Life bunch; said they could vanish when they liked, and they did vanish, too, and a hundred thousand of my dollars vanished with them. I knew Jupiter Jesus out in Denver; saw him for weeks on end; and he was just a common crook. So was the Patagonian Prophet; you bet he's made a bolt for Patagonia. No, I'm through with all that; from now on I only believe what I see. I believe they call it being an atheist."

"I guess you got me wrong," said the man from Oklahoma, almost eagerly. "I guess I'm as much of an atheist as you are. No supernatural or superstitious stuff in our movement; just plain science. The only real right science is just health, and the only real right health is just breathing. Fill your lungs with the wide air of the prairie and you could blow all your old eastern cities into the sea. You could just puff away their biggest men like thistledown. That's what we do in the new movement out home: we breathe. We don't pray; we breathe."

"Well, I suppose you do," said the secretary, wearily; he had a keen, intelligent face which could hardly conceal the weariness; but he had listened to the two monologues with the admirable patience and politeness (so much in contrast with the legends of impatience and insolence) with which such monologues are listened to in America.

"Nothing supernatural," continued Alboin, "just the great natural fact behind all the supernatural fancies. What did the Jews want with a God except to breathe into man's nostrils the breath of life? We do the breathing into our own nostrils out in Oklahoma. What's the meaning of the very word Spirit? It's just the Greek for breathing exercises. Life, progress, prophecy; it's all breath."

"Some would allow it's all wind," said Vandam; "but I'm glad you've got rid of the divinity stunt, anyhow."

The keen face of the secretary, rather pale against his red hair, showed a flicker of some odd feeling suggestive of a secret bitterness.

"I'm not glad," he said, "I'm just sure. You seem to like being atheists; so you may be just believing what you like to believe. But I wish to God there were a God; and there ain't. It's just my luck."

Without a sound or stir they all became almost creepily conscious at this moment that the group, halted outside Wynd's door, had silently grown from three figures to four. How long the fourth figure had stood there none of the earnest disputants could tell, but he had every appearance of waiting respectfully and even timidly for the opportunity to say something urgent. But to their nervous sensibility he seemed to have sprung up suddenly and silently like a mushroom. And indeed, he looked rather like a big, black mushroom, for he was quite short and his small, stumpy figure was eclipsed by his big, black clerical hat; the resemblance might have been more complete if mushrooms were in the habit of carrying umbrellas, even of a shabby and shapeless sort.

Fenner, the secretary, was conscious of a curious additional surprise at recognizing the figure of a priest; but when the priest turned up a round face under the round hat and innocently asked for Mr. Warren Wynd, he gave the regular negative answer rather more curtly than before. But the priest stood his ground.

"I do really want to see Mr. Wynd," he said. "It seems odd, but that's exactly what I do want to do. I don't want to speak to him. I just want to see him. I just want to see if he's there to be seen."

"Well, I tell you he's there and can't be seen," said Fenner, with increasing annoyance. "What do you mean by saying you want to see if he's there to be seen? Of course he's there. We all left him there five minutes ago and we've stood outside this door ever since."

"Well, I want to see if he's all right," said the priest.

"Why?" demanded the secretary, in exasperation.

"Because I have serious, I might say solemn reasons," said the cleric, gravely, "for doubting whether he is all right."

"Oh, Lord!" cried Vandam, in a sort of fury, "not more superstitions."

"I see I shall have to give my reasons," observed the little cleric, gravely. "I suppose I can't expect you even to let me look through the crack of a door till I tell you the whole story."

He was silent a moment as in reflection, and then went on without noticing the wondering faces around him. "I was walking outside along the front of the colonnade when I saw a very ragged man running hard round the corner at the end of the crescent. He came pounding along the pavement towards me, revealing a great, raw-boned figure and a face I knew. It was the face of a wild Irish fellow I once helped a little; I will not tell you his name. When he saw me he staggered, calling me by mine and saying, 'Saints alive, it's Father

Brown; you're the only man whose face could frighten me to-day.' I knew he meant he'd been doing some wild thing or other, and I don't think my face frightened him much, for he was soon telling me about it. And a very strange thing it was. He asked me if I knew Warren Wynd, and I said no, though I knew he lived near the top of these flats. He said, 'That's a man who thinks he's a saint of God; but if he knew what I was saying of him he should be ready to hang himself.' And he repeated hysterically more than once, 'Yes, ready to hang himself.' I asked him if he'd done any harm to Wynd and his answer was rather a queer one. He said: 'I took a pistol and I loaded it with neither shot nor slug, but only with a curse.' As far as I could make out, all he had done was to go down that little alley between this building and the big warehouse, with an old pistol loaded with a blank charge, and merely fire it against the wall, as if that would bring down the building. 'But as I did it,' he said, 'I cursed him with the great curse, that the justice of God should take him by the hair and the vengeance of hell by the heels, and he should be torn asunder like Judas and the world know him no more.' Well, it doesn't matter now what else I said to the poor, crazy fellow; he went away quieted down a little, and I went round to the back of the building to inspect. And sure enough, in the little alley at the foot of this wall there lay a rusty antiquated pistol; I know enough about pistols to know it had been loaded only with a little powder; there were the black marks of powder and smoke on the wall, and even the mark of the muzzle, but not even a dent of any bullet. He had left no trace of destruction; he had left no trace of anything, except those black marks and that black curse he had hurled into heaven. So I came back here to ask for this Warren Wynd and find out if he's all right."

Fenner the secretary laughed. "I can soon settle that

difficulty for you. I assure you he's quite all right; we left him writing at his desk only a few minutes ago. He was alone in his flat; it's a hundred feet up from the street, and so placed that no shot could have reached him, even if your friend hadn't fired blank. There's no other entrance to this place but this door, and we've been standing outside it ever since."

"All the same," said Father Brown, gravely, "I should like to look in and see."

"Well, you can't," retorted the other. "Good Lord, you don't tell me you think anything of the curse."

"You forget," said the millionaire, with a slight sneer, "the reverend gentleman's whole business is blessings and cursings. Come, sir, if he's been cursed to hell, why don't you bless him back again? What's the good of your blessings if they can't beat an Irish larrykin's curse."

"Does anybody believe such things now?" protested the Westerner.

"Father Brown believes a good number of things, I take it," said Vandam, whose temper was suffering from the past snub and the present bickering. "Father Brown believes a hermit crossed a river on a crocodile conjured out of nowhere, and then he told the crocodile to die, and it sure did. Father Brown believes that some blessed saint or other died, and had his dead body turned into three dead bodies, to be served out to three parishes that were all bent on figuring as his home-town. Father Brown believes that a saint hung his cloak on a sunbeam, and another used his for a boat to cross the Atlantic. Father Brown believes the holy donkey had six legs and the house at Lorretto [sic] flew through the air. He believes in hundreds of stone virgins winking and weeping all day long. It's nothing to him to believe that a man might escape through the keyhole or vanish out of a locked room. I reckon he doesn't take much stock of the laws of nature."[4]

"Anyhow, I have to take stock in the laws of Warren Wynd," said the secretary, wearily, "and it's his rule that he's to be left alone when he says so. Wilson will tell you just the same," for the large servant who had been sent for the pamphlet, passed placidly down the corridor even as he spoke, carrying the pamphlet, but serenely passing the door. "He'll go and sit on the bench by the floor-clerk and twiddle his thumbs till he's wanted; but he won't go in before then; and nor will I. I reckon we both know which side our bread is buttered; and it'd take a good many of Father Brown's saints and angels to make us forget it."

"As for saints and angels—" began the priest.

"It's all nonsense," repeated Fenner. "I don't want to say anything offensive, but that sort of thing may be very well for crypts and cloisters and all sorts of moonshiny places. But ghosts can't get through a closed door in an American hotel."

"But men can open a door, even in an American hotel," replied Father Brown, patiently. "And it seems to me the simplest thing would be to open it."

"It would be simple enough to lose me my job," answered the secretary, "and Warren Wynd doesn't like his secretaries so simple as that. Not simple enough to believe in the sort of fairy tales you seem to believe in."

"Well," said the priest gravely, "it is true enough that I believe in a good many things that you probably don't. But it would take a considerable time to explain all the things I

[4] Vandam is ridiculing popular Catholic folklore and legend, as that of Saint Teilo, whose body was multiplied to satisfy three claimants; Saint Goar, who (among others) used a sunbeam to hang up his cloak; Saint Raymund, who sailed to Barcelona on his cloak; the Virgin Mary's home being flown to Loreto by angels to save it from the Turks; and so on.

believe in, and all the reasons I have for thinking I'm right. It would take about two seconds to open that door and prove I am wrong."

Something in the phrase seemed to please the more wild and restless spirit of the man from the West.

"I'll allow I'd love to prove you wrong," said Alboin, striding suddenly past them, "and I will."

He threw open the door of the flat and looked in. The first glimpse showed that Warren Wynd's chair was empty. The second glance showed that his room was empty also.

Fenner, electrified with energy in his turn, dashed past the other into the apartment.

"He's in his bedroom," he said curtly, "he must be."

As he disappeared into the inner chamber the other men stood in the empty outer room staring about them. The severity and simplicity of its fittings, which had already been noted, returned on them with a rigid challenge. Certainly in this room there was no question of hiding a mouse, let alone a man. There were no curtains and, what is rare in American arrangements, no cupboards. Even the desk was no more than a plain table with a shallow drawer and a tilted lid. The chairs were hard and high-backed skeletons. A moment after the secretary reappeared at the inner door, having searched the two inner rooms. A staring negation stood in his eyes, and his mouth seemed to move in a mechanical detachment from it as he said sharply: "He didn't come out through here?"

Somehow the others did not even think it necessary to answer that negation in the negative. Their minds had come up against something like the blank wall of the warehouse that stared in at the opposite window, gradually turning from white to grey as dusk slowly descended with the advancing afternoon. Vandam walked over to the window-sill against which he had leant half an hour before and looked out of the open window. There was no pipe or fire-escape, no shelf or foothold of any kind on the sheer fall to the little by-street below, there was nothing on the similar expanse of wall that rose many stories above. There was even less variation on the other side of the street; there was nothing whatever but the wearisome expanse of whitewashed wall. He peered downwards, as if expecting to see the vanished philanthropist lying in a suicidal wreck on the path. He could see nothing but one small dark object which, though diminished by distance, might well be the pistol that the priest had found lying there. Meanwhile, Fenner had walked to the other window, which looked out from a wall equally blank and inaccessible, but looking out over a small ornamental park instead of a side street. Here a clump of trees interrupted the actual view of the ground; but they reached but a little way up the huge human cliff. Both turned back into the room and faced each other in the gathering twilight, where the last silver gleams of daylight on the shiny tops of desks and tables were rapidly turning grey. As if the twilight itself irritated him, Fenner touched the switch and the scene sprang into the startling distinctness of electric light.

"As you said just now," said Vandam grimly, "there's no shot from down there could hit him, even if there was a shot in the gun. But even if he was hit with a bullet he wouldn't have just burst like a bubble."

The secretary, who was paler than ever, glanced irritably at the bilious visage of the millionaire.

"What's got you started on those morbid notions? Who's talking about bullets and bubbles? Why shouldn't he be alive?"

"Why not indeed?" replied Vandam smoothly. "If you'll tell me where he is, I'll tell you how he got there."

After a pause the secretary muttered, rather sulkily: "I suppose you're right. We're right up against the very thing we were talking about. It'd be a queer thing if you or I ever came to think there was anything in cursing. But who could have harmed Wynd shut up in here?"

Mr. Alboin, of Oklahoma, had been standing rather astraddle in the middle of the room, his white, hairy halo as well as his round eyes seeming to radiate astonishment. At this point he said, abstractedly, with something of the irrelevant impudence of an *enfant terrible*:

"You didn't cotton to him much, did you, Mr. Vandam?"

Mr. Vandam's long yellow face seemed to grow longer as it grew more sinister, while he smiled and answered quietly:

"If it comes to these coincidences, it was you, I think, who said that a wind from the West would blow away our big men like thistledown."

"I know I said it would," said the Westerner, with candour; "but all the same, how the devil could it?"

The silence was broken by Fenner saying with an abruptness amounting to violence:

"There's only one thing to say about this affair. It simply hasn't happened. It can't have happened."

"Oh, yes," said Father Brown out of the corner, "it has happened all right."

They all jumped; for the truth was they had all forgotten the insignificant little man who had originally induced them to open the door. And the recovery of memory went with a sharp reversal of mood; it came back to them with a rush that they had all dismissed him as a superstitious dreamer for even hinting at the very thing that had since happened before their eyes.

"Snakes!" cried the impetuous Westerner, like one speaking before he could stop himself. "Suppose there were something in it, after all!"

"I must confess," said Fenner, frowning at the table, "that his reverence's anticipations were apparently well founded. I don't know whether he has anything else to tell us."

"He might possibly tell us," said Vandam, sardonically, "what the devil we are to do now."

The little priest seemed to accept the position in a modest, but matter-of-fact manner. "The only thing I can think of," he said, "is first to tell the authorities of this place, and then to see if there were any more traces of my man who let off the pistol. He vanished round the other end of the Crescent where the little garden is. There are seats there, and it's a favourite place for tramps."

Direct consultations with the headquarters of the hotel, leading to indirect consultations with the authorities of the police, occupied them for a considerable time; and it was already nightfall when they went out under the long, classical curve of the colonnade. The crescent looked as cold and hollow as the moon after which it was named, and the moon itself was rising luminous but spectral behind the black tree-tops when they turned the corner by the little public garden. Night veiled much of what was merely urban and artificial about the place; and as they melted into the shadows of the trees they had a strange feeling of having suddenly travelled many hundred miles from their homes. When they had walked in silence for a little, Alboin, who really had something elemental about him, suddenly exploded.

"I give up," he cried; "I hand in my checks. I never thought I should come to such things; but what happens when the things come to you? I beg your pardon, Father Brown; I reckon I'll just come across, so far as you and your fairytales are concerned. After this, it's me for the fairytales. Why, you said yourself, Mr. Vandam, that you're an atheist

and only believe what you see. Well, what was it you did see?
Or rather, what was it you didn't see?"

"I know," said Vandam and nodded in a gloomy fashion.

"Oh, it's partly all this moon and trees that get on one's
nerves," said Fenner obstinately. "Trees always look queer by
moonlight, with their branches crawling about. Look at
that—"

Yes," said Father Brown, standing still and peering at the
moon through a tangle of trees. "That's a very queer branch
up there."

When he spoke again he only said:

"I thought it was a broken branch."

But this time there was a catch in his voice that unaccount-
ably turned his hearers cold. Something that looked rather
like a dead branch was certainly dependent in a limp fashion
from the tree that showed dark against the moon; but it was
not a dead branch. When they came close to it to see what it
was, Fenner sprang away again with a ringing oath. Then he
ran in again and loosened a rope from the neck of a dingy
little body dangling with drooping plumes of grey hair.
Somehow he knew that the body was a dead body before he
managed to take it down from the tree. A very long coil of
rope was wrapped round and round the branches, and a
comparatively short length of it hung from the fork of the
branch to the body. A large garden tub was rolled a yard or so
from under the feet, like the stool kicked away from the feet
of a suicide.

"Oh, my God," said Alboin, so that it seemed as much a
prayer as an oath. "What was it that man said about him?—'If
he knew, he would be ready to hang himself.' Wasn't that
what he said, Father Brown?"

"Yes," said Father Brown.

"Well," said Vandam in a hollow voice, "I never thought to

see or say such a thing. But what can one say except that the curse has worked?"

Fenner was standing with hands covering his face; and the priest laid a hand on his arm and said, gently, "Were you very fond of him?"

The secretary dropped his hands and his white face was ghastly under the moon.

"I hated him like hell," he said; "and if he died by a curse it might have been mine."

The pressure of the priest's hand on his arm tightened; and the priest said, with an earnestness he had hardly yet shown: "It wasn't your curse; pray be comforted."

The police of the district had considerable difficulty in dealing with the four witnesses who were involved in the case. All of them were reputable, and even reliable people in the ordinary sense; and one of them was a person of considerable power and importance: Silas Vandam of the Oil Trust. The first police officer who tried to express scepticism about his story struck sparks from the steel of that magnate's mind very rapidly indeed.

"Don't you talk to me about sticking to the facts," said the millionaire with asperity. "I've stuck to a good many facts before you were born and a few of the facts have stuck to me. I'll give you the facts all right if you've got the sense to take 'em down correctly."

The policeman in question was youthful and subordinate, and had a hazy idea that the millionaire was too political to be treated as an ordinary citizen; so he passed him and his companions on to a more stolid superior, one Inspector Collins, a grizzled man with a grimly comfortable way of talking; as one who was genial but would stand no nonsense.

"Well, well," he said, looking at the three figures before

him with twinkling eyes, "this seems to be a funny sort of a tale."

Father Brown had already gone about his daily business; but Silas Vandam had suspended even the gigantic business of the markets for an hour or so to testify to his remarkable experience. Fenner's business as secretary had ceased in a sense with his employer's life; and the great Art Alboin, having no business in New York or anywhere else, except the spreading of the Breath of Life or religion of the Great Spirit, had nothing to draw him away at the moment from the immediate affair. So they stood in a row in the inspector's office, prepared to corroborate each other.

"Now I'd better tell you to start with," said the inspector cheerfully, "that it's no good for anybody to come to me with any miraculous stuff. I'm a practical man and a policeman, and that sort of thing is all very well for priests and parsons. This priest of yours seems to have got you all worked up about some story of a dreadful death and judgment; but I'm going to leave him and his religion out of it altogether. If Wynd came out of that room, somebody let him out. And if Wynd was found hanging on that tree, somebody hung him there."

"Quite so," said Fenner; "but as our evidence is that nobody let him out, the question is how could anybody have hung him there?"

"How could anybody have a nose on his face?" asked the inspector. "He had a nose on his face and he had a noose round his neck. Those are facts; and as I say, I'm a practical man and go by the facts. It can't have been done by a miracle, so it must have been done by a man."

Alboin had been standing rather in the background; and indeed his broad figure seemed to form a natural background to the leaner and more vivacious men in front of him. His white head was bowed with a certain abstraction; but as the inspector said the last sentence, he lifted it, shaking his hoary mane in a leonine fashion, and looking dazed but awakened. He moved forward into the centre of the group; and they had a vague feeling that he was even vaster than before. They had been only too prone to take him for a fool or a mountebank; but he was not altogether wrong when he said that there was in him a certain depth of lungs and life, like a west wind stored up in its strength, which might some day puff lighter things away.

"So you're a practical man, Mr. Collins," he said, in a voice at once soft and heavy. "It must be the second or third time you've mentioned in this little conversation that you are a practical man; so I can't be mistaken about that. And a very interesting little fact it is for anybody engaged in writing your life, letters, and table-talk, with portrait at the age of five, daguerreotype of your grandmother and views of the old home-town; and I'm sure your biographer won't forget to mention it, along with the fact that you had a pug nose with a pimple on it, and were nearly too fat to walk. And as you're a practical man, perhaps you would just go on practising till you've brought Warren Wynd to life again, and found out exactly how a practical man gets through a deal door.[5] But I think you've got it wrong. You're not a practical man. You're a practical joke; that's what you are. The Almighty was having a bit of fun with us when he thought of you."

With a characteristic sense of drama he went sailing towards the door before the astonished inspector could reply; and no after-recriminations could rob him of a certain appearance of triumph.

"I think you were perfectly right," said Fenner. "If those are practical men, give me priests."

[5] A "deal door", in Art Alboin's usage, and Chesterton's, is a door made of pine or fir timber.

Another attempt was made to reach an official version of the event, when the official authorities fully realized who were the backers of the story, and what were the implications of it. Already it had broken out in the Press in its most sensationally and even shamelessly psychic form. Interviews with Vandam on his marvellous adventure, articles about Father Brown and his mystical intuitions, soon led those who feel responsible for guiding the public to wish to guide it into a wiser channel. Next time the inconvenient witnesses were approached in a more indirect and tactful manner. They were told, almost in an airy fashion, that Professor Vair was very much interested in such abnormal experiences; was especially interested in their own astonishing case. Professor Vair was a psychologist of great distinction; he had been known to take a detached interest in criminology; it was only some little time afterwards that they discovered that he was in any way connected with the police.

Professor Vair was a courteous gentleman, quietly dressed in pale grey clothes, with an artistic tie and a fair, pointed beard; he looked more like a landscape painter to anyone not acquainted with a certain special type of don. He had an air not only of courtesy, but of frankness.

"Yes, yes, I know," he said smiling; "I can guess what you must have gone through. The police do not shine in inquiries of a psychic sort, do they? Of course, dear old Collins said he only wanted the facts. What an absurd blunder! In a case of this kind we emphatically do *not* only want the facts. It is even more essential to have the fancies."

"Do you mean," asked Vandam gravely, "that all that we call the facts were merely fancies?"

"Not at all," said the professor; "I only mean that the police are stupid in thinking they can leave out the psychological element in these things. Well, of course, the psychological element is everything in everything, though it is only just beginning to be understood. To begin with, take the element called personality. Now I have heard of this priest, Father Brown, before; and he is one of the most remarkable men of our time. Men of that sort carry a sort of atmosphere with them; and nobody knows how much his nerves and even his very senses are affected by it for the time being. People are hypnotized—yes, hypnotized; for hypnotism, like everything else, is a matter of degree; it enters slightly into all daily conversation; it is not necessarily conducted by a man in evening-dress on a platform in a public hall. Father Brown's religion has always understood the psychology of atmospheres, and knows how to appeal to everything simultaneously; even, for instance, to the sense of smell. It understands those curious effects produced by music on animals and human beings; it can—"

"Hang it," protested Fenner, "you don't think he walked down the corridor carrying a church organ?"

"He knows better than to do that," said Professor Vair laughing. "He knows how to concentrate the essence of all these spiritual sounds and sights, and even smells, in a few restrained gestures; in an art or school of manners. He could contrive so to concentrate your minds on the supernatural by his mere presence, that natural things slipped off your minds to left and right unnoticed. Now you know," he proceeded with a return to cheerful good sense, "that the more we study it the more queer the whole question of human evidence becomes. There is not one man in twenty who really observes things at all. There is not one man in a hundred who observes them with real precision; certainly not one in a hundred who can first observe, then remember and finally describe. Scientific experiments have been made again and again showing that men under a strain have thought a door was shut when it was open, or open when it was shut. Men have differed about the number of doors or windows in a wall just in front of them. They have suffered optical illusions in broad daylight. They have done this even without the hypnotic effect of personality; but here we have a very powerful and persuasive personality bent upon fixing only one picture on your minds; the picture of the wild Irish rebel shaking his pistol at the sky and firing that vain volley, whose echoes were the thunders of heaven."

"Professor," cried Fenner, "I'd swear on my deathbed that door never opened."

"Recent experiments," went on the professor, quietly, "have suggested that our consciousness is not continuous, but is a succession of very rapid impressions like a cinema; it is possible that somebody or something may, so to speak, slip in or out between the scenes. It acts only in the instant while the curtain is down. Probably the patter of conjurers and all forms of sleight of hand depend on what we may call these black flashes of blindness between the flashes of sight. Now this priest and preacher of transcendental notions had filled you with a transcendental imagery; the image of the Celt like a Titan shaking the tower with his curse.[6] Probably he accompanied it with some slight but compelling gesture, pointing your eyes and minds in the direction of the unknown destroyer below. Or perhaps something else happened, or somebody else passed by."

"Wilson the servant," grunted Alboin, "went down the hallway to wait on the bench, but I guess he didn't distract us much."

"You never know how much," replied Vair; "it might have

[6] Professor Vair alludes to the Greek myth of the rebel Titan Prometheus, whose defiant curse of Jupiter ("in yon ethereal tower") was dramatized in Act I of Shelley's *Prometheus Unbound* (1819).

been that or more likely your eyes following some gesture of the priest as he told his tale of magic. It was in one of those black flashes that Mr. Warren Wynd slipped out of his door and went to his death. That is the most probable explanation. It is an illustration of the new discovery. The mind is not a continuous line, but rather a dotted line."

"Very dotted," said Fenner feebly. "Not to say dotty."

"You don't really believe," asked Vair, "that your employer was shut up in a room like a box?"

"It's better than believing that I ought to be shut up in a room like a padded cell," answered Fenner. "That's what I complain of in your suggestions, professor. I'd as soon believe in a priest who believes in a miracle, as disbelieve in any man having any right to believe in a fact. The priest tells me that a man can appeal to a God I know nothing about, to avenge him by the laws of some higher justice that I know nothing about. There's nothing for me to say except that I know nothing about it. But at least if the poor Paddy's prayer and pistol could be heard in a higher world, that higher world might act in some way that seems odd to us. But you ask me to disbelieve the facts of this world as they appear to my own five wits. According to you, a whole procession of Irishmen carrying blunderbusses may have walked through this room while we were talking, so long as they took care to tread on the blind spots in our minds. Miracles of the monkish sort, like materializing a crocodile or hanging a cloak on a sunbeam, seem quite sane compared to you."

"Oh, well," said Professor Vair, rather curtly, "if you are resolved to believe in your priest and his miraculous Irishman, I can say no more. I'm afraid you have not had an opportunity of studying psychology."

"No," said Fenner dryly, "but I've had an opportunity of studying psychologists."

And, bowing politely, he led his deputation out of the room and did not speak till he got into the street; then he addressed them rather explosively.

"Raving lunatics!" cried Fenner in a fume. "What the devil do they think is to happen to the world if nobody knows whether he's seen anything or not? I wish I'd blown his silly head off with a blank charge, and then explained that I did it in a blind flash. Father Brown's miracle may be miraculous or no, but he said it would happen and it did happen. All these blasted cranks can do is to see a thing happen and then say it didn't. Look here, I think we owe it to the padre to testify to his little demonstration. We're all sane, solid men who never believed in anything. We weren't drunk. We weren't devout. It simply happened just as he said it would."

"I quite agree," said the millionaire. "It may be the beginning of mighty big things in the spiritual line; but anyhow, the man who's in the spiritual line himself, Father Brown, has certainly scored over this business."

A few days afterwards Father Brown received a very polite note signed Silas T. Vandam, and asking him if he could attend at a stated hour at the apartment which was the scene of the disappearance in order to take steps for the establishment of that marvellous occurrence. The occurrence itself had already begun to break out in the newspapers, and was being taken up everywhere by the enthusiasts of occultism. Father Brown saw the flaring posters inscribed "Suicide of Vanishing Man," and "Man's Curse Hangs Philanthropist," as he passed towards Moon Crescent and mounted the steps on the way to the elevator. He found the little group much as he left it, Vandam, Alboin, and the secretary; but there was an entirely new respectfulness and even reverence in their tone towards himself. They were standing by Wynd's desk, on which lay a large paper and writing materials, as they turned to greet him.

"Father Brown," said the spokesman, who was the white-haired Westerner somewhat sobered with his responsibility, "we asked you here in the first place to offer our apologies and our thanks. We recognize that it was you that spotted the spiritual manifestation from the first. We were hard-shell sceptics, all of us; but we realize now that a man must break that shell to get at the great things behind the world. You stand for those things; you stand for that super-normal explanation of things; and we have to hand it to you. And in the second place, we feel that this document would not be complete without your signature. We are notifying the exact facts to the Psychical Research Society, because the newspaper accounts are not what you might call exact. We've stated how the curse was spoken out in the street; how the man was sealed up here in a room like a box; how the curse dissolved him straight into thin air, and in some unthinkable way materialized him as a suicide hoisted on a gallows. That's all we can say about it; but all that we know, and have seen with our own eyes. And as you were the first to believe in the miracle, we all feel that you ought to be the first to sign."

"No, really," said Father Brown, in embarrassment. "I don't think I should like to do that."

"You mean you'd rather not sign first?"

"I mean I'd rather not sign at all," said Father Brown, modestly. "You see, it doesn't quite do for a man in my position to joke about miracles."

"But it was you who said it was a miracle," said Alboin, staring.

"I'm so sorry," said Father Brown; "I'm afraid there's some mistake. I don't think I ever said it was a miracle. All I said was that it might happen. What you said was that it couldn't happen, because it would be a miracle if it did. And then it did. And so you said it was a miracle. But I never said a word about miracles or magic or anything of the sort from beginning to end."

"But I thought you believed in miracles," broke out the secretary.

"Yes," answered Father Brown, "I believe in miracles. I believe in man-eating tigers, but I don't see them running about everywhere. If I want any miracles, I know where to get them."

"I can't understand your taking this line, Father Brown," said Vandam, earnestly. "It seems so narrow; and you don't look narrow to me, though you are a parson. Don't you see a miracle like this will knock all materialism endways? It will just tell the whole world in big print that spiritual powers can work and do work. You'll be serving religion as no parson ever served it yet."

The priest had stiffened a little and seemed in some strange way clothed with unconscious and impersonal dignity, for all his stumpy figure. "Well," he said, "you wouldn't suggest I should serve religion by what I know to be a lie? I don't know precisely what you mean by the phrase; and, to be quite candid, I'm not sure you do. Lying may be serving religion; I'm sure it's not serving God. And since you are harping so insistently on what I believe, wouldn't it be as well if you had some sort of notion of what it is?"

"I don't think I quite understand," observed the millionaire, curiously.

"I don't think you do," said Father Brown, with simplicity. "You say this thing was done by spiritual powers. What spiritual powers? You don't think the holy angels took him and hung him on a garden tree, do you? And as for the unholy angels—no, no, no. The men who did this did a wicked thing, but they went no further than their own wickedness; they weren't wicked enough to be dealing with spiritual powers. I know something about Satanism, for my sins; I've been forced to know. I know what it is, what it practically always is. It's proud and it's sly. It likes to be superior; it loves to horrify the innocent with things half understood, to make children's flesh creep. That's why it's so fond of mysteries and initiations and secret societies and all the rest of it. Its eyes are turned inwards, and however grand and grave it may look, it's always hiding a small, mad smile." He shuddered suddenly, as if caught in an icy draught of air. "Never mind about them; they've got nothing to do with this, believe me. Do you think that poor, wild Irishman of mine, who ran raving down the street, who blurted out half of it when he first saw my face, and ran away for fear he should blurt out more, do you think Satan confides any secrets to him? I admit he joined in a plot, probably in a plot with two other men worse than himself; but for all that, he was just in an everlasting rage when he rushed down the lane and let off his pistol and his curse."

"But what on earth does all this mean?" demanded Vandam. "Letting off a toy pistol and a twopenny curse wouldn't do what was done, except by a miracle. It wouldn't make Wynd disappear like a fairy. It wouldn't make him reappear a quarter of a mile away with a rope round his neck."

"No," said Father Brown, sharply, "but what would it do?"

"And still I don't follow you," said the millionaire gravely.

"I say, what would it do?" repeated the priest, showing, for the first time, a sort of animation verging on annoyance. "You keep on repeating that a blank pistol-shot wouldn't do this, and wouldn't do that; that if that was all, the murder wouldn't happen or the miracle wouldn't happen. It doesn't seem to occur to you to ask what would happen. What would happen to you, if a lunatic let off a firearm without rhyme or reason right under your window? What's the very first thing that would happen?"

Vandam looked thoughtful. "I guess I should look out of the window," he said.

"Yes," said Father Brown, "you'd look out of the window. That's the whole story. It's a sad story, but it's finished now; and there were extenuating circumstances."

"Why should looking out of the window hurt him?" asked Alboin. "He didn't fall out, or he'd have been found in the lane."

"No," said Father Brown, in a low voice. "He didn't fall. He rose." There was something in his voice like the groan of a gong, a note of doom, but otherwise he went on steadily:

"He rose, but not on wings; not on the wings of any holy or unholy angels. He rose at the end of a rope, exactly as you saw him in the garden; a noose dropped over the head the moment it was poked out of the window. Don't you remember Wilson, that big servant of his, a man of huge strength, while Wynd was the lightest of little shrimps? Didn't Wilson go to the floor above to get a pamphlet, to a room full of luggage corded in coils and coils of rope? Has Wilson been seen since that day? I fancy not."

"Do you mean," asked the secretary, "that Wilson whisked him clean out of his own window like a trout on a line?"

"Yes," said the other, "and let him down again out of the other window into the park, where the third accomplice hooked him on to a tree. Remember the lane was always empty; remember the wall opposite was quite blank; remember it was all over in five minutes after the Irishman gave the signal with the pistol. There were three of them in it of course; and I wonder whether you can all guess who they were."

They were all three staring at the plain, square window and the blank, white wall beyond; and nobody answered.

"By the way," went on Father Brown, "don't think I blame you for jumping to preternatural conclusions. The reason's very simple, really. You all swore you were hard-shelled materialists; and as a matter of fact you were all balanced on the very edge of belief—of belief in almost anything. There are thousands balanced on it to-day; but it's a sharp, uncomfortable edge to sit on. You won't rest till you believe something; that's why Mr. Vandam went through new religions with a tooth-comb and Mr. Alboin quotes Scripture for his religion of breathing exercises, and Mr. Fenner grumbles at the very God he denies. That's where you all split; it's natural to believe in the supernatural. It never feels natural to accept only natural things. But though it wanted only a touch to tip you into preternaturalism about these things, these things really were only natural things. They were not only natural, they were almost unnaturally simple. I suppose there never was quite so simple a story as this."

Fenner laughed and then looked puzzled. "I don't understand one thing," he said. "If it was Wilson, how did Wynd come to have a man like that on such intimate terms? How did he come to be killed by a man he'd seen every day for years? He was famous as being a judge of men."

Father Brown thumped his umbrella on the ground with an emphasis he rarely showed.

"Yes," he said, almost fiercely. "That was how he came to be killed. He was killed for just that. He was killed for being a judge of men."

They all stared at him, but he went on almost as if they were not there.

"What is any man that he should be a judge of men?" he demanded. "These three were the tramps that once stood before him and were dismissed rapidly right and left to one place or another; as if for them there were no cloak of courtesy, no stages of intimacy, no free will in friendship. And twenty years has not exhausted the indignation born of that unfathomable insult in that moment when he dared to know them at a glance."

"Yes," said the secretary; "I understand . . . and I understand how it is that you understand—all sorts of things."

"Well, I'm blamed if I understand," cried the breezy Western gentleman boisterously. "Your Wilson and your Irishman seem to be just a couple of cut-throat murderers who killed their benefactor. I've no use for a black and bloody assassin of that sort in my morality, whether it's religion or not."

"He was a black and bloody assassin, no doubt," said Fenner, quietly. "I'm not defending him; but I suppose it's Father Brown's business to pray for all men, even for a man like—"

"Yes," assented Father Brown, "it's my business to pray for all men, even for a man like Warren Wynd."

The Resurrection of Father Brown

THERE was a brief period during which Father Brown enjoyed, or rather did not enjoy, something like fame. He was a nine days' wonder in the newspapers; he was even a common topic of controversy in the weekly reviews; his exploits were narrated eagerly and inaccurately in any number of clubs and drawing-rooms, especially in America. Incongruous and indeed incredible as it may seem to any one who knew him, his adventures as a detective were even made the subject of short stories appearing in magazines.

Strangely enough, this wandering limelight struck him in the most obscure, or at least the most remote, of his many places of residence. He had been sent out to officiate, as something between a missionary and a parish priest, in one of those sections of the northern coast of South America, where strips of country still cling insecurely to European powers, or are continually threatening to become independent republics, under the gigantic shadow of President Monroe. The population was red and brown with pink spots; that is, it was Spanish-American, and largely Spanish-American-Indian, but there was a considerable and increasing infiltration of

"The Resurrection of Father Brown" first appeared as the lead story in *The Incredulity of Father Brown*, published in June 1926.

Americans of the northern sort—Englishmen, Germans and the rest. And the trouble seems to have begun when one of these visitors, very recently landed and very much annoyed at having lost one of his bags, approached the first building of which he came in sight; which happened to be the mission-house and chapel attached to it, in front of which ran a long veranda and a long row of stakes, up which were trained the black twisted vines, their square leaves red with autumn. Behind them, also in a row, a number of human beings sat almost as rigid as the stakes, and coloured in some fashion like the vines. For while their broad brimmed hats were as black as their unblinking eyes, the complexions of many of them might have been made out of the dark red timber of those transatlantic forests. Many of them were smoking very long thin black cigars; and in all that group the smoke was almost the only moving thing. The visitor would probably have described them as natives, though some of them were very proud of Spanish blood. But he was not one to draw any fine distinction between Spaniards and Red Indians, being rather disposed to dismiss people from the scene when once he had convicted them of being native to it.

He was a newspaper man from Kansas City, a lean, light-haired man with what Meredith called an adventurous nose; one could almost fancy it found its way by feeling its way and moved like the proboscis of an ant-eater. His name was Snaith, and his parents, after some obscure meditation, had called him Saul, a fact which he had the good feeling to conceal as far as possible. Indeed, he had ultimately compromised by calling himself Paul, though by no means for the same reason that had affected the Apostle of the Gentiles. On the contrary, so far as he had any views on such things, the name of the persecutor would have been more appropriate; for he regarded organized religion with the conventional contempt which can be learnt more easily from Ingersoll than from Voltaire.[1] And this was, as it happened, the not very important side of his character which he turned towards the mission station and the groups in front of the veranda. Something in their shameless repose and indifference inflamed his own fury of efficiency; and as he could get no particular answer to his first questions, he began to do all the talking himself.

Standing out there in the strong sunshine, a spick and span figure in his Panama hat and neat clothes, his grip-sack held in a steely grip, he began to shout at the people in the shadow. He began to explain to them very loudly why they were lazy and filthy and bestially ignorant and lower than the beasts that perish, in case this problem should have previously exercised their minds.[2] In his opinion it was the deleterious influence of priests that had made them so miserably poor and so hopelessly oppressed that they were able to sit in the shade and smoke and do nothing.

"And a mighty soft crowd you must be at that," he said, "to be bullied by these stuck-up josses because they walk about in their mitres and their tiaras and their gold copes and other glad rags, looking down on everybody else like dirt—being bamboozled by crowns and canopies and sacred umbrellas like a kid at a pantomime; just because a pompous old High Priest of Mumbo-Jumbo looks as if he was the lord of the earth. What about you? What do you look like, you poor simps? I tell you that's why you're way-back in barbarism and can't read or write and—"

At this point the High Priest of Mumbo-Jumbo came in an

---

[1] Though a superb orator, the American freethinker Robert Ingersoll (1833–99) had neither the intellect nor the scholarship of the brilliant French rationalist Voltaire (1694–1778).

[2] Ironically for him, Snaith's harangue echoes the 49th Psalm, "Man that is in honour, and understandeth not, is like the beasts that perish."

undignified hurry out of the door of the mission house, not looking very like a lord of the earth, but rather like a bundle of black second-hand clothes buttoned round a short bolster in the semblance of a guy.[3] He was not wearing his tiara, supposing him to possess one, but a shabby broad hat not very dissimilar from those of the Spanish Indians, and it was thrust to the back of his head with a gesture of botheration. He seemed just about to speak to the motionless natives when he caught sight of the stranger and said quickly:

"Oh, can I be of any assistance? Would you like to come inside?"

Mr. Paul Snaith came inside; and it was the beginning of a considerable increase of that journalist's information on many things. Presumably his journalistic instinct was stronger than his prejudices, as, indeed, it often is in clever journalists; and he asked a good many questions, the answers to which interested and surprised him. He discovered that the Indians could read and write, for the simple reason that the priest had taught them; but that they did not read or write any more than they could help, from a natural preference for more direct communications. He learned that these strange people, who sat about in heaps in the veranda without stirring a hair, could work quite hard on their own patches of land; especially those of them who were more than half Spanish; and he learned with still more astonishment that they all had patches of land that were really their own. That much was part of a stubborn tradition that seemed quite native to natives. But in that also the priest had played a certain part; and by doing so had taken perhaps what was his first and last part in politics, if it was only local politics. There had recently swept through that region

[3] The priest's shabby appearance resembles the straw-stuffed effigies burned all over England on Guy Fawkes Day, November 5, to celebrate the exposure of the infamous "Gunpowder Plot" of 1605.

one of those fevers of atheist and almost anarchist Radicalism which break out periodically in countries of the Latin culture, generally beginning in a secret society and generally ending in a civil war and in very little else. The local leader of the iconoclastic party was a certain Alvarez, a rather picturesque adventurer of Portuguese nationality but, as his enemies said, of partly negro origin, the head of any number of lodges and temples of initiation of the sort that in such places clothe even atheism with something mystical. The leader on the more conservative side was a much more commonplace person, a very wealthy man named Mendoza, the owner of many factories and quite respectable, but not very exciting. It was the general opinion that the cause of law and order would have been entirely lost if it had not adopted a more popular policy of its own, in the form of securing land for the peasants; and this movement had mainly originated from the little mission station of Father Brown.

While he was talking to the journalist, Mendoza, the Conservative leader, came in. He was a stout, dark man, with a bald head like a pear and a round body also like a pear; he was smoking a very fragrant cigar, but he threw it away, perhaps a little theatrically, when he came into the presence of the priest, as if he had been entering church; and bowed with a curve that in so corpulent a gentleman seemed quite improbable. He was always exceedingly serious in his social gestures, especially towards religious institutions. He was one of those laymen who are much more ecclesiastical than ecclesiastics. It embarrassed Father Brown a good deal, especially when carried thus into private life.

"I think I am an anti-clerical," Father Brown would say with a faint smile; "but there wouldn't be half so much clericalism if they would only leave things to the clerics."

"Why, Mr. Mendoza," exclaimed the journalist with a new

animation, "I think we have met before. Weren't you at the Trade Congress in Mexico last year?"

The heavy eyelids of Mr. Mendoza showed a flutter of recognition, and he smiled in his slow way. "I remember."

"Pretty big business done there in an hour or two," said Snaith with relish. "Made a good deal of difference to you, too, I guess."

"I have been very fortunate," said Mendoza modestly.

"Don't you believe it!" cited the enthusiastic Snaith. "Good fortune comes to the people who know when to catch hold; and you caught hold good and sure. But I hope I'm not interrupting your business?"

"Not at all," said the other. "I often have the honour of calling on the padre for a little talk. Merely for a little talk."

It seemed as if this familiarity between Father Brown and a successful and even famous man of business completed the reconciliation between the priest and the practical Mr. Snaith. He felt, it might be supposed, a new respectability clothe the station and the mission, and was ready to overlook such occasional reminders of the existence of religion as a chapel and a presbytery can seldom wholly avoid. He became quite enthusiastic about the priest's programme—at least on its secular and social side; and announced himself ready at any moment to act in the capacity of live wire for its communication to the world at large. And it was at this point that Father Brown began to find the journalist rather more troublesome in his sympathy than in his hostility.

Mr. Paul Snaith set out vigorously to feature Father Brown. He sent long and loud eulogies on him across the continent to his newspaper in the Middle West. He took snapshots of the unfortunate cleric in the most commonplace occupations and exhibited them in gigantic photographs in the gigantic Sunday papers of the United States. He turned his sayings into slogans, and was continually presenting the world with "A Message" from the reverend gentleman in South America. Any stock less strong and strenuously receptive than the American race would have become very much bored with Father Brown. As it was, he received handsome and eager offers to go on a lecturing tour in the States; and when he declined the terms were raised with expressions of respectful wonder. A series of stories about him, like the stories of Sherlock Holmes, were, by the instrumentality of Mr. Snaith, planned out and put before the hero with requests for his assistance and encouragement. As the priest found they had started, he could offer no suggestion except that they should stop. And this in turn was taken by Mr. Snaith as the text for a discussion on whether Father Brown should disappear temporarily over a cliff, in the manner of Dr. Watson's hero.[4] To all these demands the priest had patiently to reply in writing, saying that he would consent on such terms to the temporary cessation of the stories and begging that a considerable interval might occur before they began again. The notes he wrote grew shorter and shorter; and as he wrote the last of them, he sighed.

Needless to say, this strange boom in the North reacted on the little outpost in the South where he had expected to live in so lonely an exile. The considerable English and American population already on the spot began to be proud of possessing so widely advertised a person. American tourists, of the sort who land with a loud demand for Westminster Abbey, landed on that distant coast with a loud demand for Father Brown. They were within measurable distance of running

[4] A reference to "The Final Problem" (1892), in which Dr. Watson chronicles the seemingly fatal plunge of Sherlock Holmes at Reichenbach Falls; but Holmes survived, and his further adventures were published after an interval of ten years.

excursion trains named after him, and bringing crowds to see him as if he were a public monument. He was especially troubled by the active and ambitious new traders and shop-keepers of the place, who were perpetually pestering him to try their wares and to give them testimonials. Even if the testimonials were not forthcoming, they would prolong the correspondence for the purpose of collecting autographs. As he was a good-natured person they got a good deal of what they wanted out of him; and it was in answer to a particular request from a Frankfort wine-merchant named Eckstein that he wrote hastily a few words on a card, which were to prove a terrible turning-point in his life.

Eckstein was a fussy little man with fuzzy hair and pince-nez, who was wildly anxious that the priest should not only try some of his celebrated medicinal port, but should let him know where and when he would drink it, in acknowledging its receipt. The priest was not particularly surprised at the request, for he was long past surprise at the lunacies of advertisement. So he scribbled something down and turned to other business which seemed a little more sensible. He was again interrupted, by a note from no less a person than his political enemy Alvarez, asking him to come to a conference at which it was hoped that a compromise on an outstanding question might be reached; and suggesting an appointment that evening at a café just outside the walls of the little town. To this also he sent a message of acceptance by the rather florid and military messenger who was waiting for it; and then, having an hour or two before him, sat down to attempt to get through a little of his own legitimate business. At the end of the time he poured himself out a glass of Mr. Eckstein's remarkable wine and, glancing at the clock with a humorous expression, drank it and went out into the night.

Strong moonlight lay on the little Spanish town, so that when he came to the picturesque gateway, with its rather rococo arch and the fantastic fringe of palms beyond it, it looked rather like a scene in a Spanish opera. One long leaf of palm with jagged edges, black against the moon, hung down on the other side of the arch, visible through the archway, and had something of the look of the jaw of a black crocodile. The fancy would not have lingered in his imagination but for something else that caught his naturally alert eye. The air was deathly still, and there was not a stir of wind; but he distinctly saw the pendent palm-leaf move.

He looked around him and realized that he was alone. He had left behind the last houses, which were mostly closed and shuttered, and was walking between two long blank walls built of large and shapeless but flattened stones, tufted here and there with the queer prickly weeds of that region—walls which ran parallel all the way to the gateway. He could not see the lights of the café outside the gate; probably it was too far away. Nothing could be seen under the arch but a wider expanse of large-flagged pavement, pale in the moon, with the straggling prickly pear here and there. He had a strong sense of the smell of evil; he felt queer physical oppression; but he did not think of stopping. His courage, which was considerable, was perhaps even less strong a part of him than his curiosity. All his life he had been led by an intellectual hunger for the truth, even of trifles. He often controlled it in the name of proportion; but it was always there. He walked straight through the gateway, and on the other side a man sprang like a monkey out of the treetop and struck at him with a knife. At the same moment another man came crawling swiftly along the wall and, whirling a cudgel round his head, brought it down. Father Brown turned, staggered, and sank in a heap; but as he sank there dawned on his round face an expression of mild and immense surprise.

There was living in the same little town at this time another young American, particularly different from Mr. Paul Snaith. His name was John Adams Race, and he was an electrical engineer, employed by Mendoza to fit out the old town with all the new conveniences. He was a figure far less familiar in satire and international gossip than that of the American journalist. Yet, as a matter of fact, America contains a million men of the moral type of Race to one of the moral type of Snaith. He was exceptional in being exceptionally good at his job, but in every other way he was very simple. He had begun life as a druggist's assistant in a Western village and risen by sheer work and merit; but he still regarded his home town as the natural heart of the habitable world. He had been taught a very Puritan or purely Evangelical sort of Christianity from the Family Bible at his mother's knee; and in so far as he had time to have any religion, that was still his religion. Amid all the dazzling lights of the latest and even wildest discoveries, when he was at the very edge and extreme of experiment, working miracles of light and sound like a god creating new stars and solar systems, he never for a moment doubted that the things "back home" were the best things in the world; his mother and the Family Bible and the quiet and quaint morality of his village. He had as serious and noble a sense of the sacredness of his mother as if he had been a frivolous Frenchman. He was quite sure the Bible religion was really the right thing; only he vaguely missed it wherever he went in the modern world. He could hardly be expected to sympathize with the religious externals of Catholic countries; and in a dislike of mitres and croziers he sympathized with Mr. Snaith, though not in so cocksure a fashion. He had no liking for the public bowings and scrapings of Mendoza, and certainly no temptation to the masonic mysticism of the atheist Alvarez. Perhaps all that semi-tropical life was too coloured for him, shot with Indian red and Spanish gold. Anyhow, when he said there was nothing to touch his home town, he was not boasting. He really meant that there was somewhere something plain and unpretentious and touching, which he really respected more than anything else in the world. Such being the mental attitude of John Adams Race in a South American station, there had been growing on him for some time a curious feeling, which contradicted all his prejudices and for which he could not account. For the truth was this: that the only thing he had ever met in his travels that in the least reminded him of the old wood-pile and the provincial proprieties and the Bible on his mother's knee was (for some inscrutable reason) the round face and black clumsy umbrella of Father Brown.

He found himself insensibly watching that commonplace and even comic black figure as it went bustling about; watching it with an almost morbid fascination; as if it were a walking riddle or contradiction. He had found something he could not help liking in the heart of everything he hated; it was as if he had been horribly tormented by lesser demons and then found that the Devil was quite an ordinary person.

Thus it happened that, looking out of his window on that moonlit night, he saw the Devil go by, the demon of unaccountable blamelessness, in his broad black hat and long black coat, shuffling along the street towards the gateway, and saw it with an interest which he could not himself understand. He wondered where the priest was going, and what he was really up to; and remained gazing out into the moonlit street long after the little black figure had passed. And then he saw something else that intrigued him further. Two other men whom he recognized passed across his window as across a lighted stage. A sort of blue limelight of the moon ran in a spectral halo round the big bush of hair that stood erect on the head of little Eckstein, the wine-seller, and it outlined a taller and darker figure with an eagle profile and a queer old-fashioned and very top-heavy black hat, which seemed to make the whole outline still more bizarre, like a shape in a shadow pantomime. Race rebuked himself for allowing the moon to play such tricks with his fancy; for on a second glance he recognized the black Spanish side-whiskers and high-featured face of Dr. Calderon, a worthy medical man of the town, whom he had once found attending professionally on Mendoza. Still, there was something in the way the men were whispering to each other and peering up the street that struck him as peculiar. On a sudden impulse he leapt over the low window-sill and himself went bareheaded up the road, following their trail. He saw them disappear under the dark archway; and a moment after there came a dreadful cry from beyond; curiously loud and piercing, and all the more blood-curdling to Race because it said something very distinctly in some tongue that he did not know.

The next moment there was a rushing of feet, more cries, and then a confused roar of rage or grief that shook the turrets and tall palm trees of the place; there was a movement in the mob that had gathered, as if they were sweeping backwards through the gateway. And then the dark archway resounded with a new voice, this time intelligible to him and falling with the note of doom, as someone shouted through the gateway:

"Father Brown is dead!"

He never knew what prop gave way in his mind, or why something on which he had been counting suddenly failed him; but he ran towards the gateway and was just in time to meet his countryman, the journalist Snaith, coming out of the dark entrance, deadly pale and snapping his fingers nervously.

"It's quite true," said Snaith, with something which for him approached to reverence. "He's a goner. The doctor's been looking at him, and there's no hope. Some of these damned Dagos clubbed him as he came through the gate— God knows why. It'll be a great loss to the place."

Race did not or perhaps could not reply, but ran on under the arch to the scene beyond. The small black figure lay where it had fallen on the wilderness of wide stones starred here and there with green thorn; and the great crowd was being kept back, chiefly by the mere gestures of one gigantic figure in the foreground. For there were many there who swayed hither and thither at the mere movement of his hand, as if he had been a magician.

Alvarez, the dictator and demagogue, was a tall, swaggering figure, always rather flamboyantly clad, and on this occasion he wore a green uniform with embroideries like silver snakes crawling all over it, with an order round his neck hung on a very vivid maroon ribbon. His close curling hair was already grey, and in contrast his complexion, which his friends called olive and his foes octoroon, looked almost literally golden, as if it were a mask moulded in gold. But his large-featured face, which was powerful and humorous, was at this moment properly grave and grim. He had been waiting, he explained, for Father Brown at the café, when he had heard a rustle and a fall and, coming out, had found the corpse lying on the flagstones.

"I know what some of you are thinking," he said, looking round proudly, "and if you are afraid of me, as you are, I will say it for you. I am an atheist; I have no god to call on for those who will not take my word. But I tell you in the name of every root of honour that may be left to a soldier and a man, that I had no part in this. If I had the men here that did it, I would rejoice to hang them on that tree."

"Naturally we are glad to hear you say so," said old Mendoza stiffly and solemnly, standing by the body of his fallen coadjutor. "This blow has been too appalling for us to say what else we feel at present. I suggest that it will be more decent and proper if we remove my friend's body and break up this irregular meeting. I understand," he added gravely to the doctor, "that there is unfortunately no doubt."

"There is no doubt," said Dr. Calderon.

John Race went back to his lodgings sad and with a singular sense of emptiness. It seemed impossible that he should miss a man whom he never knew. He learned that the funeral was to take place next day; for all felt that the crisis should be past as quickly as possible, for fear of riots that were hourly growing more probable. When Snaith had seen the row of Red Indians sitting in the veranda, they might have been a row of ancient Aztec images carved in red wood. But he had not seen them as they were when they heard that the priest was dead.

Indeed they would certainly have risen in revolution and lynched the republican leader, if they had not been immediately blocked by the direct necessity of behaving respectfully to the coffin of their own religious leader. The actual assassins, whom it would have been most natural to lynch, seemed to have vanished into thin air. Nobody knew their names; and nobody would ever know whether the dying man had even seen their faces. That strange look of surprise that was apparently his last look on earth might have been the recognition of their faces. Alvarez repeated violently that it was no work of his, and attended the funeral, walking behind the coffin in his splendid silver and green uniform with a sort of bravado of reverence.

Behind the veranda a flight of stone steps scaled a very steep green bank, fenced by a cactus-hedge, and up this the coffin was laboriously lifted to the ground above, and placed temporarily at the foot of the great gaunt crucifix that dominated the road and guarded the consecrated ground. Below in the road were great seas of people lamenting and telling their beads; an orphan population that had lost a father. Despite all these symbols that were provocative enough to him, Alvarez behaved with restraint and respect; and all would have gone well, as Race told himself, had the others only let him alone.

Race told himself bitterly that old Mendoza had always looked like an old fool and had now very conspicuously and completely behaved like an old fool. By a custom common in simpler societies, the coffin was left open and the face uncovered, bringing the pathos to the point of agony for all those simple people. This, being consonant to tradition, need have done no harm; but some officious person had added to it the custom of the French free-thinkers, of having speeches by the graveside. Mendoza proceeded to make a speech; a rather long speech, and the longer it was the longer and lower sank John Race's spirits and sympathies with the religious ritual involved. A list of saintly attributes, apparently of the most antiquated sort, was rolled out with the dilatory dullness of an after-dinner speaker who does not know how to sit down. That was bad enough; but Mendoza had also the ineffable stupidity to start reproaching and even taunting his political opponents. In three minutes he had succeeded in making a scene and a very extraordinary scene it was.

"We may well ask," he said, looking around him pompously, "we may well ask where such virtues can be found among those who have madly abandoned the creed of their fathers. It is when we have atheists among us, atheist leaders, nay sometimes even atheist rulers, that we find their infamous philosophy bearing fruit in crimes like this. If we ask who murdered this holy man, we shall assuredly find—"

Africa of the forests looked out of the eyes of Alvarez the hybrid adventurer; and Race fancied he could see suddenly that the man was after all a barbarian, who could not control himself to the end; one might guess that all his "illuminated" transcendentalism had a touch of Voodoo. Anyhow, Mendoza could not continue, for Alvarez had sprung up and was shouting back at him and shouting him down, with infinitely superior lungs.

"Who murdered him?" he roared. "Your God murdered him! His own God murdered him! According to you, he murders all his faithful and foolish servants—as he murdered *that* one," and he made a violent gesture, not towards the coffin but the crucifix.

Seeming to control himself a little, he went on in a tone still angry but more argumentative: "I don't believe it, but you do. Isn't it better to have no God than one that robs you in this fashion? I at least am not afraid to say there is none. There is no power in all this blind and brainless universe that can hear your prayer or return your friend. Though you beg Heaven to raise him, he will not rise. Though I dare Heaven to raise him, he will not rise. Here and now I will put it to the test—I defy the God who is not there to waken the man who sleeps for ever."

There was a shock of silence, and the demagogue had made his sensation.

"We might have known," cited Mendoza in a thick gobbling voice, "when we allowed such men as you—"

A new voice cut into his speech; a high and shrill voice with a Yankee accent.

"Stop! Stop!" cried Snaith the journalist, "something's up! I swear I saw him move."

He went racing up the steps and rushed to the coffin, while the mob below swayed with indescribable frenzies. The next moment he had turned a face of amazement over his shoulder and made a signal with his finger to Dr. Calderon, who hastened forward to confer with him. When the two men stepped away again from the coffin, all could see that the position of the head had altered. A roar of excitement rose from the crowd and seemed to stop suddenly, as if cut off in mid-air; for the priest in the coffin gave a groan and raised himself on one elbow, looking with bleared and blinking eyes at the crowd.

John Adams Race, who had hitherto known only miracles of science, never found himself able in after years to describe the topsy-turvydom of the next few days. He seemed to have burst out of the world of time and space, and to be living in the impossible. In half an hour the whole of that town and district had been transformed into something never known for a thousand years; a mediaeval people turned to a mob of monks by a staggering miracle; a Greek city where the god had descended among men. Thousands prostrated themselves in the road; hundreds took vows on the spot; and even the outsiders, like the two Americans, were able to think and speak of nothing but the prodigy. Alvarez himself was shaken, as well he might be; and sat down, with his head upon his hands.

And in the midst of all this tornado of beatitude was a little man struggling to be heard. His voice was small and faint, and the noise was deafening. He made weak little gestures that seemed more those of irritation than anything else. He came to the edge of the parapet above the crowd, waving it to be quiet, with movements rather like the flap of the short wings of a penguin. There was something a little more like a lull in the noise; and then Father Brown for the first time reached the utmost stretch of the indignation that he could launch against his children.

"Oh, you *silly* people," he said in a high and quavering voice; "Oh, you silly, *silly* people."

Then he suddenly seemed to pull himself together, made a bolt for the steps with his more normal gait, and began hurriedly to descend.

"Where are you going, Father?" said Mendoza, with more than his usual veneration.

"To the telegraph office," said Father Brown hastily. "What? No, of course it's not a miracle. Why should there be a miracle? Miracles are not so cheap as all that."

And he came tumbling down the steps, the people flinging themselves before him to implore his blessing.

"Bless you, bless you," said Father Brown hastily. "God bless you all and give you more sense."

And he scuttled away with extraordinary rapidity to the telegraph office, where he wired to his Bishop's secretary: "There is some mad story about a miracle here; hope his lordship not give authority. Nothing in it."

As he turned away from this effort, he tottered a little with the reaction, and John Race caught him by the arm.

"Let me see you home," he said; "you deserve more than these people are giving you."

John Race and the priest were seated in the presbytery; the table was still piled up with the papers with which the latter had been wrestling the day before;[5] the bottle of wine and the emptied wine-glass still stood where he had left them.

"And now," said Father Brown almost grimly, "I can begin to think."

"I shouldn't think too hard just yet," said the American.

[5] In the American editions, this phrase reads "papers with which the latter had been wrestling that afternoon."

"You must be wanting a rest. Besides, what are you going to think about?"

"I have pretty often had the task of investigating murders, as it happens," said Father Brown. "Now I have got to investigate my own murder."

"If I were you," said Race, "I should take a little wine first."

Father Brown stood up and filled himself another glass, lifted it, looked thoughtfully into vacancy and put it down again. Then he sat down once more and said:

"Do you know what I felt like when I died? You may not believe it, but my feeling was one of overwhelming astonishment."

"Well," answered Race, "I suppose you were astonished at being knocked on the head."

Father Brown leaned over to him and said in a low voice:

"I was astonished at not being knocked on the head."

Race looked at him for a moment as if he thought the knock on the head had been only too effective; but he only said: "What do you mean?"

"I mean that when that man brought his bludgeon down with a great swipe, it stopped at my head and did not even touch it. In the same way the other fellow made as if to strike me with a knife, but he never gave me a scratch. It was just like play-acting. I think it was. But then followed the extraordinary thing."

He looked thoughtfully at the papers on the table for a moment and then went on:

"Though I had not even been touched with knife or stick, I began to feel my legs doubling up under me and my very life failing. I knew I was being struck down by something, but it was not by those weapons. Do you know what I think it was?"

And he pointed to the wine on the table.

Race picked up the wine-glass and looked at it and smelt it. "I think you are right," he said. "I began as a druggist and studied chemistry. I couldn't say for certain without an analysis, but I think there's something very unusual in this stuff. There are drugs by which the Asiatics produce a temporary sleep that looks like death."

"Quite so," said the priest calmly. "The whole of this miracle was faked, for some reason or other. That funeral scene was staged—and timed. I think it is part of that raving madness of publicity that has got hold of Snaith; but I can hardly believe he would go quite so far, merely for that. After all, it's one thing to make copy out of me and run me as a sort of sham Sherlock Holmes, and—"

Even as the priest spoke his face altered. His blinking eyelids shut suddenly and he stood up as if he were choking. Then he put one wavering hand as if groping his way towards the door.

"Where are you going?" asked the other in some wonder.

"If you ask me," said Father Brown, who was quite white, "I was going to pray. Or rather, to praise."

"I'm not sure I understand. What is the matter with you?"

"I was going to praise God for having so strangely and so incredibly saved me—saved me by an inch."

"Of course," said Race, "I am not of your religion; but believe me, I have religion enough to understand that. Of course you would thank God for saving you from death."

"No," said the priest. "Not from death. From disgrace."

The other sat staring; and the priest's next words broke out of him with a sort of cry.

"And if it had only been my disgrace! But it was the disgrace of all I stand for; the disgrace of the Faith that they went about to encompass. What it might have been! The most huge and horrible scandal ever launched against us since the last lie was choked in the throat of Titus Oates."[6]

"What on earth are you talking about?" demanded his companion.

"Well, I had better tell you at once," said the priest; and sitting down, he went on more composedly: "It came to me in a flash when I happened to mention Snaith and Sherlock Holmes. Now I happen to remember what I wrote about his absurd scheme; it was the natural thing to write, and yet I think they had ingeniously manoeuvered me into writing just those words. They were something like 'I am ready to die and come to life again like Sherlock Holmes, if that is the best way.' And the moment I thought of that, I realized that I had been made to write all sorts of things of that kind, all pointing to the same idea. I wrote, as if to an accomplice, saying that I would drink the drugged wine at a particular time. Now, don't you see?"

Race sprang to his feet still staring: "Yes," he said, "I think I begin to see."

"*They* would have boomed the miracle. Then *they* would have bust up the miracle. And what is the worst, they would have proved that *I* was in the conspiracy. It would have been *our* sham miracle. That's all there is to it; and about as near hell as you and I will ever be, I hope."

Then he said, after a pause, in quite a mild voice:

"They certainly would have got quite a lot of good copy out of me."

Race looked at the table and said darkly: "How many of these brutes were in it?"

---

[6] Father Brown is referring to the Titus Oates who, in 1678, invented the details of a "Popish Plot" to murder the king, burn London, and massacre Protestants. Not until 1681, after 35 Catholics had been executed for treason, was the conspiracy exposed as a fraud.

Father Brown shook his head. "More than I like to think of," he said; "but I hope some of them were only tools. Alvarez might think that all's fair in war, perhaps; he has a queer mind. I'm very much afraid that Mendoza is an old hypocrite; I never trusted him and he hated my action in an industrial matter. But all that will wait; I have only got to thank God for the escape. And especially that I wired at once to the Bishop."

John Race appeared to be very thoughtful.

"You've told me a lot I didn't know," he said at last, "and I feel inclined to tell you the only thing you don't know. I can imagine how those fellows calculated well enough. They thought any man alive, waking up in a coffin to find himself canonized like a saint, and made into a walking miracle for everyone to admire, would be swept along with his worshippers and accept the crown of glory that fell on him out of the sky. And I reckon their calculation was pretty practical psychology, as men go. I've seen all sorts of men in all sorts of places; and I tell you frankly I don't believe there's one man in a thousand who could wake up like that with all his wits about him; and while he was still almost talking in his sleep, would have the sanity and the simplicity and the humility to—" He was much surprised to find himself moved, and his level voice wavering.

Father Brown was gazing abstractedly, and in a rather cock-eyed fashion, at the bottle on the table. "Look here," he said, "what about a bottle of real wine?"

The Man with Two Beards

THIS tale was told by Father Brown to Professor Crake, the celebrated criminologist, after dinner at a club, where the two were introduced to each other as sharing a harmless hobby of murder and robbery. But, as Father Brown's version rather minimized his own part in the matter, it is here re-told in a more impartial style. It arose out of a playful passage of arms, in which the professor was very scientific and the priest rather sceptical.

"My good sir," said the professor in remonstrance. "Don't you believe that criminology is a science?"

"I'm not sure," replied Father Brown. "Do you believe that hagiology is a science?"

"What's that?" asked the specialist sharply.

"No, it's not the study of hags, and has nothing to do with burning witches," said the priest, smiling. "It's the study of holy things, saints and so on. You see, the Dark Ages tried to make a science about good people. But our own humane and enlightened age is only interested in a science about bad ones. Yet, I think our general experience is that every conceivable

"The Man with Two Beards" first appeared in the United States in the April 1925 issue of *Harper's* magazine and in England in the May 1925 issue of *Cassell's* magazine.

sort of man has been a saint. And I suspect you will find, too, that every conceivable sort of man has been a murderer."

"Well, we believe murderers can be pretty well classified," observed Crake. "The list sounds rather long and dull; but I think it's exhaustive. First, all killing can be divided into rational and irrational, and we'll take the last first, because they are much fewer. There is such a thing as homicidal mania, or love of butchery in the abstract. There is such a thing as irrational antipathy, though it's very seldom homicidal. Then we come to the true motives; of these, some are less rational in the sense of being merely romantic and retrospective. Acts of pure revenge are acts of hopeless revenge. Thus, a lover will sometimes kill a rival he could never supplant, or a rebel assassinate a tyrant after the conquest is complete. But, more often, even these acts have a rational expectation. They are hopeful murders. They fall into the larger section of the second division, of what we may call prudential crimes. These, again, fall chiefly under two descriptions. A man kills either in order to obtain what the other man possesses, either by theft or inheritance, or to stop the other man from acting in some way: as in the case of killing a blackmailer or a political opponent, or, in the case of a rather more passive obstacle, a husband or wife whose continued functioning, as such, interferes with other things. We believe that classification is pretty thoroughly thought out and, properly applied, covers the whole ground. But I'm afraid that it perhaps sounds rather dull; I hope I'm not boring you."

"Not at all," said Father Brown. "If I seemed a little absent-minded I must apologize; the truth is, I was thinking of a man I once knew. He was a murderer; but I can't see where he fits into your museum of murderers. He was not mad, nor did he like killing. He did not hate the man he killed; he hardly knew him, and certainly had nothing to avenge on him. The other man did not possess anything that he could possibly want. The other man was not behaving in any way which the murderer wanted to stop. The murdered man was not in a position to hurt, or hinder, or even affect the murderer in any way. There was no woman in the case. There were no politics in the case. This man killed a fellow-creature who was practically a stranger, and that for a very strange reason; which is possibly unique in human history."

And so, in his own more conversational fashion, he told the story. The story may well begin in a sufficiently respectable setting, at the breakfast table of a worthy though wealthy suburban family named Bankes, where the normal discussion of the newspaper had, for once, been silenced by the discussion about a mystery nearer home. Such people are sometimes accused of gossip about their neighbours, but they are in that matter almost inhumanly innocent. Rustic villagers tell tales about their neighbours, true and false; but the curious culture of the modern suburb will believe anything it is told in the papers about the wickedness of the Pope, or the martyrdom of the King of the Cannibal Islands, and, in the excitement of these topics, never knows what is happening next door. In this case, however, the two forms of interest actually coincided in a coincidence of thrilling intensity. Their own suburb had actually been mentioned in their favourite newspaper. It seemed to them like a new proof of their own existence when they saw the name in print. It was almost as if they had been unconscious and invisible before; and now they were as real as the King of the Cannibal Islands.

It was stated in the paper that a once-famous criminal, known as Michael Moonshine, and many other names that were presumably not his own, had recently been released after a long term of imprisonment for his numerous burglaries;

that his whereabouts was being kept quiet, but that he was believed to have settled down in the suburb in question, which we will call for convenience Chisham. A résumé of some of his famous and daring exploits and escapes was given in the same issue. For it is a character of that kind of press, intended for that kind of public, that it assumes that its readers have no memories. While the peasant will remember an outlaw like Robin Hood or Rob Roy for centuries,[1] the clerk will hardly remember the name of the criminal about whom he argued in trams and tubes two years before. Yet, Michael Moonshine had really shown some of the heroic rascality of Rob Roy or Robin Hood. He was worthy to be turned into legend and not merely into news. He was far too capable a burglar to be a murderer. But his terrific strength and the ease with which he knocked policemen over like ninepins, stunned people, and bound and gagged them, gave something almost like a final touch of fear or mystery to the fact that he never killed them. People almost felt that he would have been more human if he had.

Mr. Simon Bankes, the father of the family, was at once better read and more old-fashioned than the rest. He was a sturdy man, with a short grey beard and a brow barred with wrinkles. He had a turn for anecdotes and reminiscence; and he distinctly remembered the days when Londoners had lain awake listening for Mike Moonshine, as they did for Spring-heeled Jack. Then there was his wife, a thin, dark lady. There was a sort of acid elegance about her, for her family had much more money than her husband's, if rather less education; and she even possessed a very valuable emerald necklace upstairs,

[1] The references are to Britain's two foremost outlaw-heroes, medieval England's Robin Hood, who plundered his Norman overlords, and Scotland's eighteenth-century Robert MacGregor (Rob Roy), who harried the Duke of Montrose.

that gave her a right to prominence in a discussion about thieves. There was his daughter, Opal, who was also thin and dark and supposed to be psychic—at any rate, by herself; for she had little domestic encouragement. Spirits of an ardently astral turn will be well advised not to materialize as members of a large family. There was her brother John, a burly youth, particularly boisterous in his indifference to her spiritual development; and otherwise distinguishable only by his interest in motor-cars. He seemed to be always in the act of selling one car and buying another; and by some process, hard for the economic theorist to follow, it was always possible to buy a much better article by selling the one that was damaged or discredited. There was his brother Philip, a young man with dark curly hair, distinguished by his attention to dress; which is doubtless part of the duty of a stockbroker's clerk, but, as the stockbroker was prone to hint, hardly the whole of it. Finally, there was present at this family scene his friend, Daniel Devine, who was also dark and exquisitely dressed, but bearded in a fashion that was somewhat foreign, and therefore, for many, slightly menacing.

It was Devine who had introduced the topic of the newspaper paragraph, tactfully insinuating so effective an instrument of distraction at what looked like the beginning of a small family quarrel; for the psychic lady had begun the description of a vision she had had of pale faces floating in empty night outside her window, and John Bankes was trying to roar down this revelation of a higher state with more than his usual heartiness.

But the newspaper reference to their new, and possibly alarming neighbour, soon put both controversialists out of court.

"How frightful," cried Mrs. Bankes. "He must be quite a new-comer; but who can he possibly be?"

"I don't know any particularly new-comers," said her husband, "except Sir Leopold Pulman, at Beechwood House."

"My dear," said the lady, "how absurd you are—Sir Leopold!" Then, after a pause, she added: "If anybody suggested his secretary now—that man with the whiskers; I've always said, ever since he got the place Philip ought to have had—"

"Nothing doing," said Philip languidly, making his sole contribution to the conversation. "Not good enough."

"The only one I know," observed Devine, "is that man called Carver, who is stopping at Smith's Farm. He lives a very quiet life, but he's quite interesting to talk to. I think John has had some business with him."

"Knows a bit about cars," conceded the monomaniac John. "He'll know a bit more when he's been in my new car."

Devine smiled slightly; everybody had been threatened with the hospitality of John's new car. Then he added reflectively:

"That's a little what I feel about him. He knows a lot about motoring and travelling, and the active ways of the world, and yet he always stays at home pottering about round old Smith's beehives. Says he's only interested in bee culture, and that's why he's staying with Smith. It seems a very quiet hobby for a man of his sort. However, I've no doubt John's car will shake him up a bit."

As Devine walked away from the house that evening, his dark face wore an expression of concentrated thought. His thoughts would, perhaps, have been worthy of our attention, even at this stage; but it is enough to say, that their practical upshot was a resolution to pay an immediate visit to Mr. Carver at the house of Mr. Smith. As he was making his way thither he encountered Barnard, the secretary at Beechwood House, conspicuous by his lanky figure and the large side

whiskers which Mrs. Bankes counted among her private
wrongs. Their acquaintance was slight, and their conversation
brief and casual; but Devine seemed to find in it food for
further cogitation.

"Look here," he said abruptly, "excuse my asking, but is it
true that Lady Pulman has some very famous jewellery up at
her House? I'm not a professional thief, but I've just heard
there's one hanging about."

"I'll get her to give an eye to them," answered the secretary.
"To tell the truth, I've ventured to warn her about them already myself. I hope she has attended to it."

As they spoke, there came the hideous cry of a motor-horn
just behind, and John Bankes came to a stop beside them,
radiant at his own steering-wheel. When he heard of
Devine's destination he claimed it as his own, though his tone
suggested rather an abstract relish for offering people a ride.
The ride was consumed in continuous praises of the car, now
mostly in the matter of its adaptability to weather.

"Shuts up as tight as a box," he said, "and opens as easy—
as easy as opening your mouth."

Devine's mouth, at the moment, did not seem so easy to
open, and they arrived at Smith's farm to the sound of a so-
liloquy. Passing the outer gate, Devine found the man he was
looking for without going into the house. The man was
walking about in the garden, with his hands in his pockets,
wearing a large, limp, straw hat; a man with a long face and a
large chin. The wide brim cut off the upper part of his face
with a shadow that looked a little like a mask. In the background was a row of sunny beehives, along which an elderly
man, presumably Mr. Smith, was moving accompanied by a
short, commonplace-looking companion in black clerical
costume.

"I say," burst in the irrepressible John, before Devine could offer any polite greeting, "I've brought her round to give you a little run. You see if she isn't better than a 'Thunderbolt.' "[2]

Mr. Carver's mouth set into a smile that may have been meant to be gracious, but looked rather grim. "I'm afraid I shall be too busy for pleasure this evening," he said.

"How doth the little busy bee," observed Devine, equally enigmatically.[3] "Your bees must be very busy if they keep you at it all night. I was wondering if—"

"Well," demanded Carver, with a certain cool defiance.

"Well, they say we should make hay while the sun shines," said Devine. "Perhaps you make honey while the moon shines."

There came a flash from the shadow of the broad-brimmed hat, as the whites of the man's eyes shifted and shone.

"Perhaps there is a good deal of moonshine in the business," he said; "but I warn you my bees do not only make honey. They sting."

"*Are* you coming along in the car?" insisted the staring John. But Carver, though he threw off the momentary air of sinister significance with which he had been answering Devine, was still positive in his polite refusal.

"I can't possibly go," he said. "Got a lot of writing to do. Perhaps you'd be kind enough to give some of my friends a run, if you want a companion. This is my friend, Mr. Smith. Father Brown."

[2] The *Thunderbolt* was a massive eight-wheeled racing car designed in the 1920s by the American George Evston to break the prevailing land-speed record.

[3] Devine's enigmatic observation is a quotation from "Against Idleness and Mischief" by Isaac Watts (1674–1748), an English theologian now chiefly remembered for his hymns: "How doth the little busy bee improve each shining hour, and gather honey all the day from every opening flower!"

"Of course," cried Bankes; "let 'em all come."

"Thank you very much," said Father Brown. "I'm afraid I shall have to decline; I've got to go on to Benediction in a few minutes."

"Mr. Smith is your man, then," said Carver, with something almost like impatience. "I'm sure Smith is longing for a motor ride."

Smith, who wore a broad grin, bore no appearance of longing for anything. He was an active little old man with a very honest wig; one of those wigs that look no more natural than a hat. Its tinge of yellow was out of keeping with his colourless complexion. He shook his head and answered with amiable obstinacy:

"I remember I went over this road ten years ago—in one of those contraptions. Came over in it from my sister's place at Holmgate, and never been over that road in a car since. It was rough going, I can tell you."

"Ten years ago!" scoffed John Bankes. "Two thousand years ago you went in an ox wagon. Do you think cars haven't changed in ten years—and roads, too, for that matter? In my little bus you don't know the wheels are going round. You think you're just flying."

"I'm sure Smith wants to go flying," urged Carver. "It's the dream of his life. Come, Smith, go over to Holmgate and see your sister. You know you ought to go and see your sister. Go over and stay the night if you like."

"Well, I generally walk over, so I generally do stay the night," said old Smith. "No need to trouble the gentleman to-day, particularly."

"But think what fun it will be for your sister to see you arrive in a car!" cried Carver. "You really ought to go. Don't be so selfish."

"That's it," assented Bankes, with buoyant benevolence.

"Don't you be selfish. It won't hurt you. You aren't afraid of it, are you?"

"Well," said Mr. Smith, blinking thoughtfully, "I don't want to be selfish, and I don't think I'm afraid. I'll come with you if you put it that way."

The pair drove off, amid waving salutations that seemed somehow to give the little group the appearance of a cheering crowd. Yet Devine and the priest only joined in it out of courtesy, and they both felt it was the dominating gesture of their host that gave it its final air of farewell. The detail gave them a curious sense of the pervasive force of his personality.

The moment the car was out of sight he turned to them with a sort of boisterous apology and said: "Well!"

He said it with that curious heartiness which is the reverse of hospitality. That extreme geniality is the same as a dismissal.

"I must be going," said Devine. "We must not interrupt the busy bee. I'm afraid I know very little about bees; sometimes I can hardly tell a bee from a wasp."

"I've kept wasps, too," answered the mysterious Mr. Carver.

When his guests were a few yards down the street, Devine said rather impulsively to his companion: "Rather an odd scene that, don't you think?"

"Yes," replied Father Brown. "And what do you think about it?"

Devine looked at the little man in black, and something in the gaze of his great, grey eyes seemed to renew his impulse.

"I think," he said, "that Carver was very anxious to have the house to himself tonight. I don't know whether you had any such suspicions?"

"I may have my suspicions," replied the priest, "but I'm not sure whether they're the same as yours."

That evening, when the last dusk was turning into dark in the gardens round the family mansion, Opal Bankes was moving through some of the dim and empty rooms, with even more than her usual abstraction; and anyone who had looked at her closely would have noted that her pale face had more than its usual pallor. Despite its bourgeois luxury, the house as a whole had a rather unique shade of melancholy. It was the sort of immediate sadness that belongs to things that are old rather than ancient. It was full of faded fashions, rather than historic customs; of the order and ornament that is just recent enough to be recognized as dead. Here and there, Early Victorian coloured glass tinted the twilight; the high ceilings made the long rooms look narrow; and at the end of the long room down which she was walking was one of those round windows, to be found in the buildings of its period. As she came to about the middle of the room, she stopped, and then suddenly swayed a little, as if some invisible hand had struck her on the face.

An instant after there was the noise of knocking on the front door, dulled by the closed doors between. She knew that the rest of the household were in the upper parts of the house; but she could not have analysed the motive that made her go to the front door herself. On the door-step stood a dumpy and dingy figure in black, which she recognized as the Roman Catholic priest, whose name was Brown. She knew him only slightly; but she liked him. He did not encourage her psychic views, quite the contrary; but he discouraged them as if they mattered and not as if they did not matter. It was not so much that he did not sympathize with her opinions, as that he did sympathize but did not agree. All this was in some sort of chaos in her mind as she found herself saying, without greeting, or waiting to hear his business:

"I'm so glad you've come. I've seen a ghost."

"There's no need to be distressed about that," he said. "It often happens. Most of the ghosts aren't ghosts, and the few that may be won't do you any harm. Was it any ghost in particular?"

"No," she admitted, with a vague feeling of relief, "it wasn't so much the thing itself as an atmosphere of awful decay, a sort of luminous ruin. It was a face. A face at the window. But it was pale and goggling, and looked like the picture of Judas."

"Well, some people do look like that," reflected the priest, "and I dare say they look in at windows, sometimes. May I come in and see where it happened?"

When she returned to the room with the visitor, however, other members of the family had assembled, and those of a less psychic habit had thought it convenient to light the lamps. In the presence of Mrs. Bankes, Father Brown assumed a more conventional civility, and apologized for his intrusion.

"I'm afraid it is taking a liberty with your house, Mrs. Bankes," he said. "But I think I can explain how the business happens to concern you. I was up at the Pulman's place just now, when I was rung up and asked to come round here to meet a man who is coming to communicate something that may be of some moment to you. I should not have added myself to the party, only I am wanted, apparently, because I am a witness to what has happened up at Beechwood. In fact, it was I who had to give the alarm."

"What has happened?" repeated the lady.

"There has been a robbery up at Beechwood House," said Father Brown, gravely; "a robbery, and what I fear is worse, Lady Pulman's jewels have gone; and her unfortunate secretary, Mr. Barnard, was picked up in the garden, having evidently been shot by the escaping burglar."

"That man," ejaculated the lady of the house. "I believe he was—"

She encountered the grave gaze of the priest, and her words suddenly went from her; she never knew why.

"I communicated with the police," he went on, "and with another authority interested in this case; and they say that even a superficial examination has revealed foot-prints and finger-prints and other indications of a well-known criminal."

At this point, the conference was for a moment disturbed by the return of John Bankes, from what appeared to be an abortive expedition in the car. Old Smith seemed to have been a disappointing passenger, after all.

"Funked it, after all, at the last minute," he announced with noisy disgust. "Bolted off while I was looking at what I thought was a puncture. Last time I'll take one of these yokels—"

But his complaints received small attention in the general excitement that gathered round Father Brown and his news.

"Somebody will arrive in a moment," went on the priest, with the same air of weighty reserve, "who will relieve me of this responsibility. When I have confronted you with him I shall have done my duty as a witness in a serious business. It only remains for me to say that a servant up at Beechwood House told me that she had seen a face at one of the windows—"

"I saw a face," said Opal, "at one of our windows."

"Oh, you are always seeing faces," said her brother John roughly.

"It is as well to see facts even if they are faces," said Father Brown equably, "and I think the face you saw—"

Another knock at the front door sounded through the house, and a minute afterwards the door of the room opened and another figure appeared. Devine half-rose from his chair at the sight of it.

It was a tall, erect figure, with a long, rather cadaverous face, ending in a formidable chin. The brow was rather bald, and the eyes bright and blue, which Devine had last seen obscured with a broad straw hat.

"Pray don't let anybody move," said the man called Carver, in clear and courteous tones. But to Devine's disturbed mind the courtesy had an ominous resemblance to that of a brigand who holds a company motionless with a pistol.

"Please sit down, Mr. Devine," said Carver; "and, with Mrs. Bankes's permission, I will follow your example. My presence here necessitates an explanation. I rather fancy you suspected me of being an eminent and distinguished burglar."

"I did," said Devine grimly.

"As you remarked," said Carver, "it is not always easy to know a wasp from a bee."

After a pause, he continued: "I can claim to be one of the more useful, though equally annoying, insects. I am a detective, and I have come down here to investigate an alleged renewal of the activities of the criminal calling himself Michael Moonshine. Jewel robberies were his speciality; and there has just been one of them at Beechwood House, which, by all the technical tests, is obviously his work. Not only do the prints correspond, but you may possibly know that when he was last arrested, and it is believed on other occasions also, he wore a simple but effective disguise of a red beard and a pair of large horn-rimmed spectacles."

Opal Bankes leaned forward fiercely.

"That was it," she cried in excitement, "that was the face I saw, with great goggles and a red, ragged beard like Judas. I thought it was a ghost."

"That was also the ghost the servant at Beechwood saw," said Carver, dryly.

He laid some papers and packages on the table, and began carefully to unfold them. "As I say," he continued, "I was sent down here to make inquiries about the criminal plans of this man, Moonshine. That is why I interested myself in bee-keeping and went to stay with Mr. Smith."

There was a silence, and then Devine started and spoke: "You don't seriously mean to say that nice old man——"

"Come, Mr. Devine," said Carver, with a smile, "you be-lieved a beehive was only a hiding-place for me. Why shouldn't it be a hiding-place for him?"

Devine nodded gloomily, and the detective turned back to his papers. "Suspecting Smith, I wanted to get him out of the way and go through his belongings; so I took advantage of Mr. Bankes's kindness in giving him a joy ride. Searching his house, I found some curious things to be owned by an innocent old rustic interested only in bees. This is one of them."

From the unfolded paper he lifted a long, hairy object al-most scarlet in colour—the sort of sham beard that is worn in theatricals.

Beside it lay an old pair of heavy horn-rimmed spectacles.

"But I also found something," continued Carver, "that more directly concerns this house, and must be my excuse for intruding to-night. I found a memorandum, with notes of the names and conjectural value of various pieces of jewellery in the neighbourhood. Immediately after the note of Lady Pulman's tiara was the mention of an emerald necklace be-longing to Mrs. Bankes."

Mrs. Bankes, who had hitherto regarded the invasion of her house with an air of supercilious bewilderment, suddenly grew attentive. Her face suddenly looked ten years older and much more intelligent. But before she could speak the impetuous John had risen to his full height like a trumpeting elephant.

"And the tiara's gone already," he roared; "and the necklace—I'm going to see about that necklace!"

"Not a bad idea," said Carver, as the young man rushed from the room; "though, of course, we've been keeping our eyes open since we've been here. Well, it took me a little time to make out the memorandum, which was in cipher, and Father Brown's telephone message from the House came as I was near the end. I asked him to run round here first with the news, and I would follow; and so—"

His speech was sundered by a scream. Opal was standing up and pointing rigidly at the round window.

"There it is again!" she cried.

For a moment they all saw something—something that cleared the lady of the charges of lying and hysteria not uncommonly brought against her. Thrust out of the slate-blue darkness without, the face was pale, or, perhaps, blanched by pressure against the glass; and the great, glaring eyes, encircled as with rings, gave it rather the look of a great fish out of the dark-blue sea nosing at the port hole of a ship. But the gills or fins of the fish were a coppery red; they were, in truth, fierce red whiskers and the upper part of a red beard. The next moment it had vanished.

Devine had taken a single stride towards the window when a shout resounded through the house, a shout that seemed to shake it. It seemed almost too deafening to be distinguishable as words; yet it was enough to stop Devine in his stride, and he knew what had happened.

"Necklace gone!" shouted John Bankes, appearing huge and heaving in the doorway, and almost instantly vanishing again with the plunge of a pursuing hound.

"Thief was at the window just now!" cried the detective, who had already darted to the door, following the headlong John, who was already in the garden.

"Be careful," wailed the lady, "they have pistols and things."

"So have I," boomed the distant voice of the dauntless John out of the dark garden.

Devine had, indeed, noticed as the young man plunged past him that he was defiantly brandishing a revolver, and hoped there would be no need for him to so defend himself. But even as he had the thought, came the shock of two shots, as if one answered the other, and awakened a wild flock of echoes in that still suburban garden. They flapped into silence.

"Is John dead?" asked Opal in a low, shuddering voice.

Father Brown had already advanced deeper into the darkness, and stood with his back to them, looking down at something. It was he who answered her.

"No," he said, "it is the other."

Carver had joined him, and for a moment the two figures, the tall and the short, blocked out what view the fitful and stormy moonlight would allow. Then they moved to one side, and the others saw the small, wiry figure lying slightly twisted, as if with its last struggle. The false red beard was thrust upwards, as if scornfully, at the sky, and the moon shone on the great sham spectacles of the man who had been called Moonshine.

"What an end," muttered the detective, Carver. "After all his adventures, to be shot almost by accident by a stockbroker in a suburban garden."

The stockbroker, himself, naturally regarded his own triumph with more solemnity, though not without nervousness.

"I had to do it," he gasped, still panting with exertion. "I'm sorry; he fired at me."

"There will have to be an inquest, of course," said Carver, gravely. "But I think there will be nothing for you to worry about. There's a revolver fallen from his hand with one shot discharged; and he certainly didn't fire after he'd got yours."

By this time they had assembled again in the room, and the detective was getting his papers together for departure. Father Brown was standing opposite to him, looking down at the table, as if in a brown study. Then he spoke abruptly:

"Mr. Carver, you have certainly worked out a very complete case in a very masterly way. I rather suspected your professional business; but I never guessed you would link everything up together so quickly—the bees and the beard and the spectacles and the cipher and the necklace and everything."

"Always satisfactory to get a case really rounded off," said Carver.

"Yes," said Father Brown, still looking at the table. "I admire it very much." Then he added with a modesty verging on nervousness: "It's only fair to you to say that I don't believe a word of it."

Devine leaned forward with sudden interest. "Do you mean you don't believe he is Moonshine, the burglar?"

"I know he is the burglar, but he didn't burgle," answered Father Brown. "I know he didn't come here, or to the great house, to steal jewels, or get shot getting away with them. Where are the jewels?"

"Where they generally are in such cases," said Carver. "He's either hidden them or passed them on to a confederate. This was not a one-man job. Of course, my people are searching the garden and warning the district."

"Perhaps," suggested Mrs. Bankes, "the confederate stole

the necklace while Moonshine was looking in at the window."

"Why was Moonshine looking in at the window?" asked Father Brown quietly. "Why should he want to look in at the window?"

"Well, what do you think?" cried the cheery John.

"I think," said Father Brown, "that he never did want to look in at the window."

"Then why did he do it?" demanded Carver. "What's the good of talking in the air like that? We've seen the whole thing acted before our very eyes."

"I've seen a good many things acted before my eyes that I didn't believe in," replied the priest. "So have you, on the stage and off."

"Father Brown," said Devine, with a certain respect in his tones, "will you tell us why you can't believe your eyes?"

"Yes, I will try to tell you," answered the priest. Then he said gently: "You know what I am and what we are. We don't bother you much. We try to be friends with all our neighbours. But you can't think we do nothing. You can't think we know nothing. We mind our own business; but we know our own business, and we know our own people. I knew this dead man very well indeed; I was his confessor, and his friend. So far as a man can, I knew his mind when he left that garden to-day; and his mind was like a glass hive full of golden bees. It's an under-statement to say his reformation was sincere. He was one of those great penitents who manage to make more out of penitence than others can make out of virtue. I say I was his confessor; but, indeed, it was I who went to him for comfort. It did me good to be near so good a man. And when I saw him lying there dead in the garden, it seemed to me as if certain strange words that were said of old were spoken over him aloud in my ear.

They might well be; for if ever a man went straight to heaven, it might be he."

"Hang it all," said John Bankes restlessly, "after all, he was a convicted thief."

"Yes," said Father Brown, "and only a convicted thief has ever in this world heard that assurance: 'This night shalt thou be with Me in Paradise.' "

Nobody seemed to know what to do with the silence that followed, until Devine said, abruptly, at last:

"Then how in the world would you explain it all?"

The priest shook his head. "I can't explain it at all, just yet," he said, simply. "I can see one or two odd things, but I don't understand them. As yet, I've nothing to go on to prove the man's innocence, except the man. But I'm quite sure I'm right."

He sighed, and put out his hand for his big, black hat. As he removed it he remained gazing at the table with rather a new expression, his round, straight-haired head cocked at a new angle. It was rather as if some curious animal had come out of his hat, as out of the hat of a conjurer. But the others, looking at the table, could see nothing there but the detective's documents and the tawdry old property beard and spectacles.

"Lord bless us," muttered Father Brown, "and he's lying outside dead, in a beard and spectacles." He swung round suddenly upon Devine. "Here's something to follow up, if you want to know. *Why did he have two beards?*"

With that he bustled in his undignified way out of the room; but Devine was now devoured with curiosity, and pursued him into the front garden.

"I can't tell you now," said Father Brown. "I'm not sure, and I'm bothered about what to do. Come round and see me to-morrow, and I may be able to tell you the whole thing. It may already be settled for me, and—did you hear that noise?"

"A motor-car starting," remarked Devine.

"Mr. John Bankes's motor-car," said the priest. "I believe it goes very fast."

"He certainly is of that opinion," said Devine, with a smile.

"It will go far, as well as fast, to-night," said Father Brown.

"And what do you mean by that?" demanded the other.

"I mean it will not return," replied the priest. "John Bankes suspected something of what I knew from what I said. John Bankes has gone and the emeralds and all the other jewels with him."

Next day, Devine found Father Brown moving to and fro in front of the row of beehives, sadly, but with a certain serenity.

"I've been telling the bees," he said. "You know one has to tell the bees![4] 'Those singing masons building roofs of gold.' What a line!"[5] Then more abruptly: "He would like the bees looked after."

"I hope he doesn't want the human beings neglected, when the whole swarm is buzzing with curiosity," observed the young man. "You were quite right when you said that Bankes was gone with the jewels; but I don't know how you knew, or even what there was to be known."

Father Brown blinked benevolently at the beehives and said:

"One sort of stumbles on things, and there was one stumbling-block at the start. I was puzzled by poor Barnard being shot up at Beechwood House. Now, even when Michael was a master criminal, he made it a point of honour, even a point of vanity, to succeed without any killing. It seemed extraordi-

---

[4] Father Brown's reference is to the American John Greenleaf Whittier's poem "Telling the Bees" (1852) and to the folk-belief that a death in the family would drive the bees off unless the bees were told.

[5] The line is Shakespeare's, from *Henry V* (1:2:198).

nary that when he had become a sort of saint, he should go out of his way to commit the sin he had despised when he was a sinner. The rest of the business puzzled me to the last; I could make nothing out of it, except that it wasn't true. Then I had a belated gleam of sense when I saw the beard and goggles, and remembered the thief had come in another beard, with other goggles. Now, of course, it was just possible that he had duplicates; but it was at least a coincidence that he used neither the old glasses nor the old beard, both in good repair. Again, it was just possible that he went out without them, and had to procure new ones; but it was unlikely. There was nothing to make him go motoring with Bankes at all; if he was really going burgling, he could have taken his outfit easily in his pocket. Besides, beards don't grow on bushes. He would have found it hard to get such things anywhere in the time.

"No, the more I thought of it the more I felt there was something funny about his having a completely new outfit. And then the truth began to dawn on me by reason, which I knew already by instinct. He never did go out with Bankes with any intention of putting on the disguise. He never did put on the disguise. Somebody else manufactured the disguise at leisure, and then put it on him."

"Put it on him!" repeated Devine. "How the devil could they?"

"Let us go back," said Father Brown, "and look at the thing through another window—the window through which the young lady saw the ghost."

"The ghost!" repeated the other, with a slight start.

"She called it the ghost," said the little man, with composure, "and perhaps she was not so far wrong. It's quite true that she is what they call psychic. Her only mistake is in thinking that being psychic is being spiritual. Some animals are psychic; anyhow, she is a sensitive, and she was right when she felt that the face at the window had a sort of horrible halo of deathly things."

"You mean—" began Devine.

"I mean it was a dead man who looked in at the window," said Father Brown. "It was a dead man who crawled round more than one house, looking in at more than one window. Creepy, wasn't it? But in one way it was the reverse of a ghost; for it was not the antic of the soul freed from the body. It was the antic of the body freed from the soul."

He blinked again at the beehive and continued: "But, I suppose, the shortest explanation is to take it from the standpoint of the man who did it. You know the man who did it. John Bankes."

"The very last man I should have thought of," said Devine.

"The very first man I thought of," said Father Brown; "in so far as I had any right to think of anybody. My friend, there are no good or bad social types or trades. Any man can be a murderer like poor John; any man, even the same man, can be a saint like poor Michael. But if there is one type that tends at times to be more utterly godless than another, it is that rather brutal sort of business man. He has no social ideal, let alone religion; he has neither the gentleman's traditions nor the trade unionist's class loyalty. All his boasts about getting good bargains were practically boasts of having cheated people. His snubbing of his sister's poor little attempts at mysticism was detestable. Her mysticism was all nonsense; but he only hated spiritualism because it was spirituality. Anyhow, there's no doubt he was the villain of the piece; the only interest is in a rather original piece of villainy. It was really a new and unique motive for murder. It was the motive of using the corpse as a stage property—a sort of hideous doll or dummy. At the start he conceived a plan of killing Michael in the motor, merely to take him home and pretend to have killed him in the garden. But all sorts of fantastic finishing touches followed quite naturally from the primary fact; that he had at his disposal in a closed car at night the dead body of a recognized and recognizable burglar. He could leave his finger-prints and foot-prints; he could lean the familiar face against windows and take it away. You will notice that Moonshine ostensibly appeared and vanished while Bankes was ostensibly out of the room looking for the emerald necklace.

"Finally, he had only to tumble the corpse on to the lawn, fire a shot from each pistol, and there he was. It might never have been found out but for a guess about the two beards."

"Why had your friend Michael kept the old beard?" Devine said thoughtfully. "That seems to me questionable."

"To me, who knew him, it seems quite inevitable," replied Father Brown. "His whole attitude was like that wig that he wore. There was no disguise about his disguises. He didn't want the old disguise any more, but he wasn't frightened of it; he would have felt it false to destroy the false beard. It would have been like hiding; and he was not hiding. He was not hiding from God; he was not hiding from himself. He was in the broad daylight. If they'd taken him back to prison, he'd still have been quite happy. He was not whitewashed, but washed white. There was something very strange about him; almost as strange as the grotesque dance of death through which he was dragged after he was dead. When he moved to and fro smiling among these beehives, even then, in a most radiant and shining sense, he was dead. He was out of the judgment of this world."

There was a short pause, and then Devine shrugged his shoulders and said: "It all comes back to bees and wasps looking very much alike in this world, doesn't it?"

The Curse of the Golden Cross

Six people sat round a small table, seeming almost as incongruous and accidental as if they had been shipwrecked separately on the same small desert island. At least the sea surrounded them; for in one sense their island was enclosed in another island, a large and flying island like Laputa.[1] For the little table was one of many little tables dotted about in the dining saloon of that monstrous ship the *Moravia*, speeding through the night and the everlasting emptiness of the Atlantic. The little company had nothing in common except that all were travelling from America to England. Two of them at least might be called celebrities; others might be called obscure, and in one or two cases even dubious.

The first was the famous Professor Smaill, an authority on certain archaeological studies touching the later Byzantine Empire.[2] His lectures, delivered in an American University,

---

"The Curse of the Golden Cross" first appeared in the May 1925 issue of *Nash's* magazine, followed by its publication in the United States in the July 11, 1925, issue of *Collier's* magazine.

[1] Laputa is the flying island in part III of *Gulliver's Travels* (1726), in which the author, Jonathan Swift, satirizes scientific quackery, visionary theorizing, and a preoccupation with abstractions.

[2] The Byzantine Empire, Smaill's specialty, was the eastern half of the

were accepted as of the first authority even in the most authoritative seats of learning in Europe. His literary works were so steeped in a mellow and imaginative sympathy with the European past, that it often gave strangers a start to hear him speak with an American accent. Yet he was in his way very American; he had long fair hair brushed back from a big square forehead, long straight features and a curious mixture of preoccupation with a poise of potential swiftness, like a lion pondering absent-mindedly on his next leap.

There was only one lady in the group; and she was (as the journalists often said of her) a host in herself; being quite prepared to play hostess, not to say empress, at that or any other table. She was Lady Diana Wales, the celebrated lady traveller in tropical and other countries; but there was nothing rugged or masculine about her appearance at dinner. She was herself handsome in an almost tropical fashion, with a mass of hot and heavy red hair; she was dressed in what the journalists call a daring fashion, but her face was intelligent and her eyes had that bright and rather prominent appearance which belongs to the eyes of ladies who ask questions at political meetings.

The other four figures seemed at first like shadows in this shining presence; but they showed differences on a close view. One of them was a young man entered on the ship's register as Paul T. Tarrant. He was an American type which might be more truly called an American antitype. Every nation probably has an antitype; a sort of extreme exception that proves the national rule. Americans really respect work, rather as Europeans respect war. There is a halo of heroism about it; and he who shrinks from it is less than a man. The

divided Roman Empire; it prospered after Rome fell and survived until the capture of Constantinople by the Turks in 1453.

antitype is evident through being exceedingly rare. He is the
dandy or dude; the wealthy waster who makes a weak villain
for so many American novels. Paul Tarrant seemed to have
nothing whatever to do but to change his clothes, which he
did about six times a day; passing into paler or richer shades
of his suit of exquisite light grey, like the delicate silver
changes of the twilight. Unlike most Americans, he culti-
vated very carefully a short curly beard; and unlike most dan-
dies, even of his own type, he seemed rather sulky than
showy. Perhaps there was something almost Byronic about
his silence and his gloom.[3]

The next two travellers were naturally classed together;
merely because they were both English lecturers returning
from an American tour. One of them was described as
Leonard Smyth, apparently a minor poet, but something of a
major journalist; long-headed, light-haired, perfectly dressed
and perfectly capable of looking after himself. The other was
a rather comic contrast, being short and broad, with a black
walrus moustache, and as taciturn as the other was talkative.
But as he had been both charged with robbing and praised for
rescuing a Roumanian Princess threatened by a jaguar in his
travelling menagerie, and had thus figured in a fashionable
case, it was naturally felt that his views on God, progress, his
own early life, and the future of Anglo-American relations
would be of great interest and value to the inhabitants of
Minneapolis and Omaha. The sixth and most insignificant
figure was that of a little English priest going by the name of
Brown. He listened to the conversation with respectful attention, and he was at that moment forming the impression that
there was one rather curious thing about it.

---

[3] The reference is to the melancholy English poet George Gordon,
Lord Byron (1788–1824), who was almost as famed for posturing and self-
dramatization as for his poetry.

"I suppose those Byzantine studies of yours, Professor," Leonard Smyth was saying, "would throw some light on this story of a tomb found somewhere on the south coast; near Brighton, isn't it? Brighton's a long way from Byzantium, of course. But I read something about the style of burying or embalming or something being supposed to be Byzantine."

"Byzantine studies certainly have to reach a long way," replied the Professor dryly. "They talk about specialists; but I think the hardest thing on earth is to specialize. In this case, for instance: how can a man know anything about Byzantium till he knows everything about Rome before it and about Islam after it? Most Arab arts were old Byzantine arts. Why, take algebra—"

"But I won't take algebra," cried the lady decisively. "I never did and I never do. But I'm awfully interested in embalming. I was with Gatton, you know, when he opened the Babylonian tombs. Ever since then I found mummies and preserved bodies and all that perfectly thrilling. Do tell us about this one."

"Gatton was an interesting man," said the Professor. "They were an interesting family. That brother of his who went into Parliament was much more than an ordinary politician. I never understood the Fascisti till he made that speech about Italy."

"Well, we're not going to Italy on this trip," said Lady Diana persistently, "and I believe you're going to that little place where they've found the tomb. In Sussex, isn't it?"

"Sussex is pretty large, as these little English sections go," replied the Professor. "One might wander about in it for a goodish time; and it's a good place to wander in. It's wonderful how large those low hills seem when you're on them."

There was an abrupt accidental silence; and then the lady said, "Oh, I'm going on deck," and rose, the men rising with her. But the Professor lingered, and the little priest was the last to leave the table, carefully folding up his napkin. And as they were thus left alone together the Professor said suddenly to his companion:

"What would you say was the point of that little talk?"

"Well," said Father Brown smiling, "since you ask me, there was something that amused me a little. I may be wrong; but it seemed to me that the company made three attempts to get you to talk about an embalmed body said to be found in Sussex. And you, on your side, very courteously offered to talk—first about algebra, and then about the Fascisti, and then about the landscape of the Downs."

"In short," replied the Professor, "you thought I was ready to talk about any subject but that one. You were quite right."

The Professor was silent for a little time, looking down at the tablecloth; then he looked up and spoke with that swift impulsiveness that suggested the lion's leap.

"See here, Father Brown," he said, "I consider you about the wisest and whitest man I ever met."

Father Brown was very English. He had all the normal national helplessness about what to do with a serious and sincere compliment suddenly handed to him to his face, in the American manner. His reply was a meaningless murmur; and it was the Professor who proceeded, with the same staccato earnestness:

"You see, up to a point it's all simple enough. A Christian tomb of the Dark Ages, apparently that of a bishop, has been found under a little church at Dulham on the Sussex coast. The Vicar happens to be a good bit of an archaeologist himself and has been able to find out a good deal more than I know yet. There was a rumour of the corpse being embalmed in a way peculiar to Greeks and Egyptians but unknown in the West, especially at that date. So Mr. Walters (that is the

Vicar) naturally wonders about Byzantine influences. But he also mentions something else, that is of even more personal interest to me."

His long grave face seemed to grow even longer and graver as he frowned down at the table-cloth. His long finger seemed to be tracing patterns on it like the plans of dead cities and their temples and tombs.

"So I'm going to tell you, and nobody else, why it is I have to be careful about mentioning that matter in mixed company; and why, the more eager they are to talk about it, the more cautious I have to be. It is also stated that in the coffin is a chain with a cross, common enough to look at, but with a certain secret symbol on the back found on only one other cross in the world. It is from the arcana of the very earliest Church and is supposed to indicate St. Peter setting up his See at Antioch before he came to Rome. Anyhow, I believe there is but one other like it, and it belongs to me. I hear there is some story about a curse on it; but I take no notice of that. But whether or no there is a curse, there really is, in one sense, a conspiracy; though the conspiracy should only consist of one man."

"Of one man?" repeated Father Brown almost mechanically.

"Of one madman, for all I know," said Professor Smaill. "It's a long story and in some ways a silly one."

He paused again, still tracing plans like architectural drawings with his finger on the cloth, and then resumed:

"Perhaps I had better tell you about it from the beginning, in case you see some little point in the story that is meaningless to me. It began years and years ago, when I was conducting some investigations on my own account in the antiquities of Crete and the Greek islands. I did a great deal of it practically single-handed; sometimes with the most rude and temporary help from the inhabitants of the place, and sometimes literally alone. It was under the latter circumstances that I found a maze of subterranean passages which led at last to a heap of rich refuse, broken ornaments and scattered gems which I took to be the ruins of some sunken altar, and in which I found the curious gold cross. I turned it over, and on the back of it I saw the Ichthus or fish, which was an early Christian symbol, but of a shape and pattern rather different from that commonly found; and, as it seemed to me, more realistic—more as if the archaic designer had meant it to be not merely a conventional enclosure or nimbus, but to look a little more like a real fish. It seemed to me that there was a flattening towards one end of it that was not like mere mathematical decoration, but rather like a sort of rude or even savage zoology.

"In order to explain very briefly why I thought this find important, I must tell you the point of the excavation. For one thing, it had something of the nature of an excavation of an excavation. We were on the track not only of antiquities, but of the antiquarians of antiquity. We had reason to believe, or some of us thought we had reason to believe, that these underground passages, mostly of the Minoan period, like that famous one which is actually identified with the labyrinth of the Minotaur, had not really been lost and left undisturbed for all the ages between the Minotaur and the modern explorer.[4] We believed that these underground places, I might almost say these underground towns and villages, had already been penetrated during the intervening period by some persons prompted by some motive. About the motive there were different schools of thought: some holding that the Emperors

[4] Smaill refers to bronze-age Crete and legends of King Minos, whose celebrated labyrinth was the lair of the Minotaur, a monstrous half-man, half-bull.

had ordered an official exploration out of mere scientific curiosity; others that the furious fashion in the later Roman Empire for all sorts of lurid Asiatic superstitions had started some nameless Manichaean sect or other rioting in the caverns in orgies that had to be hidden from the face of the sun. I belong to the group which believed that these caverns had been used in the same way as the catacombs. That is, we believed that, during some of the persecutions which spread like a fire over the whole Empire, the Christians had concealed themselves in these ancient pagan labyrinths of stone. It was therefore with a thrill as sharp as a thunderclap that I found and picked up the fallen golden cross and saw the design upon it; and it was with still more of a shock of felicity that, on turning to make my way once more outwards and upwards into the light of day, I looked up at the walls of bare rock that extended endlessly along the low passages, and saw scratched in yet ruder outline, but if possible more unmistakable, the shape of the Fish.

"Something about it made it seem as if it might be a fossil fish or some rudimentary organism fixed for ever in a frozen sea. I could not analyse this analogy, otherwise unconnected with a mere drawing scratched or scrawled upon the stone, till I realized that I was saying in my subconscious mind that the first Christians must have seemed something like fish, dumb and dwelling in a fallen world of twilight and silence, dropped far below the feet of men and moving in dark and twilight and a soundless world.

"Everyone walking along stone passages knows what it is to be followed by phantom feet. The echo follows flapping or clapping behind or in front, so that it is almost impossible for the man who is really lonely to believe in his loneliness. I had got used to the effects of this echo and had not noticed it much for some time past, when I caught sight of the symbolical shape scrawled on the wall of rock. I stopped, and at the same instant it seemed as if my heart stopped, too; for my own feet had halted, but the echo went marching on.

"I ran forward, and it seemed as if the ghostly footsteps ran also, but not with that exact imitation which marks the material reverberation of a sound. I stopped again, and the steps stopped also; but I could have sworn they stopped an instant too late; I called out a question; and my cry was answered; but the voice was not my own.

"It came round the corner of a rock just in front of me; and throughout that uncanny chase I noticed that it was always at some such angle of the crooked path that it paused and spoke. The little space in front of me that could be illuminated by my small electric torch was always as empty as an empty room. Under these conditions I had a conversation with I know not whom, which lasted all the way to the first white gleam of daylight, and even there I could not see in what fashion he vanished into the light of day. But the mouth of the labyrinth was full of many openings and cracks and chasms, and it would not have been difficult for him to have somehow darted back and disappeared again into the underworld of the caves. I only know that I came out on the lonely steps of a great mountain like a marble terrace, varied only with a green vegetation that seemed somehow more tropical than the purity of the rock, like that Oriental invasion that has spread sporadically over the fall of classic Hellas. I looked out on a sea of stainless blue, and the sun shone steadily on utter loneliness and silence; and there was not a blade of grass stirred with a whisper of flight nor the shadow of a shadow of man.

"It had been a terrible conversation; so intimate and so individual and in a sense so casual. This being, bodiless, faceless, nameless and yet calling me by my name, had talked to me in those crypts and cracks where we were buried alive with no more passion or melodrama than if we had been sitting in two armchairs at a club. But he had told me also that he would unquestionably kill me or any other man who came into the possession of the cross with the mark of the fish. He told me frankly he was not fool enough to attack me there in the labyrinth, knowing I had a loaded revolver, and that he ran as much risk as I. But he told me equally calmly that he would plan my murder with the certainty of success, with every detail developed and every danger warded off, with the sort of artistic perfection that a Chinese craftsman or an Indian embroiderer gives to the artistic work of a lifetime. Yet he was no Oriental; I am certain he was a white man. I suspect that he was a countryman of my own.

"Since then I have received from time to time signs and symbols and queer impersonal messages that have made me certain at least that if the man is a maniac he is a monomaniac. He is always telling me, in this airy and detached way, that the preparations for my death and burial are proceeding satisfactorily; and that the only way in which I can prevent their being crowned with a comfortable success is to give up the relic in my possession—the unique cross that I found in the cavern. He does not seem to have any religious sentiment or fanaticism on the point; he seems to have no passion but the passion of a collector of curiosities. That is one of the things that makes me feel sure he is a man of the West and not of the East. But this particular curiosity seems to have driven him quite crazy.

"And then came this report, as yet unsubstantiated, about the duplicate relic found on an embalmed body in a Sussex tomb. If he had been a maniac before, this news turned him into a demoniac possessed of seven devils. That there should be one of them belonging to another man was bad enough, but that there should be two of them and neither belonging to him was a torture not to be borne. His mad messages began to come thick and fast like showers of poisoned arrows; and each cried out more confidently than the last that death would strike me at the moment when I stretched out my unworthy hand towards the cross in the tomb.

"'You will never know me,' he wrote, 'you will never say my name; you will never see my face; you will die and never know who has killed you. I may be in any form among those about you; but I shall be in that alone at which you have forgotten to look.'

"From those threats I deduce that he is quite likely to shadow me on this expedition; and try to steal the relic or do me some mischief for possessing it. But as I never saw the man in my life, he may be almost any man I meet. Logically speaking, he may be any of the waiters who wait on me at table. He may be any of the passengers who sit with me at table."

"He may be me," said Father Brown, with cheerful contempt for grammar.

"He may be anybody else," answered Smaill seriously. "That is what I meant by what I said just now. You are the only man I feel sure is not the enemy."

Father Brown again looked embarrassed; then he smiled and said, "Well, oddly enough, I'm not. What we have to consider is any chance of finding out if he really is here before he—before he makes himself unpleasant."

"There is one chance of finding out, I think," remarked the Professor rather grimly. "When we get to Southhampton I shall take a car at once along the coast; I should be glad if you would come with me, but in the ordinary sense, of course, our little party will break up. If any one of them turns up again in that little churchyard on the Sussex coast, we shall know who he really is."

The Professor's programme was duly carried out, at least to

the extent of the car and its cargo in the form of Father Brown. They coasted along the road with the sea on one side and the hills of Hampshire and Sussex on the other; nor was there visible to the eye any shadow of pursuit. As they approached the village of Dulham only one man crossed their path who had any connexion with the matter in hand; a journalist who had just visited the church and been courteously escorted by the Vicar through the new excavated chapel; but his remarks and notes seemed to be of the ordinary newspaper sort. But Professor Smaill was perhaps a little fanciful, and could not dismiss the sense of something odd and discouraging in the attitude and appearance of the man, who was tall and shabby, hook-nosed and hollow-eyed, with moustaches that drooped with depression. He seemed anything but enlivened by his late experiment as a sightseer; indeed, he seemed to be striding as fast as possible from the sight, when they stopped him with a question.

"It's all about a curse," he said; "a curse on the place, according to the guide-book or the parson or the oldest inhabitant or whoever is the authority; and really, it feels jolly like it. Curse or no curse, I'm glad to have got out of it."

"Do you believe in curses?" asked Smaill curiously.

"I don't believe in anything; I'm a journalist," answered the melancholy being—"Boon, of the *Daily Wire*. But there's a something creepy about that crypt; and I'll never deny I felt a chill." And he strode on towards the railway station with a further accelerated pace.

"Looks like a raven or a crow, that fellow," observed Smaill as they turned towards the churchyard. "What is it they say about a bird of ill omen?"[5]

[5] Smaill's reference is to augury, an ancient form of divination through omens, in which the bird of ill omen, the owl, raven, or crow, foretells death.

They entered the churchyard slowly, the eyes of the American antiquary lingering luxuriantly over the isolated roof of the lych gate and the large unfathomable black growth of the yew looking like night itself defying the broad daylight. The path climbed up amid heaving levels of turf in which the gravestones were tilted at all angles like stone rafts tossed on a green sea, till it came to the ridge beyond which the great grey sea itself ran like an iron bar, with pale lights in it like steel. Almost at their feet the tough rank grass turned into a tuft of sea-holly and ended in grey and yellow sand; and a foot or two from the holly, and outlined darkly against the steely sea, stood a motionless figure. But for its dark grey clothing it might almost have been the statue on some sepulchral monument. But Father Brown instantly recognized something in the elegant stoop of the shoulders and the rather sullen outward thrust of the short beard.

"Gee!" exclaimed the professor of archaeology, "it's that man Tarrant, if you call him a man. Did you think, when I spoke on the boat, that I should ever get so quick an answer to my question?"

"I thought you might get too many answers to it," answered Father Brown.

"Why, how do you mean?" inquired the Professor, darting a look at him over his shoulder.

"I mean," answered the other mildly, "that I thought I heard voices behind the yew-tree. I don't think Mr. Tarrant is so solitary as he looks. I might even venture to say, so solitary as he likes to look."

Even as Tarrant turned slowly round in his moody manner, the confirmation came. Another voice, high and rather hard, but none the less feminine, was saying with experienced raillery:

"And how was I to know he would be here?"

It was borne in upon Professor Smaill that this gay observation was not addressed to him; so he was forced to conclude in some bewilderment, that yet a third person was present. As Lady Diana Wales came out radiant and resolute as ever from the shadow of the yew, he noted grimly that she had a living shadow of her own. The lean dapper figure of Leonard Smyth, that insinuating man of letters, appeared immediately behind her own flamboyant form, smiling, his head a little on one side like a dog's.

"Snakes!" muttered Smaill. "Why, they're all here! Or all except that little showman with the walrus whiskers."

He heard Father Brown laughing softly beside him; and indeed the situation was becoming something more than laughable. It seemed to be turning topsy-turvy and tumbling about their ears like a pantomime trick; for even while the Professor had been speaking, his words had received the most comical contradiction. The round head with the grotesque black crescent of moustache had appeared suddenly and seemingly out of a hole in the ground. An instant afterwards they realized that the hole was in fact a very large hole, leading to a ladder which descended into the bowels of the earth; that it was in fact the entrance to the subterranean scene they had come to visit. The little man had been the first to find the entrance and had already descended a rung or two of the ladder before he put his head out again to address his fellow-travellers. He looked like some particularly preposterous Grave-digger in a burlesque of *Hamlet*.[6] He only said thickly behind his thick moustaches, "It is down here." But it came to the rest of the company with a start of realization that, though they had sat opposite him at meal-times for a week, they had hardly ever heard him speak before; and that though

[6] A reference to Act 5, Scene 1, of Shakespeare's play, in which the gravedigger typically delivers his lines from a trap door in the stage.

he was supposed to be an English lecturer, he spoke with a
rather occult foreign accent.

"You see, my dear Professor," cried Lady Diana with tren-
chant cheerfulness, "your Byzantine mummy was simply too
exciting to be missed. I simply had to come along and see it;
and I'm sure the gentlemen felt just the same. Now you must
tell us all about it."

"I do not know all about it," said the Professor gravely, not
to say grimly. "In some respects I don't even know what it's all
about. It certainly seems odd that we should have all met
again so soon; but I suppose there are no limits to the modern
thirst for information. But if we are all to visit the place it
must be done in a responsible way and, if you will forgive me,
under responsible leadership. We must notify whoever is in
charge of the excavations; we shall probably at least have to
put our names in a book."

Something rather like a wrangle followed on this collision
between the impatience of the lady and the suspicions of the
archaeologist; but the latter's insistence on the official rights
of the Vicar and the local investigation ultimately prevailed;
the little man with the moustaches came reluctantly out of his
grave again and silently acquiesced in a less impetuous descent. Fortunately, the clergyman himself appeared at this
stage, a grey-haired, good-looking gentleman with a droop
accentuated by double eyeglasses; and while rapidly establish-
ing sympathetic relations with the Professor as a fellow anti-
quarian, he did not seem to regard his rather motley group of
companions with anything more hostile than amusement.

"I hope you are none of you superstitious," he said pleasantly. "I ought to tell you, to start with, that there are supposed to be all sorts of bad omens and curses hanging over
our devoted heads in this business. I have just been decipher-
ing a Latin inscription which was found over the entrance to

the chapel; and it would seem that there are no less than three curses involved; a curse for entering the sealed chamber, a double curse for opening the coffin, and a triple and most terrible curse for touching the gold relic found inside it. The two first maledictions I have already incurred myself," he added with a smile, "but I fear that even you will have to incur the first and mildest of them if you are to see anything at all. According to the story, the curses descend in a rather lingering fashion, at long intervals and on later occasions. I don't know whether that is any comfort to you." And the Reverend Mr. Walters smiled once more in his drooping and benevolent manner.

"Story," repeated Professor Smaill, "why, what story is that?"

"It is rather a long story and varies, like other local legends," answered the Vicar. "But it is undoubtedly contemporary with the time of the tomb; and the substance of it is embodied in the inscription and is roughly this: Guy de Gisors, a lord of the manor here early in the thirteenth century, had set his heart on a beautiful black horse in the possession of an envoy from Genoa, which that practical merchant prince would not sell except for a huge price. Guy was driven by avarice to the crime of pillaging the shrine and, according to one story, even killing the bishop, who was then resident there. Anyhow, the bishop uttered a curse which was to fall on anybody who should continue to withhold the gold cross from its resting-place in his tomb, or should take steps to disturb it when it had returned there. The feudal lord raised the money for the horse by selling the gold relic to a goldsmith in the town; but on the first day he mounted the horse the animal reared and threw him in front of the church porch, breaking his neck. Meanwhile the goldsmith, hitherto wealthy and prosperous, was ruined by a series of inexplicable accidents, and fell into the power of a Jew money-lender living in the manor. Eventually the unfortunate goldsmith, faced with nothing but starvation, hanged himself on an apple-tree. The gold cross, with all his other goods, his house, shop, and tools, had long ago passed into the possession of the money-lender. Meanwhile, the son and heir of the feudal lord, shocked by the judgment on his blasphemous sire, had become a religious devotee in the dark and stern spirit of those times, and conceived it his duty to persecute all heresy and unbelief among his vassals. Thus the Jew in his turn who had been cynically tolerated by the father, was ruthlessly burnt by order of the son; so that he, in his turn, suffered for the possession of the relic; and after these three judgments, it was returned to the bishop's tomb; since when no eye has seen and no hand has touched it."

Lady Diana Wales seemed to be more impressed than might have been expected.

"It really gives one rather a shiver," she said, "to think that we are going to be the first, except the Vicar."

The pioneer with the big moustaches and the broken English did not descend after all by his favourite ladder, which indeed had only been used by some of the workmen conducting the excavation; for the clergyman led them round to a larger and more convenient entrance about a hundred yards away, out of which he himself had just emerged from his investigations underground. Here the descent was by a fairly gradual slope with no difficulties save the increasing darkness; for they soon found themselves moving in single file down a tunnel as black as pitch, and it was some little time before they saw a glimmer of light ahead of them. Once during that silent march there was a sound like a catch in somebody's breath, it was impossible to say whose; and once there was an oath like a dull explosion, and it was in an unknown tongue.

They came out in a circular chamber like a basilica in a ring of round arches; for that chapel had been built before the first pointed arch of the Gothic had pierced our civilization like a spear. A glimmer of greenish light between some of the pillars marked the place of the other opening into the world above, and gave a vague sense of being under the sea, which was intensified by one or two other incidental and perhaps fanciful resemblances. For the dog-tooth pattern of the Norman was faintly traceable round all the arches, giving them, above the cavernous darkness, something of the look of the mouths of monstrous sharks.[7] And in the centre the dark bulk of the tomb itself, with its lifted lid of stone, might almost have been the jaws of some such leviathan.

Whether out of a sense of fitness or from the lack of more modern appliances, the clerical antiquary had arranged for the illumination of the chapel only by four tall candles in big wooden candlesticks standing on the floor. Of these only one was alight when they entered, casting a faint glimmer over the mighty architectural forms. When they had all assembled, the clergyman proceeded to light the three others, and the appearance and contents of the great sarcophagus came more clearly into view.

All eyes went first to the face of the dead, preserved across all those ages in the lines of life by some secret Eastern process, it was said, inherited from heathen antiquity and unknown to the simple graveyards of our own island. The Professor could hardly repress an exclamation of wonder; for, though the face was as pale as a mask of wax, it looked otherwise like a sleeping man who had but that moment closed his eyes. The face was of the ascetic, perhaps even the fanatical type, with a high framework of bones; the figure was clad in

[7] The archways of many Norman castles were decorated with one or more rows of chevrons, giving the saw-tooth effect referred to here.

a golden cope and gorgeous vestments, and high up on the breast, at the base of the throat, glittered the famous gold cross upon a short gold chain, or rather necklace. The stone coffin had been opened by lifting the lid of it at the head and propping it aloft upon two strong wooden shafts or poles, hitched above under the edge of the upper slab and wedged below into the corners of the coffin behind the head of the corpse. Less could therefore be seen of the feet or the lower part of the figure, but the candle-light shone full on the face; and in contrast with its tones of dead ivory the cross of gold seemed to stir and sparkle like a fire.

Professor Smaill's big forehead had carried a big furrow of reflection, or possibly of worry, ever since the clergyman had told the story of the curse. But feminine intuition, not untouched by feminine hysteria, understood the meaning of his brooding immobility better than did the men around him. In the silence of that candle-lit cavern Lady Diana cried out suddenly:

"Don't touch it, I tell you!"

But the man had already made one of his swift leonine movements, leaning forward over the body. The next instant they all darted, some forward and some backward, but all with a dreadful ducking motion as if the sky were falling.

As the Professor laid a finger on the gold cross, the wooden props, that bent very slightly in supporting the lifted lid of stone, seemed to jump and straighten themselves with a jerk. The lip of the stone slab slipped from its wooden perch; and in all their souls and stomachs came a sickening sense of down-rushing ruin, as if they had all been flung off a precipice. Smaill had withdrawn his head swiftly, but not in time; and he lay senseless beside the coffin, in a red puddle of blood from scalp or skull. And the old stone coffin was once more closed as it had been for centuries; save that one or two sticks or splinters stuck in the crevice, horribly suggestive of bones crunched by an ogre. The leviathan had snapped its jaws of stone.

Lady Diana was looking at the wreck with eyes that had an electric glare as of lunacy; her red hair looked scarlet against the pallor of her face in the greenish twilight. Smyth was looking at her, still with something dog-like in the turn of his head; but it was the expression of a dog who looks at a master whose catastrophe he can only partly understand. Tarrant and the foreigner had stiffened in their usual sullen attitudes; but their faces had turned the colour of clay. The Vicar seemed to have fainted. Father Brown was kneeling beside the fallen figure, trying to test its condition.

Rather to the general surprise, the Byronic lounger, Paul Tarrant, came forward to help him.

"He'd better be carried up into the air," he said. "I suppose there's just a chance for him."

"He isn't dead," said Father Brown in a low voice, "but I think it's pretty bad; you aren't a doctor by any chance?"

"No; but I've had to pick up a good many things in my time," said the other. "But never mind about me just now. My real profession would probably surprise you."

"I don't think so," replied Father Brown, with a slight smile. "I thought of it about halfway through the voyage. You are a detective shadowing somebody. Well, the cross is safe from thieves now, anyhow."

While they were speaking Tarrant had lifted the frail figure of the fallen man with easy strength and dexterity, and was carefully carrying him towards the exit. He answered over his shoulder: "Yes, the cross is safe enough."

"You mean that nobody else is," replied Brown. "Are you thinking of the curse, too?"

Father Brown went about for the next hour or two under

a burden of frowning perplexity that was something beyond the shock of the tragic accident. He assisted in carrying the victim to the little inn opposite the church, interviewed the doctor, who reported the injury as serious and threatening, though not certainly fatal, and carried the news to the little group of travellers who had gathered round the table in the inn parlour. But wherever he went the cloud of mystification rested on him and seemed to grow darker the more deeply he pondered. For the central mystery was growing more and more mysterious, actually in proportion as many of the minor mysteries began to clear themselves up in his mind. Exactly in proportion as the meaning of individual figures in that motley group began to explain itself, the thing that had happened grew more and more difficult to explain. Leonard Smyth had come merely because Lady Diana had come; and Lady Diana had come merely because she chose. They were engaged in one of those floating society flirtations that are all the more silly for being semi-intellectual. But the lady's romanticism had a superstitious side to it; and she was pretty well prostrated by the terrible end of her adventure. Paul Tarrant was a private detective, possibly watching the flirtation, for some wife or husband; possibly shadowing the foreign lecturer with the moustaches, who had much the air of an undesirable alien. But if he or anybody else had intended to steal the relic, the intention had been finally frustrated. And to all mortal appearance, what had frustrated it was either an incredible coincidence or the intervention of the ancient curse.

As he stood in unusual perplexity in the middle of the village street, between the inn and the church, he felt a mild shock of surprise at seeing a recently familiar but rather unexpected figure advancing up the street. Mr. Boon, the journalist, looking very haggard in the sunshine, which showed up his shabby raiment like that of a scarecrow, had his dark and deep-set eyes (rather close together on either side of the long drooping nose) fixed on the priest. The latter looked twice before he realized that the heavy dark moustache hid something like a grin or at least a grim smile.

"I thought you were going away," said Father Brown a little sharply. "I thought you left by that train two hours ago."

"Well, you see I didn't," said Boon.

"Why have you come back?" asked the priest almost sternly.

"This is not the sort of little rural paradise for a journalist to leave in a hurry," replied the other. "Things happen too fast here to make it worth while to go back to a dull place like London. Besides, they can't keep me out of the affair—I mean this second affair. It was I that found the body, or at any rate the clothes. Quite suspicious conduct on my part, wasn't it? Perhaps you think I wanted to dress up in his clothes. Shouldn't I make a lovely parson?"

And the lean and long-nosed mountebank suddenly made an extravagant gesture in the middle of the market-place, stretching out his arms and spreading out his dark-gloved hands in a sort of burlesque benediction and saying, "Oh, my dear brethren and sisters, for I would embrace you all. . . ."

"What on earth are you talking about?" cried Father Brown, and rapped the stones slightly with his stumpy umbrella, for he was a little less patient than usual.

"Oh, you'll find out all about it if you ask that picnic party of yours at the inn," replied Boon scornfully. "That man Tarrant seems to suspect me merely because I found the clothes; though he only came up a minute too late to find them himself. But there are all sorts of mysteries in this business. The little man with the big moustaches may have more in him than meets the eye. For that matter, I don't see why you shouldn't have killed the poor fellow yourself."

Father Brown did not seem in the least annoyed at the suggestion, but he seemed exceedingly bothered and bewildered by the remark.

"Do you mean," he asked with simplicity, "that it was I who tried to kill Professor Smaill?"

"Not at all," said the other, waving his hand with the air of one making a handsome concession. "Plenty of dead people for you to choose among. Not limited to Professor Smaill. Why, didn't you know somebody else had turned up, a good deal deader than Professor Smaill? And I don't see why you shouldn't have done him in, in a quiet way. Religious differences, you know . . . lamentable disunion of Christendom. . . . I suppose you've always wanted to get the English parishes back."

"I'm going back to the inn," said the priest quietly; "you say the people there know what you mean, and perhaps *they* may be able to say it."

In truth, just afterwards his private perplexities suffered a momentary dispersal at the news of a new calamity. The moment he entered the little parlour where the rest of the company were collected, something in their pale faces told him they were shaken by something yet more recent than the accident at the tomb. Even as he entered Leonard Smyth was saying: "Where is all this going to end?"

"It will never end, I tell you," repeated Lady Diana, gazing into vacancy with glassy eyes; "it will never end till we all end. One after another the curse will take us; perhaps slowly, as the poor Vicar said; but it will take us all as it has taken him."

"What in the world has happened now?" asked Father Brown.

There was a silence, and then Tarrant said in a voice that sounded a little hollow:

"Mr. Walters, the Vicar, has committed suicide. I suppose it was the shock unhinged him. But I fear there can be no doubt about it. We've just found his black hat and clothes on a rock jutting out from the shore. He seems to have jumped into the sea. I thought he looked as if it had knocked him half-witted, and perhaps we ought to have looked after him; but there was so much to look after."

"You could have done nothing," said the lady. "Don't you see the thing is dealing doom in a sort of dreadful order? The Professor touched the cross, and he went first; the Vicar had opened the tomb, and he went second; we only entered the chapel, and we—"

"Hold on," said Father Brown, in a sharp voice he very seldom used; "this has got to stop."

He still wore a heavy though unconscious frown, but in his eyes was no longer the cloud of mystification, but a light of almost terrible understanding.

"What a fool I am!" he muttered. "I ought to have seen it long ago. The tale of the curse ought to have told me."

"Do you mean to say," demanded Tarrant, "that we can really be killed now by something that happened in the thirteenth century?"

Father Brown shook his head and answered with quiet emphasis:

"I won't discuss whether we can be killed by something that happened in the thirteenth century. But I'm jolly certain that we can't be killed by something that *never* happened in the thirteenth century, something that never happened at all."

"Well," said Tarrant, "it's refreshing to find a priest so sceptical of the supernatural as all that."

"Not at all," replied the priest calmly; "it's not the supernatural part I doubt. It's the natural part. I'm exactly in the position of the man who said, 'I can believe the impossible, but not the improbable.' "[8]

"That's what you call a paradox, isn't it?" asked the other. "It's what I call common sense, properly understood," replied Father Brown. "It really is more natural to believe a preternatural story, that deals with things we don't understand, than a natural story that contradicts things we do understand. Tell me that the great Mr. Gladstone, in his last hours, was haunted by the ghost of Parnell, and I will be agnostic about it.[9] But tell me that Mr. Gladstone, when first presented to Queen Victoria, wore his hat in her drawing-room and slapped her on the back and offered her a cigar, and I am not agnostic at all. That is not impossible; it's only incredible. But I'm much more certain it didn't happen than that Parnell's ghost didn't appear; because it violates the laws of the world I do understand. So it is with that tale of the curse. It isn't the legend that I disbelieve—it's the history."

Lady Diana had recovered a little from her trance of Cassandra,[10] and her perennial curiosity about new things began to peer once more out of her bright and prominent eyes.

"What a curious man you are!" she said. "Why should you disbelieve the history?"

"I disbelieve the history because it isn't history," answered Father Brown. "To anybody who happens to know a little about the Middle Ages, the whole story was about as probable

[8] The man who said it was Oscar Wilde in "The Decay of Lying" (1891): "Man can believe the impossible, but man can never believe the improbable."

[9] Father Brown refers to the Victorian Prime Minister William Gladstone (1809–98), who was induced by the Irish MP Charles Parnell (1846–91) to support "Home Rule" for Ireland.

[10] A reference to the trance-ridden Cassandra of Greek mythology, the unheeded prophetess of the Trojan War.

as Gladstone offering Queen Victoria a cigar. But does anybody know anything about the Middle Ages? Do you know
what a Guild was? Have you ever heard of *salvo managio suo*?
Do you know what sort of people were *Servi Regis*?[11]

"No, of course I don't," said the lady, rather crossly. "What
a lot of Latin words!"

"No, of course," said Father Brown. "If it had been
Tutankhamen[12] and a set of dried-up Africans preserved,
Heaven knows why, at the other end of the world; if it had
been Babylonia or China; if it had been some race as remote
and mysterious as the Man in the Moon, your newspapers
would have told you all about it, down to the last discovery of
a tooth-brush or a collar-stud. But the men who built your
own parish churches, and gave the names to your own towns
and trades and the very roads you walk on—it has never occurred to you to know anything about them. I don't claim to
know a lot myself, but I know enough to see that story is stuff
and nonsense from the beginning to end. It was illegal for a
money-lender to distrain on a man's shop and tools. It's exceedingly unlikely that the Guild would not have saved a man
from such utter ruin, especially if he were ruined by a Jew.
Those people had vices and tragedies of their own; they

---

[11] Father Brown is quoting from the provisions of the charter that King
John (1167–1216) gave to the burghers, under which a debt-ridden member of a craft-guild could not be deprived of his means of livelihood (*salvo
managio suo*); and Jews, to avoid persecution, could seek the protected
status of king's moneyer and royal servant (*servi regis*), for which privilege
they paid a heavy tallage (feudal tax).

[12] The 1922 excavation of the tomb of Egyptian Pharaoh Tutankhamun
("King Tut's Tomb"), laden with treasures and curses, created a newspaper
sensation and fueled a voguish fascination with Egyptology. Father
Brown's view echoes that expressed by Chesterton in his *Illustrated London
News* essay for February 17, 1923, "The New Interest in Things Egyptian"
(*Collected Works*, vol. XXXIII, pp. 44–48).

sometimes tortured and burned people. But that idea of a man, without God or hope in the world, crawling away to die because nobody cared whether he lived—that isn't a mediaeval idea. That's a product of our economic science and progress. The Jew wouldn't have been a vassal of the feudal lord. The Jews normally had a special position as servants of the King. Above all, the Jew couldn't possibly have been burned for his religion."

"The paradoxes are multiplying," observed Tarrant, "but surely you won't deny that Jews were persecuted in the Middle Ages?"

"It would be nearer the truth," said Father Brown, "to say they were the only people who weren't persecuted in the Middle Ages. If you want to satirize mediaevalism, you could make a good case by saying that some poor Christian might be burned alive for making a mistake about the Homo-ousion,[13] while a rich Jew might walk down the street openly sneering at Christ and the Mother of God. Well, that's what the story is like. It was never a story of the Middle Ages; it was never even a legend about the Middle Ages. It was made up by somebody whose notions came from novels and newspapers; and probably made up on the spur of the moment."

The others seemed a little dazed by the historical digression, and seemed to wonder vaguely why the priest emphasized it and made it so important a part of the puzzle. But Tarrant, whose trade it was to pick the practical detail out of many tangles of digression, had suddenly become alert. His bearded chin was thrust forward farther than ever, but his sullen eyes were wide awake.

[13] The reference is to heretical beliefs about the Holy Trinity. The Church Council of Nicea (A.D. 325) had used the Greek word *homoousion*, "same substance", to distinguish the Catholic Creed from that of Arius, who taught that the Son is not of the same substance as the Father.

"Ah," he said; "made up on the spur of the moment!"

"Perhaps that is an exaggeration," admitted Father Brown calmly. "I should rather say made up more casually and carelessly than the rest of an uncommonly careful plot. But the plotter did not think the details of mediaeval history would matter much to anybody. And his calculation in a general way was pretty nearly right, like most of his other calculations."

"Whose calculations? Who was right?" demanded the lady with a sudden passion of impatience. "Who is this person you are talking about? Haven't we gone through enough, without your making our flesh creep with your hes and hims?"

"I am talking about the murderer," said Father Brown.

"What murderer?" she asked sharply. "Do you mean that the poor professor was murdered?"

"Well," said the staring Tarrant gruffly into his beard, "we can't say 'murdered,' for we don't know he's killed."

"The murderer killed somebody else, who was not Professor Smaill," said the priest gravely.

"Why, whom else could he kill?" asked the other.

"He killed the Reverend John Walters, the Vicar of Dulham," replied Father Brown with precision. "He only wanted to kill those two, because they both had got hold of relics of one rare pattern. The murderer was a sort of monomaniac on the point."

"It all sounds very strange," muttered Tarrant. "Of course we can't swear that the Vicar's really dead either. We haven't seen his body."

"Oh yes, you have," said Father Brown.

There was a silence as sudden as the stroke of a gong; a silence in which that sub-conscious guesswork that was so active and accurate in the woman moved her almost to a shriek.

"That is exactly what you have seen," went on the priest. "You have seen his body. You haven't seen him, the real living man, but you have seen his body all right. You have stared at it hard by the light of four great candles; and it was not tossing suicidally in the sea but lying in state like a Prince of the Church in a shrine built before the Crusades."

"In plain words," said Tarrant, "you actually ask us to believe that the embalmed body was really the corpse of a murdered man."

Father Brown was silent for a moment; then he said almost with an air of irrelevance:

"The first thing I noticed about it was the cross; or rather the string suspending the cross. Naturally, for most of you, it was only a string of beads and nothing else in particular, but, naturally also, it was rather more in my line than yours. You remember it lay close up to the chin, with only a few beads showing, as if the whole necklet were quite short. But the beads that showed were arranged in a special way, first one and then three, and so on; in fact, I knew at a glance that it was a rosary, an ordinary rosary with a cross at the end of it. But a rosary has at least five decades and additional beads as well; and I naturally wondered where all the rest of it was. It would go much more than once round the old man's neck. I couldn't understand it at the time; and it was only afterwards I guessed where the extra length had gone to. It was coiled round and round the foot of the wooden prop that was fixed in the corner of the coffin, holding up the lid. So that when poor Smaill merely plucked at the cross, it jerked the prop out of its place and the lid fell on his skull like a club of stone."

"By George!" said Tarrant, "I'm beginning to think there's something in what you say. This is a queer story if it's true."

"When I realized that," went on Father Brown, "I could manage more or less to guess the rest. Remember, first of all, that there never was any responsible archaeological authority for anything more than investigation. Poor old Walters was an honest antiquary, who was engaged in opening the tomb to *find out* if there was any truth in the legend about embalmed bodies. The rest was all rumour, of the sort that often anticipates or exaggerates such finds. As a fact, he found the body had not been embalmed, but had fallen into dust long ago. Only while he was working there by the light of his lonely candle in that sunken chapel, the candlelight threw another shadow that was not his own."

"Ah!" cried Lady Diana with a catch in her breath; "and I know what you mean now. You mean to tell us we have met the murderer, talked and joked with the murderer, let him tell us a romantic tale, and let him depart untouched."

"Leaving his clerical disguise on a rock," assented Brown. "It is all dreadfully simple. This man got ahead of the Professor in the race to the churchyard and chapel, possibly while the Professor was talking to that lugubrious journalist. He came on the old clergyman beside the empty coffin and killed him. Then he dressed himself in the black clothes from the corpse, wrapped it in an old cope which had been among the real finds of the exploration, and put it in the coffin, arranging the rosary and the wooden support as I have described. Then, having thus set the trap for his second enemy, he went up into the daylight and greeted us all with the most amiable politeness of a country clergyman."

"He ran a considerable risk," objected Tarrant, "of somebody knowing Walters by sight."

"I admit he was half-mad," agreed Father Brown; "and I think you will admit that the risk was worth taking, for he has got off, after all."

"I'll admit he was very lucky," growled Tarrant. "And who the devil was he?"

"As you say, he was very lucky," answered Father Brown, "and not least in that respect. For that is the one thing we may never know."

He frowned at the table for a moment and then went on: "This fellow has been hovering round and threatening for years, but the one thing he was careful of was to keep the secret of who he was; and he has kept it still. But if poor Smaill recovers, as I think he will, it is pretty safe to say that you will hear more of it."

"Why, what will Professor Smaill do, do you think?" asked Lady Diana.

"I should think the first thing he would do," said Tarrant, "would be to put the detectives on like dogs after this murdering devil. I should like to have a go at him myself."

"Well," said Father Brown, smiling suddenly after his long fit of frowning perplexity, "I think I know the very first thing he ought to do."

"And what is that?" asked Lady Diana with graceful eagerness.

"He ought to apologize to all of you," said Father Brown.

It was not upon this point, however, that Father Brown found himself talking to Professor Smaill as he sat by the bedside during the slow convalescence of that eminent archaeologist. Nor indeed was it chiefly Father Brown who did the talking; for though the Professor was limited to small doses of the stimulant of conversation, he concentrated most of it upon these interviews with his clerical friend. Father Brown had a talent for being silent in an encouraging way. And Smaill was encouraged by it to talk about many strange things not always easy to talk about; such as the morbid phases of recovery and the monstrous dreams that often accompany delirium. It is often rather an unbalancing business to recover slowly from a bad knock on the head; and when the head is as

interesting a head as that of Professor Smaill even its distur-
bances and distortions are apt to be original and curious. His
dreams were like bold and big designs rather out of drawing,
as they can be seen in the strong but stiff archaic arts that he
had studied; they were full of strange saints with square and
triangular haloes, of golden outstanding crowns and glories
round dark and flattened faces, of eagles out of the east and
the high headdresses of bearded men with their hair bound
like women. Only, as he told his friend, there was one much
simpler and less entangled type that continually recurred to
his imaginative memory. Again and again all these Byzantine
patterns would fade away like the fading gold on which they
were traced as upon fire; and nothing remained but the dark
bare wall of rock on which the shining shape of the fish was
traced as with a finger dipped in the phosphorescence of
fishes. For that was the sign which he once looked up and saw,
in the moment when he first heard round the corner of the
dark passage the voice of his enemy.

"And at last," he said, "I think I have seen a meaning in
the picture and the voice; and one that I never understood
before. Why should I worry because one madman among a
million of sane men, leagued in a great society against him,
chooses to brag of persecuting me or pursuing me to death?
The man who drew in the dark catacomb the secret symbol
of Christ was persecuted in a very different fashion. He was
the solitary madman; the whole sane society was leagued together not to save but to slay him. I have sometimes fussed
and fidgeted and wondered whether this or that man was my
persecutor; whether it was Tarrant; whether it was Leonard
Smyth; whether it was any one of them! Suppose it had been
all of them! Suppose it had been all the men on the boat and
the men on the train and the men in the village. Suppose, so
far as I was concerned, they were all murderers. I thought I

had a right to be alarmed because I was creeping through the bowels of the earth in the dark and there was a man who would destroy me. What would it have been like, if the destroyer had been up in the daylight and had owned all the earth and commanded all the armies and the crowds? How if he had been able to stop all the earths or smoke me out of my hole, or kill me the moment I put my nose out in the daylight? What was it like to deal with murder on that scale? The world has forgotten these things, as until a little while ago it had forgotten war."

"Yes," said Father Brown, "but the war came. The fish may be driven underground again, but it will come up into the daylight once more. As St. Antony of Padua humorously remarked, it is only fishes who survive the Deluge."[14]

---

[14] Father Brown refers to the eloquent Franciscan (1165–1231) who, when rebuffed by the sinners of Rimini, went to the riverbank and preached a sermon to the fish, solemnly telling them that "when the great flood swallowed up the world, God preserved you only without injury or harm."

The Secret Garden

Aristide Valentin, Chief of the Paris Police, was late for his dinner, and some of his guests began to arrive before him. These were, however, reassured by his confidential servant, Ivan, the old man with a scar, and a face almost as grey as his moustaches, who always sat at a table in the entrance hall—a hall hung with weapons. Valentin's house was perhaps as peculiar and celebrated as its master. It was an old house, with high walls and tall poplars almost overhanging the Seine; but the oddity—and perhaps the police value—of its architecture was this: that there was no ultimate exit at all except through this front door, which was guarded by Ivan and the armoury. The garden was large and elaborate, and there were many exits from the house into the garden. But there was no exit from the garden into the world outside; all round it ran a tall, smooth, unscalable wall with special spikes at the top; no bad garden, perhaps, for a man to reflect in whom some hundred criminals had sworn to kill.

As Ivan explained to the guests, their host had telephoned that he was detained for ten minutes. He was, in truth, making some last arrangements about executions and such ugly

"The Secret Garden" first appeared in the October 1910 issue of *Storyteller* magazine.

things; and though these duties were rootedly repulsive to him, he always performed them with precision. Ruthless in the pursuit of criminals, he was very mild about their punishment. Since he had been supreme over French—and largely over European—policial methods, his great influence had been honourably used for the mitigation of sentences and the purification of prisons. He was one of the great humanitarian French freethinkers; and the only thing wrong with them is that they make mercy even colder than justice.

When Valentin arrived he was already dressed in black clothes and the red rosette—an elegant figure, his dark beard already streaked with grey. He went straight through his house to his study, which opened on the grounds behind. The garden door of it was open, and after he had carefully locked his box in its official place, he stood for a few seconds at the open door looking out upon the garden. A sharp moon was fighting with the flying rags and tatters of a storm, and Valentin regarded it with a wistfulness unusual in such scientific natures as his. Perhaps such scientific natures have some psychic prevision of the most tremendous problem of their lives. From any such occult mood, at least, he quickly recovered, for he knew he was late, and that his guests had already begun to arrive. A glance at his drawing-room when he entered it was enough to make certain that his principal guest was not there, at any rate. He saw all the other pillars of the little party: he saw Lord Galloway, the English Ambassador—a choleric old man with a russet face like an apple, wearing the blue ribbon of the Garter.[1] He saw Lady Galloway, slim and threadlike, with silver hair and a face sensitive and superior. He saw her daughter, Lady Margaret Graham, a pale and pretty girl with an elfish face and copper-coloured

---

[1] The ribbon informs us that Lord Galloway is a member of the Noble Order of the Garter, the most prestigious of British orders of knighthood.

hair. He saw the Duchess of Mont St. Michel, black-eyed and opulent, and with her her two daughters, black-eyed and opulent also. He saw Dr. Simon, a typical French scientist, with glasses, a pointed brown beard, and a forehead barred with those parallel wrinkles which are the penalty of superciliousness, since they come through constantly elevating the eyebrows. He saw Father Brown, of Cobhole, in Essex, whom he had recently met in England.[2] He saw—perhaps with more interest than any of these—a tall man in uniform, who had bowed to the Galloways without receiving any very hearty acknowledgment, and who now advanced alone to pay his respects to his host. This was Commandant O'Brien, of the French Foreign Legion. He was a slim yet somewhat swaggering figure, clean-shaven, dark-haired, and blue-eyed, and, as seemed natural in an officer of that famous regiment of victorious failures and successful suicides, he had an air at once dashing and melancholy. He was by birth an Irish gentleman, and in boyhood had known the Galloways—especially Margaret Graham. He had left his country after some crash of debts, and now expressed his complete freedom from British etiquette by swinging about in uniform, sabre and spurs. When he bowed to the Ambassador's family, Lord and Lady Galloway bent stiffly, and Lady Margaret looked away.

But for whatever old causes such people might be interested in each other, their distinguished host was not specially interested in them. No one of them at least was in his eyes the guest of the evening. Valentin was expecting, for special reasons, a man of world-wide fame, whose friendship he had secured during some of his great detective tours and triumphs in the United States. He was expecting Julius K. Brayne, that multimillionaire whose colossal and even crushing endow-

---

[2] The details of that recent meeting were disclosed in an earlier Father Brown story, the first: "The Blue Cross".

ments of small religions have occasioned so much easy sport and easier solemnity for the American and English papers. Nobody could quite make out whether Mr. Brayne was an atheist or a Mormon or a Christian Scientist; but he was ready to pour money into any intellectual vessel, so long as it was an untried vessel. One of his hobbies was to wait for the American Shakespeare—a hobby more patient than angling. He admired Walt Whitman, but thought that Luke P. Tanner, of Paris, Pa., was more "progressive" than Whitman any day.[3] He liked anything that he thought "progressive." He thought Valentin "progressive," thereby doing him a grave injustice.

The solid appearance of Julius K. Brayne in the room was as decisive as a dinner bell. He had this great quality, which very few of us can claim, that his presence was as big as his absence. He was a huge fellow, as fat as he was tall, clad in complete evening black, without so much relief as a watch-chain or a ring. His hair was white and well brushed back like a German's; his face was red, fierce and cherubic, with one dark tuft under the lower lip that threw up that otherwise infantile visage with an effect theatrical and even Mephistophelean.[4] Not long, however, did that *salon* merely stare at the celebrated American; his lateness had already become a domestic problem, and he was sent with all speed into the dining-room with Lady Galloway upon his arm.

Except on one point the Galloways were genial and casual enough. So long as Lady Margaret did not take the arm of that adventurer O'Brien, her father was quite satisfied; and

[3] The reference to the major American poet Walt Whitman (1819–92) is sincere enough, but "Luke P. Tanner" was invented by Chesterton for the purpose of Brayne's comparison.

[4] Mephistopheles, the devil to whom Faust sold his soul in the medieval legend, is generally presented on the stage with the triangular tuft of beard mentioned here.

she had not done so, she had decorously gone in with Dr. Simon. Nevertheless, old Lord Galloway was restless and almost rude. He was diplomatic enough during dinner, but when, over the cigars, three of the younger men—Simon the doctor, Brown the priest, and the detrimental O'Brien, the exile in a foreign uniform—all melted away to mix with the ladies or smoke in the conservatory, then the English diplomatist grew very undiplomatic indeed. He was stung every sixty seconds with the thought that the scamp O'Brien might be signalling to Margaret somehow; he did not attempt to imagine how. He was left over the coffee with Brayne, the hoary Yankee who believed in all religions, and Valentin, the grizzled Frenchman who believed in none. They could argue with each other, but neither could appeal to him. After a time this "progressive" logomarchy had reached a crisis of tedium; Lord Galloway got up also and sought the drawing-room. He lost his way in long passages for some six or eight minutes: till he heard the high-pitched, didactic voice of the doctor, and then the dull voice of the priest, followed by general laughter. They also, he thought with a curse, were probably arguing about "science and religion." But the instant he opened the *salon* door he saw only one thing—he saw what was not there. He saw that Commandant O'Brien was absent, and that Lady Margaret was absent, too.

Rising impatiently from the drawing-room, as he had from the dining-room, he stamped along the passage once more. His notion of protecting his daughter from the Irish-Algerian ne'er-do-weel had become something central and even mad in his mind. As he went towards the back of the house, where was Valentin's study, he was surprised to meet his daughter, who swept past with a white, scornful face, which was a second enigma. If she had been with O'Brien, where was O'Brien? If she had not been with O'Brien, where had she been? With a sort of senile and passionate suspicion he groped his way to the dark back parts of the mansion, and eventually found a servants' entrance that opened on to the garden. The moon with her scimitar had now ripped up and rolled away all the storm-wrack. The argent light lit up all four corners of the garden. A tall figure in blue was striding across the lawn towards the study door; a glint of moonlit silver on his facings picked him out as Commandant O'Brien.

He vanished through the French windows into the house, leaving Lord Galloway in an indescribable temper, at once virulent and vague. The blue-and-silver garden, like a scene in a theatre, seemed to taunt him with all that tyrannic tenderness against which his worldly authority was at war. The length and grace of the Irishman's stride enraged him as if he were a rival instead of a father; the moonlight maddened him. He was trapped as if by magic into a garden of troubadours, a Watteau fairyland;[5] and, willing to shake off such amorous imbecilities by speech, he stepped briskly after his enemy. As he did so he tripped over some tree or stone in the grass; looked down at it first with irritation and then a second time with curiosity. The next instant the moon and the tall poplars looked at an unusual sight—an elderly English diplomatist running hard and crying or bellowing as he ran.

His hoarse shouts brought a pale face to the study door, the beaming glasses and worried brow of Dr. Simon, who heard the nobleman's first clear words. Lord Galloway was crying: "A corpse in the grass—a bloodstained corpse." O'Brien at last had gone utterly from his mind.

"We must tell Valentin at once," said the doctor, when the other had brokenly described all that he had dared to examine. "It is fortunate that he is here"; and even as he spoke the great

[5] The reference is to French artist Jean Antoin Watteau (1684–1721), famous for his sensuous images and his enchanted and delicate landscapes.

detective entered the study, attracted by the cry. It was almost amusing to note his typical transformation; he had come with the common concern of a host and a gentleman, fearing that some guest or servant was ill. When he was told the gory fact, he turned with all his gravity instantly bright and business-like; for this, however abrupt and awful, was his business.

"Strange, gentlemen," he said, as they hurried out into the garden, "that I should have hunted mysteries all over the earth, and now one comes and settles in my own back-yard. But where is the place?" They crossed the lawn less easily, as a slight mist had begun to rise from the river; but under the guidance of the shaken Galloway they found the body sunken in deep grass—the body of a very tall and broad-shouldered man. He lay face downwards, so they could only see that his big shoulders were clad in black cloth, and that his big head was bald, except for a wisp or two of brown hair that clung to his skull like wet seaweed. A scarlet serpent of blood crawled from under his fallen face.

"At least," said Simon, with a deep and singular intonation, "he is none of our party." '

"Examine him, doctor," cried Valentin rather sharply. "He may not be dead."

The doctor bent down. "He is not quite cold, but I am afraid he is dead enough," he answered. "Just help me to lift him up."

They lifted him carefully an inch from the ground, and all doubts as to his being really dead were settled at once and frightfully. The head fell away. It had been entirely sundered from the body; whoever had cut his throat had managed to sever the neck as well. Even Valentin was slightly shocked. "He must have been as strong as a gorilla," he muttered.

Not without a shiver, though he was used to anatomical abortions, Dr. Simon lifted the head. It was slightly slashed about the neck and jaw, but the face was substantially unhurt. It was a ponderous, yellow face, at once sunken and swollen, with a hawk-like nose and heavy lids—the face of a wicked Roman emperor, with, perhaps, a distant touch of a Chinese emperor. All present seemed to look at it with the coldest eye of ignorance. Nothing else could be noted about the man except that, as they had lifted his body, they had seen underneath it the white gleam of a shirtfront defaced with a red gleam of blood. As Dr. Simon said, the man had never been of their party. But he might very well have been trying to join it, for he had come dressed for such an occasion.

Valentin went down on his hands and knees and examined with his closest professional attention the grass and ground for some twenty yards round the body, in which he was assisted less skillfully by the doctor, and quite vaguely by the English lord. Nothing rewarded their grovellings except a few twigs, snapped or chopped into very small lengths, which Valentin lifted for an instant's examination, and then tossed away.

"Twigs," he said gravely; "twigs, and a total stranger with his head cut off; that is all there is on this lawn."

There was an almost creepy stillness, and then the unnerved Galloway called out sharply:

"Who's that? Who's that over there by the garden wall?"

A small figure with a foolishly large head drew waveringly near them in the moonlit haze; looked for an instant like a goblin, but turned out to be the harmless little priest whom they had left in the drawing-room.

"I say," he said meekly, "there are no gates to this garden, do you know."

Valentin's black brows had come together somewhat crossly, as they did on principle at the sight of the cassock. But he was far too just a man to deny the relevance of the remark.

"You are right," he said. "Before we find out how he came to be killed, we may have to find out how he came to be here. Now listen to me, gentlemen. If it can be done without prejudice to my position and duty, we shall all agree that certain distinguished names might well be kept out of this. There are ladies, gentlemen, and there is a foreign ambassador. If we must mark it down as a crime, then it must be followed up as a crime. But till then I can use my own discretion. I am the head of the police; I am so public that I can afford to be private. Please Heaven, I will clear every one of my own guests before I call in my men to look for anybody else. Gentlemen, upon your honour, you will none of you leave the house till to-morrow at noon; there are bedrooms for all. Simon, I think you know where to find my man, Ivan, in the front hall; he is a confidential man. Tell him to leave another servant on guard and come to me at once. Lord Galloway, you are certainly the best person to tell the ladies what has happened, and prevent a panic. They also must stay. Father Brown and I will remain with the body."

When this spirit of the captain spoke in Valentin he was obeyed like a bugle. Dr. Simon went through to the armoury and routed out Ivan, the public detective's private detective. Galloway went to the drawing-room and told the terrible news tactfully enough, so that by the time the company assembled there the ladies were already startled and already soothed. Meanwhile the good priest and the good atheist stood at the head and foot of the dead man motionless in the moonlight, like symbolic statues of their two philosophies of death.

Ivan, the confidential man with the scar and the moustaches, came out of the house like a cannon ball, and came racing across the lawn to Valentin like a dog to his master. His livid face was quite lively with the glow of this domestic detective story, and it was with almost unpleasant eagerness that he asked his master's permission to examine the remains.

"Yes; look, if you like, Ivan," said Valentin, "but don't be long. We must go in and thrash this out in the house."

Ivan lifted the head, and then almost let it drop.

"Why," he gasped, "it's—no, it isn't; it can't be. Do you know this man, sir?"

"No," said Valentin indifferently; "we had better go inside."

Between them they carried the corpse to a sofa in the study, and then all made their way to the drawing-room.

The detective sat down at a desk quietly, and even with hesitation; but his eye was the iron eye of a judge at assize. He made a few rapid notes upon paper in front of him, and then said shortly: "Is everybody here?"

"Not Mr. Brayne," said the Duchess of Mont St. Michel, looking round.

"No," said Lord Galloway, in a hoarse, harsh voice. "And not Mr. Neil O'Brien, I fancy. I saw that gentleman walking in the garden when the corpse was still warm."

"Ivan," said the detective, "go and fetch Commandant O'Brien and Mr. Brayne. Mr. Brayne, I know, is finishing a cigar in the dining-room; Commandant O'Brien, I think, is walking up and down the conservatory. I am not sure."

The faithful attendant flashed from the room, and before anyone could stir or speak Valentin went on with the same soldierly swiftness of exposition.

"Everyone here knows that a dead man has been found in the garden, his head cut clean from his body. Dr. Simon, you have examined it. Do you think that to cut a man's throat like that would need great force? Or, perhaps, only a very sharp knife?"

"I should say that it could not be done with a knife at all," said the pale doctor.

"Have you any thought," resumed Valentin, "of a tool with which it could be done?"

"Speaking within modern probabilities, I really haven't," said the doctor, arching his painful brows. "It's not easy to hack a neck through even clumsily, and this was a very clean cut. It could be done with a battle-axe or an old headsman's axe, or an old two-handed sword."

"But, good heavens!" cried the Duchess, almost in hysterics, "there aren't any two-handed swords and battle-axes round here."

Valentin was still busy with the paper in front of him. "Tell me," he said, still writing rapidly, "could it have been done with a long French cavalry sabre?"

A low knocking came at the door, which for some unreasonable reason, curdled everyone's blood like the knocking in *Macbeth*.[6] Amid that frozen silence Dr. Simon managed to say: "A sabre—yes, I suppose it could."

"Thank you," said Valentin. "Come in, Ivan."

The confidential Ivan opened the door and ushered in Commandant Neil O'Brien, whom he had found at last pacing the garden again.

The Irish officer stood disordered and defiant on the threshold. "What do you want with me?" he cried.

"Please sit down," said Valentin in pleasant, level tones. "Why, you aren't wearing your sword! Where is it?"

"I left it on the library table," said O'Brien, his brogue deepening in his disturbed mood. "It was a nuisance, it was getting—"

---

[6] Immediately following the midnight murder in Act II of Shakespeare's play, the Macbeths (and the audience) are startled by the loud, unexpected, and insistent knocking at the castle gate.

"Ivan," said Valentin: "please go and get the Commandant's sword from the library." Then, as the servant vanished: "Lord Galloway says he saw you leaving the garden just before he found the corpse. What were you doing in the garden?" The Commandant flung himself recklessly into a chair. "Oh," he cried in pure Irish; "admirin' the moon. Communing with Nature, me bhoy."

A heavy silence sank and endured, and at the end of it came again that trivial and terrible knocking. Ivan reappeared, carrying an empty steel scabbard. "This is all I can find," he said.

"Put it on the table," said Valentin, without looking up.

There was an inhuman silence in the room, like that sea of inhuman silence round the dock of the condemned murderer. The Duchess's weak exclamations had long ago died away. Lord Galloway's swollen hatred was satisfied and even sobered. The voice that came was quite unexpected.

"I think I can tell you," cried Lady Margaret, in that clear, quivering voice with which a courageous woman speaks publicly. "I can tell you what Mr. O'Brien was doing in the garden, since he is bound to silence. He was asking me to marry him. I refused; I said in my family circumstances I could give him nothing but my respect. He was a little angry at that; he did not seem to think much of my respect. I wonder," she added, with rather a wan smile, "if he will care at all for it now. For I offer it him now. I will swear anywhere that he never did a thing like this."

Lord Galloway had edged up to his daughter, and was intimidating her in what he imagined to be an undertone. "Hold your tongue, Maggie," he said in a thunderous whisper. "Why should you shield the fellow? Where's his sword? Where's his confounded cavalry—"

He stopped because of the singular stare with which his

daughter was regarding him, a look that was indeed a lurid magnet for the whole group.

"You old fool!" she said, in a low voice without pretence of piety; "what do you suppose you are trying to prove? I tell you this man was innocent while with me. But if he wasn't innocent, he was still with me. If he murdered a man in the garden, who was it who must have seen—who must at least have known? Do you hate Neil so much as to put your own daughter—"

Lady Galloway screamed. Everyone else sat tingling at the touch of those satanic tragedies that have been between lovers before now. They saw the proud, white face of the Scotch aristocrat and her lover, the Irish adventurer, like old portraits in a dark house. The long silence was full of formless historical memories of murdered husbands and poisonous paramours.

In the centre of this morbid silence an innocent voice said: "Was it a very long cigar?"

The change of thought was so sharp that they had to look round to see who had spoken.

"I mean," said little Father Brown, from the corner of the room. "I mean that cigar Mr. Brayne is finishing. It seems nearly as long as a walking-stick."

Despite the irrelevance there was assent as well as irritation in Valentin's face as he lifted his head.

"Quite right," he remarked sharply. "Ivan, go and see about Mr. Brayne again, and bring him here at once."

The instant the factotum had closed the door, Valentin addressed the girl with an entirely new earnestness.

"Lady Margaret," he said, "we all feel, I am sure, both gratitude and admiration for your act in rising above your lower dignity and explaining the Commandant's conduct. But there is a hiatus still. Lord Galloway, I understand, met you passing from the study to the drawing-room, and it was only some minutes afterwards that he found the garden and the Commandant still walking there."

"You have to remember," replied Margaret, with a faint irony in her voice, "that I had just refused him, so we should scarcely have come back arm in arm. He is a gentleman, anyhow; and he loitered behind—and so got charged with murder."

"In those few moments," said Valentin gravely, "he might really—"

The knock came again, and Ivan put in his scarred face.

"Beg pardon, sir," he said, "but Mr. Brayne has left the house."

"Left!" cried Valentin, and rose for the first time to his feet.

"Gone. Scooted. Evaporated," replied Ivan, in humorous French. "His hat and coat are gone, too; and I'll tell you something to cap it all. I ran outside the house to find any traces of him, and I found one, and a big trace, too."

"What do you mean?" asked Valentin.

"I'll show you," said his servant, and reappeared with a flashing naked cavalry sabre, streaked with blood about the point and edge. Everyone in the room eyed it as if it were a thunderbolt; but the experienced Ivan went on quite quietly:

"I found this," he said, "flung among the bushes fifty yards up the road to Paris. In other words, I found it just where your respectable Mr. Brayne threw it when he ran away."

There was again a silence, but of a new sort. Valentin took the sabre, examined it, reflected with unaffected concentration of thought, and then turned a respectful face to O'Brien. "Commandant," he said, "we trust you will always produce this weapon if it is wanted for police examination. Meanwhile," he added, slapping the steel back in the ringing scabbard, "let me return you your sword."

At the military symbolism of the action the audience could hardly refrain from applause.

For Neil O'Brien, indeed, that gesture was the turning-point of existence. By the time he was wandering in the mysterious garden again in the colours of the morning the tragic futility of his ordinary mien had fallen from him; he was a man with many reasons for happiness. Lord Galloway was a gentleman, and had offered him an apology. Lady Margaret was something better than a lady, a woman at least, and had perhaps given him something better than an apology, as they drifted among the old flower-beds before breakfast. The whole company was more light-hearted and humane, for though the riddle of the death remained, the load of suspicion was lifted off them all, and sent flying off to Paris with the strange millionaire—a man they hardly knew. The devil was cast out of the house—he had cast himself out.

Still, the riddle remained; and when O'Brien threw himself on a garden seat beside Dr. Simon, that keenly scientific person at once resumed it. He did not get much talk out of O'Brien, whose thoughts were on pleasanter things.

"I can't say it interests me much," said the Irishman frankly, "especially as it seems pretty plain now. Apparently Brayne hated this stranger for some reason; lured him into the garden, and killed him with my sword. Then he fled to the city, tossing the sword away as he went. By the way, Ivan tells me the dead man had a Yankee dollar in his pocket. So he was a countryman of Brayne's, and that seems to clinch it. I don't see any difficulties about the business."

"There are five colossal difficulties," said the doctor quietly; "like high walls within walls. Don't mistake me. I don't doubt that Brayne did it; his flight, I fancy, proves that. But as to how he did it. First difficulty: Why should a man kill another man with a great hulking sabre, when he can almost kill him with a pocket knife and put it back in his pocket? Second difficulty: Why was there no noise or outcry? Does a man commonly see another come up waving a scimitar and offer no remarks? Third difficulty: A servant watched the front door all the evening; and a rat cannot get into Valentin's garden anywhere. How did the dead man get into the garden? Fourth difficulty: Given the same conditions, how did Brayne get out of the garden?"

"And the fifth," said Neil, with eyes fixed on the English priest, who was coming slowly up the path.

"Is a trifle, I suppose," said the doctor, "but I think an odd one. When I first saw how the head had been slashed, I supposed the assassin had struck more than once. But on examination I found many cuts across the truncated section; in other words, they were struck *after* the head was off. Did Brayne hate his foe so fiendishly that he stood sabring his body in the moonlight?"

"Horrible!" said O'Brien, and shuddered.

The little priest, Brown, had arrived while they were talking, and had waited, with characteristic shyness, till they had finished. Then he said awkwardly:

"I say, I'm sorry to interrupt. But I was sent to tell you the news!"

"News?" repeated Simon, and stared at him rather painfully through his glasses.

"Yes, I'm sorry," said Father Brown mildly. "There's been another murder, you know."

Both men on the seat sprang up, leaving it rocking.

"And, what's stranger still," continued the priest, with his dull eye on the rhododendrons, "it's the same disgusting sort; it's another beheading. They found the second head actually bleeding in the river, a few yards along Brayne's road to Paris; so they suppose that he—"

"Great Heaven!" cried O'Brien. "Is Brayne a monomaniac?"

"There are American vendettas," said the priest impassively. Then he added: "They want you to come to the library and see it."

Commandant O'Brien followed the others towards the inquest, feeling decidedly sick. As a soldier, he loathed all this secretive carnage; where were these extravagant amputations going to stop? First one head was hacked off, and then another; in this case (he told himself bitterly) it was not true that two heads were better than one. As he crossed the study he almost staggered at a shocking coincidence. Upon Valentin's table lay the coloured picture of yet a third bleeding head; and it was the head of Valentin himself. A second glance showed him it was only a Nationalist paper, called *The Guillotine*, which every week showed one of its political opponents with rolling eyes and writhing features just after execution; for Valentin was an anti-clerical of some note. But O'Brien was an Irishman, with a kind of chastity even in his sins; and his gorge rose against that great brutality of the intellect which belongs only to France. He felt Paris as a whole, from the grotesques on the Gothic churches to the gross caricatures in the newspapers. He remembered the gigantic jests of the Revolution. He saw the whole city as one ugly energy, from the sanguinary sketch lying on Valentin's table up to where, above a mountain and forest of gargoyles, the great devil grins on Notre Dame.

The library was long, low, and dark; what light entered it shot from under low blinds and had still some of the ruddy tinge of morning. Valentin and his servant Ivan were waiting for them at the upper end of a long, slightly-sloping desk, on which lay the mortal remains, looking enormous in the twilight. The big black figure and yellow face of the man found in the garden confronted them essentially unchanged. The second head, which had been fished from among the river reeds that morning, lay streaming and dripping beside it; Valentin's men were still seeking to recover the rest of this second corpse, which was supposed to be afloat. Father Brown, who did not seem to share O'Brien's sensibilities in the least, went up to the second head and examined it with his blinking care. It was little more than a mop of wet white hair, fringed with silver fire in the red and level morning light; the face, which seemed of an ugly, empurpled and perhaps criminal type, had been much battered against trees or stones as it tossed in the water.

"Good morning, Commandant O'Brien," said Valentin, with quiet cordiality. "You have heard of Brayne's last experiment in butchery, I suppose?"

Father Brown was still bending over the head with white hair, and he said, without looking up:

"I suppose it is quite certain that Brayne cut off this head, too."

"Well, it seems common sense," said Valentin, with his hands in his pockets. "Killed in the same way as the other. Found within a few yards of the other. And sliced by the same weapon which we know he carried away."

"Yes, yes; I know," replied Father Brown, submissively. "Yet, you know, I doubt whether Brayne could have cut off this head."

"Why not?" inquired Dr. Simon, with a rational stare.

"Well, doctor," said the priest, looking up blinking, "can a man cut off his own head? I don't know."

O'Brien felt an insane universe crashing about his ears; but the doctor sprang forward with impetuous practicality and pushed back the wet white hair.

"Oh, there's no doubt it's Brayne," said the priest quietly. "He had exactly that chip in the left ear."

The detective, who had been regarding the priest with steady and glittering eyes, opened his clenched mouth and said sharply: "You seem to know a lot about him, Father Brown."

"I do," said the little man simply. "I've been about with him for some weeks. He was thinking of joining our church."

The star of the fanatic sprang into Valentin's eyes; he strode towards the priest with clenched hands. "And, perhaps," he cried, with a blasting sneer: "perhaps he was also thinking of leaving all his money to your church."

"Perhaps he was," said Brown stolidly; "it is possible."

"In that case," cried Valentin, with a dreadful smile: "you may indeed know a great deal about him. About his life and about his—"

Commandant O'Brien laid a hand on Valentin's arm. "Drop that slanderous rubbish, Valentin," he said: "or there may be more swords yet."

But Valentin (under the steady, humble gaze of the priest) had already recovered himself. "Well," he said shortly: "people's private opinions can wait. You gentlemen are still bound by your promise to stay; you must enforce it on yourselves—and on each other. Ivan here will tell you anything more you want to know; I must get to business and write to the authorities. We can't keep this quiet any longer. I shall be writing in my study if there is any more news."

"Is there any more news, Ivan?" asked Dr. Simon, as the chief of police strode out of the room.

"Only one more thing, I think, sir," said Ivan, wrinkling up his grey old face, "but that's important, too, in its way. There's that old buffer you found on the lawn," and he pointed without pretence of reverence at the big black body with the yellow head. "We've found out who he is, anyhow."

"Indeed!" cried the astonished doctor; "and who is he?"

"His name was Arnold Becker," said the under-detective, "though he went by many aliases. He was a wandering sort of scamp, and is known to have been in America; so that was where Brayne got his knife into him. We didn't have much to do with him ourselves, for he worked mostly in Germany. We've communicated, of course, with the German police. But, oddly enough, there was a twin brother of his, named Louis Becker, whom we had a great deal to do with. In fact, we found it necessary to guillotine him only yesterday. Well, it's a rum thing, gentlemen, but when I saw that fellow flat on the lawn I had the greatest jump of my life. If I hadn't seen Louis Becker guillotined with my own eyes, I'd have sworn it was Louis Becker lying there in the grass. Then, of course, I remembered his twin brother in Germany, and following up the clue—"

The explanatory Ivan stopped, for the excellent reason that nobody was listening to him. The Commandant and the doctor were both staring at Father Brown, who had sprung stiffly to his feet, and was holding his temples tight like a man in sudden and violent pain.

"Stop, stop, stop!" he cried; "stop talking a minute, for I see half. Will God give me strength? Will my brain make the one jump and see all? Heaven help me! I used to be fairly good at thinking. I could paraphrase any page in Aquinas once. Will my head split—or will it see? I see half—I only see half."

He buried his head in his hands, and stood in a sort of rigid torture of thought or prayer, while the other three could only go on staring at this last prodigy of their wild twelve hours.

When Father Brown's hands fell they showed a face quite fresh and serious, like a child's. He heaved a huge sigh, and said: "Let us get this said and done with as quickly as possible. Look here, this will be the quickest way to convince you all of the truth." He turned to the doctor. "Dr. Simon," he said, "you have a strong head-piece, and I heard you this morning asking the five hardest questions about this business. Well, if you will now ask them again, I will answer them."

Simon's pince-nez dropped from his nose in his doubt and wonder, but he answered at once. "Well, the first question, you know, is why a man should kill another with a clumsy sabre at all when a man can kill with a bodkin?"

"A man cannot behead with a bodkin," said Brown, calmly, "and for *this* murder beheading was absolutely necessary."

"Why?" asked O'Brien, with interest.

"And the next question?" asked Father Brown.

"Well, why didn't the man cry out or anything?" asked the doctor; "sabres in gardens are certainly unusual."

"Twigs," said the priest gloomily, and turned to the window which looked on the scene of death. "No one saw the point of the twigs. Why should they lie on that lawn (look at it) so far from any tree? They were not snapped off; they were chopped off. The murderer occupied his enemy with some tricks with the sabre, showing how he could cut a branch in mid-air, or what not. Then, while his enemy bent down to see the result, a silent slash, and the head fell."

"Well," said the doctor slowly, "that seems plausible enough. But my next two questions will stump anyone."

The priest still stood looking critically out of the window and waited.

"You know how all the garden was sealed up like an airtight chamber," went on the doctor. "Well, how did the strange man get into the garden?"

Without turning round, the little priest answered: "There never was any strange man in the garden."

There was a silence, and then a sudden cackle of almost

childish laughter relieved the strain. The absurdity of Brown's remark moved Ivan to open taunts.

"Oh!" he cried; "then we didn't lug a great fat corpse on to a sofa last night? He hadn't got into the garden, I suppose."

"Got into the garden?" repeated Brown reflectively. "No, not entirely."

"Hang it all," cried Simon, "a man gets into a garden, or he doesn't."

"Not necessarily," said the priest, with a faint smile. "What is the next question, doctor?"

"I fancy you're ill," exclaimed Dr. Simon sharply; "but I'll ask the next question if you like. How did Brayne get out of the garden?"

"He didn't get out of the garden," said the priest, still looking out of the window.

"Didn't get out of the garden?" exploded Simon.

"Not completely," said Father Brown.

Simon shook his fists in a frenzy of French logic. "A man gets out of a garden, or he doesn't," he cried.

"Not always," said Father Brown.

Dr. Simon sprang to his feet impatiently. "I have no time to spare on such senseless talk," he cried angrily. "If you can't understand a man being on one side of the wall or the other, I won't trouble you further."

"Doctor," said the cleric very gently, "we have always got on very pleasantly together. If only for the sake of old friendship, stop and tell me your fifth question."

The impatient Simon sank into a chair by the door and said briefly: "The head and shoulders were cut about in a queer way. It seemed to be done after death."

"Yes," said the motionless priest, "it was done so as to make you assume exactly the one simple falsehood that you did assume. It was done to make you take for granted that the head belonged to the body."

The borderland of the brain, where all the monsters are made, moved horribly in the Gaelic O'Brien. He felt the chaotic presence of all the horse-men and fish-women that man's unnatural fancy has begotten. A voice older than his first fathers seemed saying in his ear: "Keep out of the monstrous garden where grows the tree with double fruit. Avoid the evil garden where died the man with two heads." Yet, while these shameful symbolic shapes passed across the ancient mirror of his Irish soul, his Frenchified intellect was quite alert, and was watching the odd priest as closely and incredulously as all the rest.

Father Brown had turned round at last, and stood against the window with his face in dense shadow; but even in that shadow they could see it was pale as ashes. Nevertheless, he spoke quite sensibly, as if there were no Gaelic souls on earth.

"Gentlemen," he said, "you did not find the strange body of Becker in the garden. You did not find any strange body in the garden. In face of Dr. Simon's rationalism, I still affirm that Becker was only partly present. Look here!" (pointing to the black bulk of the mysterious corpse) "you never saw that man in your lives. Did you ever see this man?"

He rapidly rolled away the bald, yellow head of the unknown, and put in its place the white-maned head beside it. And there, complete, unified, unmistakable, lay Julius K. Brayne.

"The murderer," went on Brown quietly, "hacked off his enemy's head and flung the sword far over the wall. But he was too clever to fling the sword only. He flung the head over the wall also. Then he had only to clap on another head to the corpse, and (as he insisted on a private inquest) you all imagined a totally new man."

"Clap on another head!" said O'Brien, staring. "What other head? Heads don't grow on garden bushes, do they?"

"No," said Father Brown huskily, and looking at his boots; "there is only one place where they grow. They grow in the basket of the guillotine, beside which the Chief of Police, Aristide Valentin, was standing not an hour before the murder. Oh, my friends, hear me a minute more before you tear me in pieces. Valentin is an honest man, if being mad for an arguable cause is honesty. But did you never see in that cold, grey eye of his that he is mad? He would do anything, *anything*, to break what he calls the superstition of the Cross. He has fought for it and starved for it, and now he has murdered for it. Brayne's crazy millions had hitherto been scattered among so many sects that they did little to alter the balance of things. But Valentin heard a whisper that Brayne, like so many scatter-brained sceptics, was drifting to us; and that was quite a different thing. Brayne would pour supplies into the impoverished and pugnacious Church of France; he would support six Nationalist newspapers like *The Guillotine*. The battle was already balanced on a point, and the fanatic took flame at the risk. He resolved to destroy the millionaire, and he did it as one would expect the greatest of detectives to commit his only crime. He abstracted the severed head of Becker on some criminological excuse, and took it home in his official box. He had that last argument with Brayne, that Lord Galloway did not hear the end of; that failing, he led him out into the sealed garden, talked about swordsmanship, used twigs and a sabre for illustration, and—"

Ivan of the Scar sprang up. "You lunatic," he yelled; "you'll go to my master now, if I take you by—"

"Why, I was going there," said Brown heavily; "I must ask him to confess, and all that."

Driving the unhappy Brown before them like a hostage or

sacrifice, they rushed together into the sudden stillness of Valentin's study. The great detective sat at his desk apparently too occupied to hear their turbulent entrance. They paused a moment, and then something in the look of that upright and elegant back made the doctor run forward suddenly. A touch and a glance showed him that there was a small box of pills at Valentin's elbow, and that Valentin was dead in his chair; and on the blind face of the suicide was more than the pride of Cato.[7]

---

[7] The reference is to Cato the Younger (95–46 B.C.), the Roman Stoic and supporter of Pompey, whose pride led him to commit suicide rather than submit to Julius Caesar.

The Flying Stars

"THE most beautiful crime I ever committed," Flambeau would say in his highly moral old age, "was also, by a singular coincidence, my last. It was committed at Christmas. As an artist I had always attempted to provide crimes suitable to the special season or landscapes in which I found myself, choosing this or that terrace or garden for a catastrophe, as if for a statuary group. Thus squires should be swindled in long rooms panelled with oak; while Jews, on the other hand, should rather find themselves unexpectedly penniless among the light and screens of the Café Riche. Thus, in England, if I wished to relieve a dean of his riches (which is not so easy as you might suppose), I wished to frame him, if I make myself clear, in the green lawns and grey towers of some cathedral town. Similarly, in France, when I had got money out of a rich and wicked peasant (which is almost impossible), it gratified me to get his indignant head relieved against a grey line of clipped poplars, and those solemn plains of Gaul over which broods the mighty spirit of Millet.[1]

"The Flying Stars" first appeared in the June 1911 issue of *Cassell's* Magazine.
[1] Flambeau is referring to Jean François Millet (1814–75), a French painter celebrated for his rural scenes and peasant subjects.

"Well, my last crime was a Christmas crime, a cheery, cosy, English middle-class crime; a crime of Charles Dickens.[2] I did it in a good old middle-class house near Putney, a house with a crescent of carriage drive, a house with a stable by the side of it, a house with the name on the two outer gates, a house with a monkey tree. Enough, you know the species. I really think my imitation of Dickens's style was dexterous and literary. It seems almost a pity I repented the same evening."

Flambeau would then proceed to tell the story from the inside; and even from the inside it was odd. Seen from the outside it was perfectly incomprehensible, and it is from the outside that the stranger must study it. From this standpoint the drama may be said to have begun when the front doors of the house with the stable opened on the garden with the monkey tree, and a young girl came out with bread to feed the birds on the afternoon of Boxing Day.[3] She had a pretty face, with brave brown eyes; but her figure was beyond conjecture, for she was so wrapped up in brown furs that it was hard to say which was hair and which was fur. But for the attractive face she might have been a small toddling bear.

The winter afternoon was reddening towards evening, and already a ruby light was rolled over the bloomless beds, filling them, as it were, with the ghosts of the dead roses. On one side of the house stood the stable, on the other an alley or

[2] Here he refers to the ability of novelist Charles Dickens (1812–70) to evoke the atmosphere and setting of a traditional English Christmas. For Chesterton's own view (that all of the comedy in Dickens expresses a Christmas-like joy) see, for example, his "Appreciations and Criticism of the Works of Charles Dickens", "Christmas Stories", *Collected Works*, vol. XV, pp. 336–41.

[3] Boxing Day is, in England and other places, the first weekday after Christmas Day and a traditional bank-holiday on which gifts and gratuities are customary.

cloister of laurels led to the larger garden behind. The young lady, having scattered bread for the birds (for the fourth or fifth time that day, because the dog ate it), passed unobtrusively down the lane of laurels and into a glimmering plantation of evergreens behind. Here she gave an exclamation of wonder, real or ritual, and looking up at the high garden wall above her, beheld it fantastically bestridden by a somewhat fantastic figure.

"Oh, don't jump, Mr. Crook," she called out in some alarm; "it's much too high."

The individual riding the party wall like an aerial horse was a tall, angular young man, with dark hair sticking up like a hair brush, intelligent and even distinguished lineaments, but a sallow and almost alien complexion. This showed the more plainly because he wore an aggressive red tie, the only part of his costume of which he seemed to take any care. Perhaps it was a symbol. He took no notice of the girl's alarmed adjuration, but leapt like a grasshopper to the ground beside her, where he might very well have broken his legs.

"I think I was meant to be a burglar," he said placidly, "and I have no doubt I should have been if I hadn't happened to be born in that nice house next door. I can't see any harm in it, anyhow."

"How can you say such things?" she remonstrated.

"Well," said the young man, "if you're born on the wrong side of the wall, I can't see that it's wrong to climb over it."

"I never know what you will say or do next," she said.

"I don't often know myself," replied Mr. Crook; "but then I am on the right side of the wall now."

"And which is the right side of the wall?" asked the young lady, smiling.

"Whichever side you are on," said the young man named Crook.

As they went together through the laurels towards the front garden a motor horn sounded thrice, coming nearer and nearer, and a car of splendid speed, great elegance, and a pale green colour swept up to the front doors like a bird and stood throbbing.

"Hullo, hullo!" said the young man with the red tie, "here's somebody born on the right side, anyhow. I didn't know, Miss Adams, that your Santa Claus was so modern as this."

"Oh, that's my godfather, Sir Leopold Fischer. He always comes on Boxing Day."

Then, after an innocent pause, which unconsciously betrayed some lack of enthusiasm, Ruby Adams added:

"He is very kind."

John Crook, journalist, had heard of that eminent City magnate; and it was not his fault if the City magnate had not heard of him; for in certain articles in *The Clarion* or *The New Age*[4] Sir Leopold had been dealt with austerely. But he said nothing and grimly watched the unloading of the motor-car, which was rather a long process. A large, neat chauffeur in green got out from the front, and a small, neat manservant in grey got out from the back, and between them they deposited Sir Leopold on the doorstep and began to unpack him, like some very carefully protected parcel. Rugs enough to stock a bazaar, furs of all the beasts of the forest, and scarves of all the colours of the rainbow were unwrapped one by one, till they revealed something resembling the human form; the form of a friendly, but foreign-looking old gentleman, with a grey goat-like beard and a beaming smile, who rubbed his big fur gloves together.

Long before this revelation was complete the two big doors of the porch had opened in the middle, and Colonel Adams

[4] At the time this story was written (1911), *The Clarion* and *The New Age* were prominent Socialist newspapers published in London.

(father of the furry young lady) had come out himself to invite his eminent guest inside. He was a tall, sunburnt and very silent man, who wore a red smoking-cap like a fez, making him look like one of the English Sirdars or Pashas in Egypt.[5] With him was his brother-in-law, lately come from Canada, a big and rather boisterous young gentleman-farmer, with a yellow beard, by name James Blount. With him also was the more insignificant figure of the priest from the neighbouring Roman church; for the colonel's late wife had been a Catholic, and the children, as is common in such cases, had been trained to follow her. Everything seemed undistinguished about the priest, even down to his name, which was Brown; yet the colonel had always found something companionable about him, and frequently asked him to such family gatherings.

In the large entrance hall of the house there was ample room even for Sir Leopold and the removal of his wraps. Porch and vestibule, indeed, were unduly large in proportion to the house, and formed, as it were, a big room with the front door at one end, and the bottom of the staircase at the other. In front of the large hall fire, over which hung the colonel's sword, the process was completed and the company, including the saturnine Crook, presented to Sir Leopold Fischer. That venerable financier, however, still seemed struggling with portions of his well-lined attire, and at length produced from a very interior tail-coat pocket, a black oval case which he radiantly explained to be his Christmas present for his goddaughter. With an unaffected vain-glory that had something disarming about it he held out the case before them all; it flew open at a touch and half-blinded them. It was just as if a

[5] *Sirdar*, a word from the Urdu language of India, means "a leader" and was used at the time of this story for the British Commander of Egyptian Armies; *pasha* (or *pacha*) is Turkish for "high-ranking official".

crystal fountain had spurted in their eyes. In a nest of orange velvet lay like three eggs, three white and vivid diamonds that seemed to set the very air on fire all round them. Fischer stood beaming benevolently and drinking deep of the astonishment and ecstasy of the girl, the grim admiration and gruff thanks of the colonel, the wonder of the whole group.

"I'll put 'em back now, my dear," said Fischer, returning the case to the tails of his coat. "I had to be careful of 'em coming down. They're the three great African diamonds called 'The Flying Stars,' because they've been stolen so often. All the big criminals are on the track; but even the rough men about in the streets and hotels could hardly have kept their hands off them. I might have lost them on the road here. It was quite possible."

"Quite natural, I should say," growled the man in the red tie. "I shouldn't blame 'em if they had taken 'em. When they ask for bread, and you don't even give them a stone, I think they might take the stone for themselves."

"I won't have you talking like that," cried the girl, who was in a curious glow. "You've only talked like that since you became a horrid what's-his-name. You know what I mean. What do you call a man who wants to embrace the chimney-sweep?"

"A saint," said Father Brown.

"I think," said Sir Leopold, with a supercilious smile, "that Ruby means a Socialist."

"A Radical does not mean a man who lives on radishes," remarked Crook, with some impatience; "and a Conservative does not mean a man who preserves jam. Neither, I assure you, does a Socialist mean a man who desires a social evening with the chimney-sweep. A Socialist means a man who wants all the chimneys swept and all the chimney-sweeps paid for it."

"But who won't allow you," put in the priest in a low voice, "to own your own soot."

Crook looked at him with an eye of interest and even respect. "Does one want to own soot?" he asked.

"One might," answered Brown, with speculation in his eye. "I've heard that gardeners use it. And I once made six children happy at Christmas when the conjuror didn't come, entirely with soot—applied externally."

"Oh, splendid," cried Ruby. "Oh, I wish you'd do it to this company."

The boisterous Canadian, Mr. Blount, was lifting his loud voice in applause, and the astonished financier his (in some considerable deprecation), when a knock sounded at the double front doors. The priest opened them, and they showed again the front garden of evergreens, monkey-tree and all, now gathering gloom against a gorgeous violet sunset. The scene thus framed was so coloured and quaint, like a back scene in a play, that they forgot for a moment the insignificant figure standing in the door. He was dusty-looking and in a frayed coat, evidently a common messenger. "Any of you gentlemen Mr. Blount?" he asked, and held forward a letter doubtfully. Mr. Blount started, and stopped in his shout of assent. Ripping up the envelope with evident astonishment he read it; his face clouded a little, and then cleared, and he turned to his brother-in-law and host.

"I'm sick at being such a nuisance, colonel," he said, with the cheery colonial convention; "but would it upset you if an old acquaintance called on me here to-night on business? In point of fact it's Florian, that famous French acrobat and comic actor; I knew him years ago out West (he was a French-Canadian by birth), and he seems to have business for me, though I hardly guess what."

"Of course, of course," replied the colonel carelessly. "My

dear chap, any friend of yours. No doubt he will prove an acquisition."

"He'll black his face, if that's what you mean," cried Blount, laughing. "I don't doubt he'd black everyone else's eyes. I don't care; I'm not refined. I like the jolly old pantomime where a man sits on his top hat."

"Not on mine, please," said Sir Leopold Fischer, with dignity.

"Well, well," observed Crook airily, "don't let's quarrel. There are lower jokes than sitting on a top hat."

Dislike of the red-tied youth, born of his predatory opinions and evident intimacy with the pretty god-child, led Fischer to say, in his most sarcastic, magisterial manner: "No doubt you have found something much lower than sitting on a top hat. What is it, pray?"

"Letting a top hat sit on you, for instance," said the Socialist.

"Now, now, now," cried the Canadian farmer with his barbarian benevolence, "don't let's spoil a jolly evening. What I say is, let's do something for the company to-night. Not blacking faces or sitting on hats, if you don't like those—but something of the sort. Why couldn't we have a proper old English pantomime—clown, columbine, and so on.[6] I saw one when I left England at twelve years old, and it's blazed in my brain like a bonfire ever since. I came back to the old country only last year, and I find the thing's extinct. Nothing but a lot of snivelling fairy plays. I want a hot poker and a policeman made into sausages, and they give me princesses moralizing by moonlight, Blue Birds, or some-

[6] The conventional improvisations of the Italian *commedia dell'arte*, with the mute romance of Harlequin and Columbine and the joking buffoonery of Clown and Pantaloon, were exported by way of France to England in 1702; thereafter these performances became an English Christmas tradition.

thing.[7] Blue Beard's more in my line, and him I liked best when he turned into the pantaloon."[8]

"I'm all for making a policeman into sausages," said John Crook. "It's a better definition of Socialism than some recently given. But surely the get-up would be too big a business."

"Not a scrap," cried Blount, quite carried away. "A harlequinade's the quickest thing we can do, for two reasons. First, one can gag to any degree; and, second, all the objects are household things—tables and towel-horses and washing baskets, and things like that."

"That's true," admitted Crook, nodding eagerly and walking about. "But I'm afraid I can't have my policeman's uniform. Haven't killed a policeman lately."

Blount frowned thoughtfully a space, and then smote his thigh. "Yes, we can!" he cried. "I've got Florian's address here, and he knows every *costumier* in London. I'll 'phone him to bring a police dress when he comes." And he went bounding away to the telephone.

"Oh, it's glorious, godfather," cried Ruby, almost dancing. "I'll be columbine and you shall be pantaloon."

The millionaire held himself stiff with a sort of heathen solemnity. "I think, my dear," he said, "you must get someone else for pantaloon."

"I will be pantaloon, if you like," said Colonel Adams, taking his cigar out of his mouth, and speaking for the first and last time.

---

[7] Blount's reference is to *The Blue Bird* (1908), a children's fable and play by the Belgian dramatist Maurice Maeterlink.

[8] Blount prefers children's theater of the less refined sort: pantomime productions of grisly folktales such as that of the wife-murdering Bluebeard or performances of the even more raucous and slapstick harlequinades.

"You ought to have a statue," cried the Canadian, as he came back, radiant, from the telephone. "There, we are all fitted. Mr. Crook shall be clown; he's a journalist and knows all the oldest jokes. I can be harlequin, that only wants long legs and jumping about. My friend Florian 'phones he's bringing the police costume; he's changing on the way. We can act it in this very hall, the audience sitting on those broad stairs opposite, one row above another. These front doors can be the back scene, either open or shut. Shut, you see an English interior. Open, a moonlit garden. It all goes by magic." And snatching a chance piece of billiard chalk from his pocket, he ran it across the hall floor, half-way between the front door and the staircase, to mark the line of the footlights.

How even such a banquet of bosh was got ready in the time remained a riddle. But they went at it with that mixture of recklessness and industry that lives when youth is in a house; and youth was in that house that night, though not all may have isolated the two faces and hearts from which it flamed. As always happens, the invention grew wilder and wilder through the very tameness of the *bourgeois* conventions from which it had to create. The columbine looked charming in an outstanding skirt that strangely resembled the large lamp-shade in the drawing-room. The clown and pantaloon made themselves white with flour from the cook, and red with rouge from some other domestic, who remained (like all true Christian benefactors) anonymous. The harlequin, already clad in silver paper out of cigar boxes, was, with difficulty, prevented from smashing the old Victorian lustre chandeliers, that he might cover himself with resplendent crystals. In fact he would certainly have done so, had not Ruby unearthed some old pantomime paste jewels she had worn at a fancy dress party as the Queen of Diamonds. Indeed, her uncle, James Blount, was getting almost out of hand in his excitement; he was like a schoolboy. He put a paper donkey's head unexpectedly on Father Brown, who bore it patiently, and even found some private manner of moving his ears. He even essayed to put the paper donkey's tail to the coat-tails of Sir Leopold Fischer. This, however, was frowned down. "Uncle is too absurd," cried Ruby to Crook, round whose shoulders she had seriously placed a string of sausages. "Why is he so wild?"

"He is harlequin to your columbine," said Crook. "I am only the clown who makes the old jokes."

"I wish you were the harlequin," she said, and left the string of sausages swinging.

Father Brown, though he knew every detail done behind the scenes, and had even evoked applause by his transformation of a pillow into a pantomime baby, went round to the front and sat among the audience with all the solemn expectation of a child at his first matinée. The spectators were few, relations, one or two local friends, and the servants; Sir Leopold sat in the front seat, his full and still fur-collared figure largely obscuring the view of the little cleric behind him; but it has never been settled by artistic authorities whether the cleric lost much. The pantomime was utterly chaotic, yet not contemptible; there ran through it a rage of improvisation which came chiefly from Crook the clown. Commonly he was a clever man, and he was inspired to-night with a wild omniscience, a folly wiser than the world, that which comes to a young man who has seen for an instant a particular expression on a particular face. He was supposed to be the clown, but he was really almost everything else, the author (so far as there was an author), the prompter, the scene-painter, the scene-shifter, and, above all, the orchestra. At abrupt intervals in the outrageous performance he would hurl himself in full costume at the piano and bang out some popular music equally absurd and appropriate.

The climax of this, as of all else, was the moment when the two front doors at the back of the scene flew open, showing the lovely moonlit garden, but showing more prominently the famous professional guest; the great Florian, dressed up as a policeman. The clown at the piano played the constabulary chorus in the "Pirates of Penzance,"[9] but it was drowned in the deafening applause, for every gesture of the great comic actor was an admirable though restrained version of the carriage and manner of the police. The harlequin leapt upon him and hit him over the helmet; the pianist playing "Where did you get that hat?"[10] he faced about in admirably simulated astonishment, and then the leaping harlequin hit him again (the pianist suggesting a few bars of "Then we had another one"[11]). Then the harlequin rushed right into the arms of the policeman and fell on top of him, amid a roar of applause. Then it was that the strange actor gave that celebrated imitation of a dead man, of which the fame still lingers round Putney. It was almost impossible to believe that a living person could appear so limp.

The athletic harlequin swung him about like a sack or twisted or tossed him like an Indian club; all the time to the most maddeningly ludicrous tunes from the piano. When the harlequin heaved the comic constable heavily off the floor the clown played "I arise from dreams of thee."[12] When he shuffled him across his back, "With my bundle on

---

[9] Gilbert and Sullivan's operetta *The Pirates of Penzance* (1880) features a chorus of constables singing "A Policeman's Lot Is Not a Happy One".

[10] The premise of "Where Did You Get That Hat?" (a popular song by J. J. Sullivan, from 1888) was, appropriately, dressing up in old clothes found in the attic.

[11] "Then We Had Another One" was a comic music-hall drinking song of the day.

[12] The lines, "I arise from dreams of thee, in the first sweet sleep of night", occur in Percy Bysshe Shelley's lyric "Indian Serenade" (1819).

my shoulder,"[13] and when the harlequin finally let fall the policeman with a most convincing thud, the lunatic at the instrument struck into a jingling measure with some words which are still believed to have been, "I sent a letter to my love and on the way I dropped it."[14]

At about this limit of mental anarchy Father Brown's view was obscured altogether; for the City magnate in front of him rose to his full height and thrust his hands savagely into all his pockets. Then he sat down nervously, still fumbling, and then stood up again. For an instant it seemed seriously likely that he would stride across the footlights; then he turned a glare at the clown playing the piano; and then he burst in silence out of the room.

The priest had only watched for a few more minutes the absurd but not inelegant dance of the amateur harlequin over his splendidly unconscious foe. With real though rude art, the harlequin danced slowly backwards out of the door into the garden, which was full of moonlight and stillness. The vamped dress of silver paper and paste, which had been too glaring in the footlights, looked more and more magical and silvery as it danced away under a brilliant moon. The audience was closing in with a cataract of applause, when Brown felt his arm abruptly touched, and he was asked in a whisper to come into the colonel's study.

He followed his summoner with increasing doubt, which was not dispelled by a solemn comicality in the scene of the study. There sat Colonel Adams, still unaffectedly dressed as a pantaloon, with the knobbed whalebone nodding above his brow, but with his poor old eyes sad enough to have sobered

---

[13] The chorus of "Off to Philadelphia" (a popular song of the day, based upon an old Irish air) begins "With my bundle on my shoulder".

[14] The words are from the familiar nursery song "A-Tisket, A-Tasket", which continues, "a little boy picked it up and put it in his pocket."

a Saturnalia. Sir Leopold Fischer was leaning against the mantelpiece and heaving with all the importance of panic.

"This is a very painful matter, Father Brown," said Adams. "The truth is, those diamonds we all saw this afternoon seem to have vanished from my friend's tail-coat pocket. And as you—"

"As I," supplemented Father Brown, with a broad grin, "was sitting just behind him—"

"Nothing of the sort shall be suggested," said Colonel Adams, with a firm look at Fischer, which rather implied that some such thing *had* been suggested. "I only ask you to give me the assistance that any gentleman might give."

"Which is turning out his pockets," said Father Brown, and proceeded to do so, displaying seven and sixpence, a return ticket, a small silver crucifix, a small breviary, and a stick of chocolate.

The colonel looked at him long, and then said, "Do you know, I should like to see the inside of your head more than the inside of your pockets. My daughter is one of your people, I know; well, she has lately—" and he stopped.

"She has lately," cried out old Fischer, "opened her father's house to a cut-throat Socialist, who says openly he would steal anything from a richer man. This is the end of it. Here is the richer man—and none the richer."

"If you want the inside of my head you can have it," said Brown rather wearily. "What it's worth you can say afterwards. But the first thing I find in that disused pocket is this; that men who mean to steal diamonds don't talk Socialism. They are more likely," he added demurely, "to denounce it."

Both the others shifted sharply, and the priest went on:

"You see, we know these people, more or less. That Socialist would no more steal a diamond than a Pyramid. We ought to look at once to the one man we don't know. The fellow acting the policeman—Florian. Where is he exactly at this minute, I wonder?"

The pantaloon sprang erect and strode out of the room. An interlude ensued, during which the millionaire stared at the priest, and the priest at his breviary; then the pantaloon returned and said, with *staccato* gravity, "The policeman is still lying on the stage. The curtain has gone up and down six times; he is still lying there."

Father Brown dropped his book and stood staring with a look of blank mental ruin. Very slowly a light began to creep back in his grey eyes, and then he made the scarcely obvious answer.

"Please forgive me, colonel, but when did your wife die?"

"My wife!" replied the staring soldier, "she died this year two months. Her brother James arrived just a week too late to see her."

The little priest bounded like a rabbit shot. "Come on!" he cried in quite unusual excitement. "Come on! We've got to go and look at that policeman!"

They rushed on to the now curtained stage, breaking rudely past the columbine and clown (who seemed whispering quite contentedly), and Father Brown bent over the prostrate comic policeman.

"Chloroform," he said as he rose; "I only guessed it just now."

There was a startled stillness, and then the colonel said slowly, "Please say seriously what all this means."

Father Brown suddenly shouted with laughter, then stopped, and only struggled with it for instants during the rest of his speech. "Gentlemen," he gasped, "there's not much time to talk. I must run after the criminal. But this great French actor who played the policeman—this clever corpse the harlequin waltzed with and dandled and threw about—he was—" His voice again failed him, and he turned his back to run.

"He was?" called Fischer inquiringly.

"A real policeman," said Father Brown, and ran away, into the dark.

There were hollows and bowers at the extreme end of that leafy garden, in which the laurels and other immortal shrubs showed against sapphire sky and silver moon, even in that midwinter, warm colours as of the south. The green gaiety of the waving laurels, the rich purple indigo of the night, the moon like a monstrous crystal, make an almost irresponsibly romantic picture; and among the top branches of the garden trees a strange figure is climbing, who looks not so much romantic as impossible. He sparkles from head to heel, as if clad in ten million moons; the real moon catches him at every movement and sets a new inch of him on fire. But he swings, flashing and successful, from the short tree in this garden to the tall, rambling tree in the other, and only stops there because a shade has slid under the smaller tree and has unmistakably called up to him.

"Well, Flambeau," says the voice, "you really look like a Flying Star; but that always means a Falling Star at last."

The silver, sparkling figure above seems to lean forward in the laurels and, confident of escape, listens to the little figure below.

"You never did anything better, Flambeau. It was clever to come from Canada (with a Paris ticket, I suppose) just a week after Mrs. Adams died, when no one was in a mood to ask questions. It was cleverer to have marked down the Flying Stars and the very day of Fischer's coming. But there's no cleverness, but mere genius, in what followed. Stealing the stones, I suppose, was nothing to you. You could have done it by sleight of hand in a hundred other ways besides that pretence of putting a paper donkey's tail to Fischer's coat. But in the rest you eclipsed yourself."

The silvery figure among the green leaves seems to linger as if hypnotised, though his escape is easy behind him; he is staring at the man below.

"Oh, yes," says the man below, "I know all about it. I know you not only forced the pantomime, but put it to a double use. You were going to steal the stones quietly; news came by an accomplice that you were already suspected, and a capable police officer was coming to rout you up that very night. A common thief would have been thankful for the warning and fled; but you are a poet. You already had the clever notion of hiding the jewels in a blaze of false stage jewellery. Now, you saw that if the dress were a harlequin's the appearance of a policeman would be quite in keeping. The worthy officer started from Putney police-station to find you, and walked into the queerest trap ever set in this world. When the front door opened he walked straight on to the stage of a Christmas pantomime, where he could be kicked, clubbed, stunned and drugged by the dancing harlequin, amid roars of laughter from all the most respectable people in Putney. Oh, you will never do anything better. And now, by the way, you might give me back those diamonds."

The green branch on which the glittering figure swung, rustled as if in astonishment; but the voice went on:

"I want you to give them back, Flambeau, and I want you to give up this life. There is still youth and honour and humour in you; don't fancy they will last in that trade. Men may keep a sort of level of good, but no man has ever been able to keep on one level of evil. That road goes down and down. The kind man drinks and turns cruel; the frank man kills and lies about it. Many a man I've known started like you to be an honest outlaw, a merry robber of the rich, and ended stamped into slime. Maurice Blum started out as an anarchist of principle, a father of the poor; he ended a greasy spy and tale-bearer that both sides used and despised. Harry Burke started his free money movement sincerely enough; now he's sponging on a half-starved sister for endless brandies and sodas. Lord Amber went into wild society in a sort of chivalry; now he's paying blackmail to the lowest vultures in London. Captain Barillon was the great gentleman-apache before your time; he died in a madhouse, screaming with fear of the "narks" and receivers that had betrayed him and hunted him down.[15] I know the woods look very free behind you, Flambeau; I know that in a flash you could melt into them like a monkey. But some day you will be an old grey monkey, Flambeau. You will sit up in your tree forest cold at heart and close to death, and the tree-tops will be very bare."

Everything continued still, as if the small man below held the other in the tree in some long invisible leash; and he went on:

"Your downward steps have begun. You used to boast of doing nothing mean, but you are doing something mean tonight. You are leaving suspicion on an honest boy with a good deal against him already; you are separating him from the woman he loves and who loves him. But you will do meaner things than that before you die."

Three flashing diamonds fell from the tree to the turf. The small man stooped to pick them up, and when he looked up again the green cage of the tree was emptied of its silver bird.

The restoration of the gems (accidentally picked up by Father Brown, of all people) ended the evening in uproarious triumph; and Sir Leopold, in his height of good humour,

---

[15] At the turn of the century, *apache* was the French journalists' name for the street brawlers of Paris, and *nark* was English slang for underworld informer.

even told the priest that though he himself had broader views, he could respect those whose creed required them to be cloistered and ignorant of this world.

The Honour of Israel Gow

A STORMY evening of olive and silver was closing in, as
Father Brown, wrapped in a grey Scotch plaid, came to
the end of a grey Scotch valley and beheld the strange castle
of Glengyle. It stopped one end of the glen or hollow like a
blind alley; and it looked like the end of the world. Rising in
steep roofs and spires of seagreen slate in the manner of the
old French-Scotch châteaux, it reminded an Englishman of
the sinister steeple-hats of witches in fairy tales; and the pine
woods that rocked round the green turrets looked, by comparison, as black as numberless flocks of ravens. This note of
a dreamy, almost a sleepy devilry, was no mere fancy from the
landscape. For there did rest on the place one of those clouds
of pride and madness and mysterious sorrow which lie more
heavily on the noble houses of Scotland than on any other of
the children of men. For Scotland has a double dose of the
poison called heredity; the sense of blood in the aristocrat,
and the sense of doom in the Calvinist.[1]

"The Honour of Israel Gow" first appeared in the April 1911 issue of
Cassell's magazine, under the title "The Strange Justice".

[1] The system of the French theologian John Calvin (1509–64) denied
that human free will is a factor in salvation, positing that God predestines
some for heaven while dooming others to hell.

The priest had snatched a day from his business at Glasgow to meet his friend Flambeau, the amateur detective, who was at Glengyle Castle with another more formal officer investigating the life and death of the late Earl of Glengyle. That mysterious person was the last representative of a race whose valour, insanity, and violent cunning had made them terrible even among the sinister nobility of their nation in the sixteenth century. None were deeper in that labyrinthine ambition, in chamber within chamber of that palace of lies that was built up around Mary Queen of Scots.[2]

The rhyme in the country-side attested the motive and the result of their machinations candidly:

> "As green sap to the simmer trees
> Is red gold to the Ogilvies."

For many centuries there had never been a decent lord in Glengyle Castle; and with the Victorian era one would have thought that all eccentricities were exhausted. The last Glengyle, however, satisfied his tribal tradition by doing the only thing that was left for him to do; he disappeared. I do not mean that he went abroad; by all accounts he was still in the castle, if he was anywhere. But though his name was in the church register and the big red Peerage, nobody ever saw him under the sun.

If anyone saw him it was a solitary man-servant, something between a groom and a gardener. He was so deaf that the more business-like assumed him to be dumb; while the more penetrating declared him to be half-witted. A gaunt,

---

[2] Chesterton's view of Queen Mary I (1516–58), who tried to restore Roman Catholicism to England, contradicted the popular notions and prevailing historical ideas of his day. To sample his views see his *Illustrated London News* essay for February 14, 1931, "The Conflict of Romance and Realism" (*Collected Works*, vol. XXXV, pages 467–71).

red-haired labourer, with a dogged jaw and chin, but quite black blue eyes, he went by the name of Israel Gow, and was the one silent servant on that deserted estate. But the energy with which he dug potatoes, and the regularity with which he disappeared into the kitchen gave people an impression that he was providing for the meals of a superior, and that the strange earl was still concealed in the castle. If society needed any further proof that he was there, the servant persistently asserted that he was not at home. One morning the provost and the minister (for the Glengyles were Presbyterian) were summoned to the castle. There they found that the gardener, groom and cook had added to his many professions that of an undertaker, and had nailed up his noble master in a coffin. With how much or how little further inquiry this odd fact was passed, did not as yet very plainly appear; for the thing had never been legally investigated till Flambeau had gone north two or three days before. By then the body of Lord Glengyle (if it was the body) had lain for some time in the little churchyard on the hill.

As Father Brown passed through the dim garden and came under the shadow of the château, the clouds were thick and the whole air damp and thundery. Against the last stripe of the green-gold sunset he saw a black human silhouette; a man in a chimney-pot hat,[3] with a big spade over his shoulder. The combination was queerly suggestive of a sexton; but when Brown remembered the deaf servant who dug potatoes, he thought it natural enough. He knew something of the Scotch peasant; he knew the respectability which might well feel it necessary to wear "blacks" for an official inquiry; he knew

[3] At the time this story was written (1911), "chimney-pot" described the gentleman's tall, cylindrical black silk hat (as did "stove-pipe" in American usage).

also the economy that would not lose an hour's digging for that. Even the man's start and suspicious stare as the priest went by were consonant enough with the vigilance and jealousy of such a type.

The great door was opened by Flambeau himself, who had with him a lean man with iron-grey hair and papers in his hand: Inspector Craven from Scotland Yard. The entrance hall was mostly stripped and empty; but the pale, sneering faces of one or two of the wicked Ogilvies looked down out of the black periwigs and blackening canvas.

Following them into an inner room, Father Brown found that the allies had been seated at a long oak table, of which their end was covered with scribbled papers, flanked with whisky and cigars. Through the whole of its remaining length it was occupied by detached objects arranged at intervals; objects about as inexplicable as any objects could be. One looked like a small heap of glittering broken glass. Another looked like a high heap of brown dust. A third appeared to be a plain stick of wood.

"You seem to have a sort of geological museum here," he said, as he sat down, jerking his head briefly in the direction of the brown dust and the crystalline fragments.

"Not a geological museum," replied Flambeau; "say a psychological museum."

"Oh, for the Lord's sake," cried the police detective, laughing, "don't let's begin with such long words."

"Don't you know what psychology means?" asked Flambeau with friendly surprise. "Psychology means being off your chump."

"Still I hardly follow," replied the official.

"Well," said Flambeau, with decision, "I mean that we've only found out one thing about Lord Glengyle. He was a maniac."

The black silhouette of Gow with his top hat and spade passed the window, dimly outlined against the darkening sky. Father Brown stared passively at it and answered:

"I can understand there must have been something odd about the man, or he wouldn't have buried himself alive—nor been in such a hurry to bury himself dead. But what makes you think it was lunacy?"

"Well," said Flambeau; "you just listen to the list of things Mr. Craven has found in the house."

"We must get a candle," said Craven, suddenly. "A storm is getting up, and it's too dark to read."

"Have you found any candles," asked Brown smiling, "among your oddities?"

Flambeau raised a grave face, and fixed his dark eyes on his friend.

"That is curious, too," he said. "Twenty-five candles, and not a trace of a candlestick."

In the rapidly darkening room and rapidly rising wind, Brown went along the table to where a bundle of wax candles lay among the other scrappy exhibits. As he did so he bent accidentally over the heap of red-brown dust; and a sharp sneeze cracked the silence.

"Hullo!" he said, "snuff!"

He took one of the candles, lit it carefully, came back and stuck it in the neck of the whisky bottle. The unrestful night air, blowing through the crazy window, waved the long flame like a banner. And on every side of the castle they could hear the miles and miles of black pine wood seething like a black sea around a rock.

"I will read the inventory," began Craven gravely, picking up one of the papers, "the inventory of what we found loose and unexplained in the castle. You are to understand that the place generally was dismantled and neglected; but one or two rooms had plainly been inhabited in a simple but not squalid style by somebody; somebody who was not the servant Gow. The list is as follows:

"First item. A very considerable hoard of precious stones, nearly all diamonds, and all of them loose, without any setting whatever. Of course, it is natural that the Ogilvies should have family jewels; but those are exactly the jewels that are almost always set in particular articles of ornament. The Ogilvies would seem to have kept theirs loose in their pockets, like coppers.

"Second item. Heaps and heaps of loose snuff, not kept in a horn, or even a pouch, but lying in heaps on the mantelpieces, on the sideboard, on the piano, anywhere. It looks as if the old gentleman would not take the trouble to look in a pocket or lift a lid.

"Third item. Here and there about the house curious little heaps of minute pieces of metal, some like steel springs and some in the form of microscopic wheels. As if they had gutted some mechanical toy.

"Fourth item. The wax candles, which have to be stuck in bottle necks because there is nothing else to stick them in. Now I wish you to note how very much queerer all this is than anything we anticipated. For the central riddle we are prepared; we have all seen at a glance that there was something wrong about the last earl. We have come here to find out whether he really lived here, whether he really died here, whether that red-haired scarecrow who did his burying had anything to do with his dying. But suppose the worst in all this, the most lurid or melodramatic solution you like. Suppose the servant really killed the master, or suppose the master isn't really dead, or suppose the master is dressed up as the servant, or suppose the servant is buried for the master; invent what Wilkie Collins tragedy you like,[4] and you still have not explained a candle without a candlestick, or why an elderly gentleman of good family should habitually spill snuff on the piano. The core of the tale we could imagine; it is the fringes that are mysterious. By no stretch of fancy can the human mind connect together snuff and diamonds and wax and loose clockwork."

"I think I see the connection," said the priest. "This Glengyle was mad against the French Revolution. He was an enthusiast for the *ancien régime*,[5] and was trying to re-enact literally the family life of the last Bourbons. He had snuff because it was the eighteenth century luxury; wax candles, because they were the eighteenth century lighting; the mechanical bits of iron represent the locksmith hobby of Louis XVI; the diamonds are for the Diamond Necklace of Marie Antoinette."[6]

Both the other men were staring at him with round eyes. "What a perfectly extraordinary notion!" cried Flambeau. "Do you really think that is the truth?"

"I am perfectly sure it isn't," answered Father Brown, "only you said that nobody could connect snuff and diamonds and clockwork and candles. I give you that connection off-hand. The real truth, I am very sure, lies deeper."

He paused a moment and listened to the wailing of the

[4] Inspector Craven refers to such novels as *The Woman in White* and other inventively plotted Gothic mysteries by the Victorian novelist Wilkie Collins (1824–89).

[5] During the French Revolution of 1789 and subsequently, the phrase *ancien régime* ("the old order") referred to the earlier system of government, the Bourbon monarchy.

[6] The perceived frivolity of King Louis XVI and the prodigality of his Queen, Marie Antoinette, as reflected in his pastimes and her jewelry (including a diamond necklace theft in which she was unjustly implicated), contributed to the popular resentment that preceded the French Revolution.

wind in the turrets. Then he said: "The late Earl of Glengyle was a thief. He lived a second and darker life as a desperate house-breaker. He did not have any candlesticks because he only used these candles cut short in the little lantern he carried. The snuff he employed as the fiercest French criminals have used pepper: to fling it suddenly in dense masses in the face of a captor or pursuer. But the final proof is in the curious coincidence of the diamonds and the small steel wheels. Surely that makes everything plain to you? Diamonds and small steel wheels are the only two instruments with which you can cut out a pane of glass."

The bough of a broken pine tree lashed heavily in the blast against the windowpane behind them, as if in parody of a burglar, but they did not turn round. Their eyes were fastened on Father Brown.

"Diamonds and small wheels," repeated Craven ruminating. "Is that all that makes you think it the true explanation?"

"I don't think it the true explanation," replied the priest placidly; "but you said that nobody could connect the four things. The true tale, of course, is something much more humdrum. Glengyle had found, or thought he had found, precious stones on his estate. Somebody had bamboozled him with those loose brilliants, saying they were found in the castle caverns. The little wheels are some diamond-cutting affair. He had to do the thing very roughly and in a small way, with the help of a few shepherds or rude fellows on these hills. Snuff is the one great luxury of such Scotch shepherds; it's the one thing with which you can bribe them. They didn't have candlesticks because they didn't want them; they held the candles in their hands when they explored the caves."

"Is that all?" asked Flambeau after a long pause. "Have we got to the dull truth at last?"

"Oh, no," said Father Brown.

As the wind died in the most distant pine woods with a long hoot as of mockery Father Brown, with an utterly impassive face, went on:

"I only suggested that because you said one could not plausibly connect snuff with clockwork or candles with bright stones. Ten false philosophies will fit the universe; ten false theories will fit Glengyle Castle. But we want the real explanation of the castle and the universe. But are there no other exhibits?"

Craven laughed, and Flambeau rose smiling to his feet and strolled down the long table.

"Items five, six, seven, etc.," he said, "are certainly more varied than instructive. A curious collection, not of lead pencils, but of the lead out of lead pencils. A senseless stick of bamboo, with the top rather splintered. It might be the instrument of the crime. Only, there isn't any crime. The only other things are a few old missals and little Catholic pictures, which the Ogilvies kept, I suppose, from the Middle Ages— their family pride being stronger than their Puritanism. We only put them in the museum because they seem curiously cut about and defaced."

The heady tempest without drove a dreadful wrack of clouds across Glengyle and threw the long room into darkness as Father Brown picked up the little illuminated pages to examine them. He spoke before the drift of darkness had passed; but it was the voice of an utterly new man.

"Mr. Craven," said he, talking like a man ten years younger, "you have got a legal warrant, haven't you, to go up and examine that grave? The sooner we do it the better, and get to the bottom of this horrible affair. If I were you I should start now."

"Now," repeated the astonished detective, "and why now?"

"Because this is serious," answered Brown; "this is not spilt snuff or loose pebbles, that might be there for a hundred reasons. There is only one reason I know of for *this* being done; and the reason goes down to the roots of the world. These religious pictures are not just dirtied or torn or scrawled over, which might be done in idleness or bigotry, by children or by Protestants. These have been treated very carefully—and very queerly. In every place where the great ornamented name of God comes in the old illuminations it has been elaborately taken out. The only other thing that has been removed is the halo round the head of the Child Jesus. Therefore, I say, let us get our warrant and our spade and our hatchet, and go up and break open that coffin."

"What *do* you mean?" demanded the London officer.

"I mean," answered the little priest, and his voice seemed to rise slightly in the roar of the gale. "I mean that the great devil of the universe may be sitting on the top tower of this castle at this moment, as big as a hundred elephants, and roaring like the Apocalypse. There is black magic somewhere at the bottom of this."

"Black magic," repeated Flambeau in a low voice, for he was too enlightened a man not to know of such things; "but what can these other things mean?"

"Oh, something damnable, I suppose," replied Brown impatiently. "How should I know? How can I guess all their mazes down below? Perhaps you can make a torture out of snuff and bamboo. Perhaps lunatics lust after wax and steel filings. Perhaps there is a maddening drug made of lead pencils! Our shortest cut to the mystery is up the hill to the grave."

His comrades hardly knew that they had obeyed and followed him till a blast of the night wind nearly flung them on their faces in the garden. Nevertheless they had obeyed him like automata; for Craven found a hatchet in his hand, and the warrant in his pocket; Flambeau was carrying the heavy spade of the strange gardener; Father Brown was carrying the little gilt book from which had been torn the name of God.

The path up the hill to the churchyard was crooked but short; only under the stress of wind it seemed laborious and long. Far as the eye could see, farther and farther as they mounted the slope, were seas beyond seas of pines, now all aslope one way under the wind. And that universal gesture seemed as vain as it was vast, as vain as if that wind were whistling about some unpeopled and purposeless planet. Through all that infinite growth of grey-blue forests sang, shrill and high, that ancient sorrow that is in the heart of all heathen things. One could fancy that the voices from the under world of unfathomable foliage were cries of the lost and wandering pagan gods: gods who had gone roaming in that irrational forest, and who will never find their way back to heaven.

"You see," said Father Brown in a low but easy tone, "Scotch people before Scotland existed were a curious lot. In fact, they're a curious lot still. But in the prehistoric times I fancy they really worshipped demons. That," he added genially, "is why they jumped at the Puritan theology."[7]

"My friend," said Flambeau, turning in a kind of fury, "what does all that snuff mean?"

"My friend," replied Brown, with equal seriousness, "there is one mark of all genuine religions: materialism. Now, devil-worship is a perfectly genuine religion."

[7] Father Brown's view is Chesterton's, who denounced Puritan theology throughout his career (because of the harsh fatalism and the denial of free will implied in the Calvinist's view of predestination). Chesterton once wrote of the "quiet street in hell, where live the children of that unique dispensation which theologians call Calvinism and Christians devil-worship" (see *Charles Dickens* in *Collected Works*, vol. XV, p. 136).

They had come up on the grassy scalp of the hill, one of the few bald spots that stood clear of the crashing and roaring pine forest. A mean enclosure, partly timber and partly wire, rattled in the tempest to tell them the border of the graveyard. But by the time Inspector Craven had come to the corner of the grave, and Flambeau had planted his spade point downwards and leaned on it, they were both almost as shaken as the shaky wood and wire. At the foot of the grave grew great tall thistles, grey and silver in their decay. Once or twice, when a ball of thistledown broke under the breeze and flew past him, Craven jumped slightly as if it had been an arrow.

Flambeau drove the blade of his spade through the whistling grass into the wet clay below. Then he seemed to stop and lean on it as on a staff.

"Go on," said the priest very gently. "We are only trying to find the truth. What are you afraid of?"

"I am afraid of finding it," said Flambeau.

The London detective spoke suddenly in a high crowing voice that was meant to be conversational and cheery. "I wonder why he really did hide himself like that. Something nasty, I suppose; was he a leper?"

"Something worse than that," said Flambeau.

"And what do you imagine," asked the other, "would be worse than a leper?"

"I don't imagine it," said Flambeau.

He dug for some dreadful minutes in silence, and then said in a choked voice, "I'm afraid of his not being the right shape."

"Nor was that piece of paper, you know," said Father Brown quietly, "and we survived even that piece of paper."[8]

Flambeau dug on with a blind energy. But the tempest had

---

[8] Here Father Brown recalls his experience with the oddly-cut sheet of paper that figured so prominently in the story of "The Wrong Shape".

shouldered away the choking grey clouds that clung to the hills like smoke and revealed grey fields of faint starlight before he cleared the shape of a rude timber coffin, and somehow tipped it up upon the turf. Craven stepped forward with his axe; a thistle-top touched him, and he flinched. Then he took a firmer stride, and hacked and wrenched with an energy like Flambeau's till the lid was torn off, and all that was there lay glimmering in the grey starlight.

"Bones," said Craven; and then he added, "but it is a man," as if that were something unexpected.

"Is he," asked Flambeau in a voice that went oddly up and down, "is he all right?"

"Seems so," said the officer huskily, bending over the obscure and decaying skeleton in the box. "Wait a minute."

A vast heave went over Flambeau's huge figure. "And now I come to think of it," he cried, "why in the name of madness shouldn't he be all right? What is it gets hold of a man on these cursed cold mountains? I think it's the black, brainless repetition; all these forests, and over all an ancient horror of unconsciousness. It's like the dream of an atheist. Pine-trees and more pine-trees and millions more pine-trees—"

"God!" cried the man by the coffin; "but he hasn't got a head."

While the others stood rigid the priest, for the first time, showed a leap of startled concern.

"No head!" he repeated. "*No head?*" as if he had almost expected some other deficiency.

Half-witted visions of a headless baby born to Glengyle, of a headless youth hiding himself in the castle, of a headless man pacing those ancient halls or that gorgeous garden, passed in panorama through their minds. But even in that stiffened instant the tale took no root in them and seemed to have no reason in it. They stood listening to the loud woods and the shrieking sky quite foolishly, like exhausted animals. Thought seemed to be something enormous that had suddenly slipped out of their grasp.

"There are three headless men," said Father Brown: "standing round this open grave."

The pale detective from London opened his mouth to speak, and left it open like a yokel, while a long scream of wind tore the sky; then he looked at the axe in his hands as if it did not belong to him, and dropped it.

"Father," said Flambeau in that infantile and heavy voice he used very seldom, "what are we to do?"

His friend's reply came with the pent promptitude of a gun going off.

"Sleep!" cried Father Brown. "Sleep. We have come to the end of the ways. Do you know what sleep is? Do you know that every man who sleeps believes in God? It is a sacrament; for it is an act of faith and it is a food. And we need a sacrament, if only a natural one. Something has fallen on us that falls very seldom on men; perhaps the worst thing that can fall on them."

Craven's parted lips came together to say, "What do you mean?"

The priest had turned his face to the castle as he answered: "We have found the truth; and the truth makes no sense."

He went down the path in front of them with a plunging and reckless step very rare with him, and when they reached the castle again he threw himself upon sleep with the simplicity of a dog.

Despite his mystic praise of slumber, Father Brown was up earlier than anyone else except the silent gardener; and was found smoking a big pipe and watching that expert at his speechless labours in the kitchen garden. Towards daybreak the rocking storm had ended in roaring rains, and the day came with a curious freshness. The gardener seemed even to have been conversing, but at sight of the detectives he planted his spade sullenly in a bed and, saying something about his breakfast, shifted along the lines of cabbages and shut himself in the kitchen. "He's a valuable man, that," said Father Brown. "He does the potatoes amazingly. Still," he added, with a dispassionate charity, "he has his faults; which of us hasn't? He doesn't dig this bank quite regularly. There, for instance," and he stamped suddenly on one spot. "I'm really very doubtful about that potato."

"And why?" asked Craven, amused with the little man's new hobby.

"I'm doubtful about it," said the other, "because old Gow was doubtful about it himself. He put his spade in methodically in every place but just this. There must be a mighty fine potato just here."

Flambeau pulled up the spade and impetuously drove it into the place. He turned up, under a load of soil, something that did not look like a potato, but rather like a monstrous, over-domed mushroom. But it struck the spade with a cold click; it rolled over like a ball, and grinned up at them.

"The Earl of Glengyle," said Brown sadly, and looked down heavily at the skull.

Then, after a momentary meditation, he plucked the spade from Flambeau, and, saying "We must hide it again," clamped the skull down in the earth. Then he leaned his little body and huge head on the great handle of the spade, that stood up stiffly in the earth, and his eyes were empty and his forehead full of wrinkles. "If one could only conceive," he muttered, "the meaning of this last monstrosity." And leaning on the large spade handle, he buried his brows in his hands, as men do in church.

All the corners of the sky were brightening into blue and

silver; the birds were chattering in the tiny garden trees; so loud it seemed as if the trees themselves were talking. But the three men were silent enough.

"Well, I give it all up," said Flambeau at last boisterously. "My brain and this world don't fit each other; and there's an end of it. Snuff, spoilt Prayer Books, and the insides of musical boxes—what—"

Brown threw up his bothered brow and rapped on the spade handle with an intolerance quite unusual with him. "Oh, tut, tut, tut, tut!" he cried. "All that is as plain as a pikestaff. I understood the snuff and clockwork, and so on, when I first opened my eyes this morning. And since then I've had it out with old Gow, the gardener, who is neither so deaf nor so stupid as he pretends. There's nothing amiss about the loose items. I was wrong about the torn mass-book, too; there's no harm in that. But it's this last business. Desecrating graves and stealing dead men's heads—surely there's harm in that? Surely there's black magic still in that? That doesn't fit in to the quite simple story of the snuff and the candles." And, striding about again, he smoked moodily.

"My friend," said Flambeau, with a grim humour, "you must be careful with me and remember I was once a criminal. The great advantage of that estate was that I always made up the story myself, and acted it as quick as I chose. This detective business of waiting about is too much for my French impatience. All my life, for good or evil, I have done things at the instant; I always fought duels the next morning; I always paid bills on the nail; I never even put off a visit to the dentist—"

Father Brown's pipe fell out of his mouth and broke into three pieces on the gravel path. He stood rolling his eyes, the exact picture of an idiot. "Lord, what a turnip I am!" he kept saying. "Lord, what a turnip!" Then, in a somewhat groggy kind of way, he began to laugh.

"The dentist!" he repeated. "Six hours in the spiritual abyss, and all because I never thought of the dentist! Such a simple, such a beautiful and peaceful thought! Friends, we have passed a night in hell; but now the sun is risen, the birds are singing, and the radiant form of the dentist consoles the world."

"I will get some sense out of this," cried Flambeau, striding forward, "if I use the tortures of the Inquisition."

Father Brown repressed what appeared to be a momentary disposition to dance on the now sunlit lawn and cried quite piteously, like a child: "Oh, let me be silly a little. You don't know how unhappy I have been. And now I know that there has been no deep sin in this business at all. Only a little lunacy, perhaps—and who minds that?"

He spun round once more, then faced them with gravity.

"This is not a story of crime," he said; "rather it is the story of a strange and crooked honesty. We are dealing with the one man on earth, perhaps, who has taken no more than his due. It is a study in the savage living logic that has been the religion of this race.

"That old local rhyme about the house of Glengyle—

'As green sap to the simmer trees
Is red gold to the Ogilvies'—

was literal as well as metaphorical. It did not merely mean that the Glengyles sought for wealth; it was also true that they literally gathered gold; they had a huge collection of ornaments and utensils in that metal. They were, in fact, misers whose mania took that turn. In the light of that fact, run through all the things we found in the castle. Diamonds without their gold rings; candles without their gold candlesticks; snuff without the gold snuff-boxes; pencil-leads without the gold pencil-cases; a walking stick without its gold top; clockwork without the gold clocks—or rather watches. And, mad as it sounds, because the halos and the name of God in the old missals were of real gold; these also were taken away."

The garden seemed to brighten, the grass to grow gayer in the strengthening sun, as the crazy truth was told. Flambeau lit a cigarette as his friend went on.

"Were taken away," continued Father Brown; "were taken away—but not stolen. Thieves would never have left this mystery. Thieves would have taken the gold snuff-boxes, snuff and all; the gold pencil-cases, lead and all. We have to deal with a man with a peculiar conscience, but certainly a conscience. I found that mad moralist this morning in the kitchen garden yonder, and I heard the whole story.

"The late Archibald Ogilvie was the nearest approach to a good man ever born at Glengyle. But his bitter virtue took the turn of the misanthrope; he moped over the dishonesty of his ancestors, from which, somehow, he generalized a dishonesty of all men. More especially he distrusted philanthropy or free-giving; and he swore if he could find one man who took his exact rights he should have all the gold of Glengyle. Having delivered this defiance to humanity he shut himself up, without the smallest expectation of its being answered. One day, however, a deaf and seemingly senseless lad from a distant village brought him a belated telegram; and Glengyle, in his acrid pleasantry, gave him a new farthing. At least he thought he had done so, but when he turned over his change he found the new farthing still there and a sovereign gone.[9] The accident offered him vistas of sneering speculation. Either way, the boy would show the greasy greed of the species. Either he would vanish, a thief stealing a coin; or he would sneak back with it virtuously, a

[9] The sovereign was a gold coin worth one pound (20 shillings). The shilling was worth 12 pence and the farthing only one-quarter of a penny.

snob seeking a reward. In the middle of that night Lord Glengyle was knocked up out of his bed—for he lived alone—and forced to open the door to the deaf idiot. The idiot brought with him, not the sovereign, but exactly nineteen shillings and eleven-pence three-farthings in change.

"Then the wild exactitude of this action took hold on the mad lord's brain like fire. He swore he was Diogenes, that had long sought an honest man, and at last had found one.[10] He made a new will, which I have seen. He took the literal youth into his huge, neglected house, and trained him up as his solitary servant and—after an odd manner—his heir. And whatever that queer creature understands, he understood absolutely his lord's two fixed ideas: first, that the letter of right is everything; and second, that he himself was to have the gold of Glengyle. So far, that is all; and that is simple. He has stripped the house of gold, and taken not a grain that was not gold; not so much as a grain of snuff. He lifted the gold leaf off an old illumination, fully satisfied that he left the rest unspoilt. All that I understood; but I could not understand this skull business. I was really uneasy about that human head buried among the potatoes. It distressed me—till Flambeau said the word.

"It will be all right. He will put the skull back in the grave, when he has taken the gold out of the tooth."

And, indeed, when Flambeau crossed the hill that morning, he saw that strange being, the just miser, digging at the desecrated grave, the plaid round his throat thrashing out in the mountain wind; the sober top hat on his head.

---

[10] Father Brown alludes to Diogenes (c. 400–325 B.C.), who wandered through Athens by day with a lantern, searching in vain for an honest man.

The Insoluble Problem

THIS queer incident, in some ways perhaps the queerest of the many that came his way, happened to Father Brown at the time when his French friend Flambeau had retired from the profession of crime and had entered with great energy and success on the profession of crime investigator. It happened that both as a thief and a thief-taker, Flambeau had rather specialized in the matter of jewel thefts, on which he was admitted to be an expert, both in the matter of identifying jewels and the equally practical matter of identifying jewel-thieves. And it was in connection with his special knowledge of this subject, and a special commission which it had won for him, that he rang up his friend the priest on the particular morning on which this story begins.

Father Brown was delighted to hear the voice of his old friend, even on the telephone; but in a general way, and especially at that particular moment, Father Brown was not very fond of the telephone. He was one who preferred to watch people's faces and feel social atmospheres, and he knew well that without these things, verbal messages are apt to be very misleading, especially from total strangers. And it

"The Insoluble Problem" first appeared in the March 1935 issue of *Storyteller* magazine.

seemed as if, on that particular morning, a swarm of total strangers had been buzzing in his ear with more or less unenlightening verbal messages; the telephone seemed to be possessed of a demon of triviality. Perhaps the most distinctive voice was one which asked him whether he did not issue regular permits for murder and theft upon the payment of a regular tariff hung up in his church; and as the stranger, on being informed that this was not the case, concluded the colloquy with a hollow laugh, it may be presumed that he remained unconvinced. Then an agitated, rather inconsequent female voice rang up requesting him to come round at once to a certain hotel he had heard of some forty-five miles on the road to a neighbouring cathedral town; the request being immediately followed by a contradiction in the same voice, more agitated and yet more inconsequent, telling him that it did not matter and that he was not wanted after all. Then came an interlude of a Press agency asking him if he had anything to say on what a Film Actress had said about Moustaches for Men; and finally yet a third return of the agitated and inconsequent lady at the hotel, saying that he was wanted, after all. He vaguely supposed that this marked some of the hesitations and panics not unknown among those who are vaguely veering in the direction of Instruction, but he confessed to a considerable relief when the voice of Flambeau wound up the series with a hearty threat of immediately turning up to breakfast.

Father Brown very much preferred to talk to a friend sitting comfortably over a pipe, but it soon appeared that his visitor was on the war-path and full of energy, having every intention of carrying off the little priest captive on some important expedition of his own. It was true that there was a special circumstance involved which might be supposed to claim the priest's attention. Flambeau had figured several times of late as successfully thwarting a theft of famous precious stones; he had torn the tiara of the Duchess of Dulwich out of the very hand of the bandit as he bolted through the garden. He laid so ingenious a trap for the criminal who planned to carry off the celebrated Sapphire Necklace, that the artist in question actually carried off the copy which he had himself planned to leave as a substitute.

Such were doubtless the reasons that had led to his being specially summoned to guard the delivery of a rather different sort of treasure; perhaps even more valuable in its mere materials, but possessing also another sort of value. A world-famous reliquary, supposed to contain a relic of St. Dorothy the martyr, was to be delivered at the Catholic monastery in a cathedral town; and one of the most famous of international jewel-thieves was supposed to have an eye on it; or rather presumably on the gold and rubies of its setting, rather than its purely hagiological importance. Perhaps there was something in this association of ideas which made Flambeau feel that the priest would be a particularly appropriate companion in his adventure; but anyhow, he descended on him, breathing fire and ambition and very voluble about his plans for preventing the theft.

Flambeau indeed bestrode the priest's hearth gigantically and in the old swaggering musketeer attitude, twirling his great moustaches.

"You can't," he cried, referring to the sixty-mile road to Casterbury. "You can't allow a profane robbery like that to happen under your very nose."

The relic was not to reach the monastery till the evening; and there was no need for its defenders to arrive earlier; for indeed a motor-journey would take them the greater part of the day. Moreover, Father Brown casually remarked that there was an inn on the road, at which he would prefer to lunch, as he had been already asked to look in there as soon as was convenient.

As they drove along through a densely wooded but sparsely inhabited landscape, in which inns and all other buildings seemed to grow rarer and rarer, the daylight began to take on the character of a stormy twilight even in the heat of noon; and dark purple clouds gathered over the dark grey forests. As is common under the lurid quietude of that kind of light, what colour there was in the landscape gained a sort of secretive glow which is not found in objects under the full sunlight; and ragged red leaves or golden or orange fungi seemed to burn with a dark fire of their own. Under such a half-light they came to a break in the woods like a great rent in a grey wall, and saw beyond, standing above the gap, the tall and rather outlandish-looking inn that bore the name of the Green Dragon.

The two old companions had often arrived together at inns and other human habitations, and found a somewhat singular state of things there; but the signs of singularity had seldom manifested themselves so early. For while their car was still some hundreds of yards from the dark green door, which matched the dark green shutters of the high and narrow building, the door was thrown open with violence and a woman with a wild mop of red hair rushed to meet them, as if she were ready to board the car in full career. Flambeau brought the car to a standstill, but almost before he had done so, she thrust her white and tragic face into the window, crying:

"Are you Father Brown?" and then almost in the same breath; "who is this man?"

"This gentleman's name is Flambeau," said Father Brown in a tranquil manner, "and what can I do for you?"

"Come into the inn," she said, with extraordinary abruptness even under the circumstances. "There's been a murder done."

They got out of the car in silence and followed her to the dark green door which opened inwards on a sort of dark green alley, formed of stakes and wooden pillars, wreathed with vine and ivy, showing square leaves of black and red and many sombre colours. This again led through an inner door into a sort of large parlour hung with rusty trophies of Cavalier arms, of which the furniture seemed to be antiquated and also in great confusion, like the inside of a lumber-room. They were quite startled for the moment; for it seemed as if one large piece of lumber rose and moved towards them; so dusty and shabby and ungainly was the man who thus abandoned what seemed like a state of permanent immobility.

Strangely enough, the man seemed to have a certain agility of politeness, when once he did move; even if it suggested the wooden joints of a courtly step-ladder or an obsequious towel-horse. Both Flambeau and Father Brown felt that they had hardly ever clapped eyes on a man who was so difficult to place. He was not what is called a gentleman; yet he had something of the dusty refinement of a scholar; there was something faintly disreputable or *déclassé* about him; and yet the smell of him was rather bookish than Bohemian. He was thin and pale, with a pointed nose and a dark pointed beard; his brow was bald, but his hair behind long and lank and stringy; and the expression of his eyes was almost entirely masked by a pair of blue spectacles. Father Brown felt that he had met something of the sort somewhere, and a long time ago; but he could no longer put a name to it.[1] The lumber he

[1] Father Brown's vague recollection of a bearded man with blue spectacles might refer to Dr. Hirsch of "The Duel of Dr. Hirsch" or possibly to the mysterious stranger in "The Head of Caesar".

sat among was largely literary lumber; especially bundles of seventeenth-century pamphlets.

"Do I understand the lady to say," asked Flambeau gravely, "that there is a murder here?"

The lady nodded her red ragged head rather impatiently; except for those flaming elf-locks she had lost some of her look of wildness; her dark dress was of a certain dignity and neatness; her features were strong and handsome; and there was something about her suggesting that double strength of body and mind which makes women powerful, particularly in contrast with men like the man in blue spectacles. Nevertheless, it was he who gave the only articulate answer, intervening with a certain antic gallantry.

"It is true that my unfortunate sister-in-law," he explained, "has almost this moment suffered a most appalling shock which we should all have desired to spare her. I only wish that I myself had made the discovery and suffered only the further distress of bringing the terrible news. Unfortunately it was Mrs. Flood herself who found her aged grandfather, long sick and bed-ridden in this hotel, actually dead in the garden; in circumstances which point only too plainly to violence and assault. Curious circumstances, I may say very curious circumstances indeed." And he coughed slightly, as if apologizing for them.

Flambeau bowed to the lady and expressed his sincere sympathies; then he said to the man: "I think you said, sir, that you are Mrs. Flood's brother-in-law."

"I am Dr. Oscar Flood," replied the other. "My brother, this lady's husband, is at present away on the Continent on business, and she is running the hotel. Her grandfather was partially paralysed and very far advanced in years. He was never known to leave his bedroom; so that really these extraordinary circumstances. . . ."

"Have you sent for a doctor or the police?" asked Flambeau.

"Yes," replied Dr. Flood, "we rang up after making the dreadful discovery; but they can hardly be here for some hours. This roadhouse stands so very remote. It is only used by people going to Casterbury or even beyond. So we thought we might ask for your valuable assistance until—"

"If we are to be of any assistance," said Father Brown, interrupting in too abstracted a manner to seem uncivil; "I should say we had better go and look at the circumstances at once."

He stepped almost mechanically towards the door; and almost ran into a man who was shouldering his way in; a big, heavy young man with dark hair unbrushed and untidy, who would nevertheless have been rather handsome save for a slight disfigurement of one eye, which gave him rather a sinister appearance.

"What the devil are you doing?" he blurted out, "telling every Tom, Dick and Harry—at least you ought to wait for the police."

"I will be answerable to the police," said Flambeau with a certain magnificence, and a sudden air of having taken command of everything. He advanced to the doorway, and as he was much bigger than the big young man, and his moustaches were as formidable as the horns of a Spanish bull, the big young man backed before him and had an inconsequent air of being thrown out and left behind, as the group swept out into the garden and up the flagged path towards the mulberry plantation. Only Flambeau heard the little priest say to the doctor: "He doesn't seem to love us really, does he? By the way, who is he?"

"His name is Dunn," said the doctor, with a certain restraint of manner. "My sister-in-law gave him the job of managing the garden, because he lost an eye in the War."

As they went through the mulberry bushes, the landscape of the garden presented that rich yet ominous effect which is found when the land is actually brighter than the sky. In the broken sunlight from behind, the tree-tops in front of them stood up like pale green flames against a sky steadily blackening with storm, through every shade of purple and violet. The same light struck strips of the lawn and garden beds; and whatever it illuminated seemed more mysteriously sombre and secret for the light. The garden bed was dotted with tulips that looked like drops of dark blood, and some of which one might have sworn were truly black; and the line ended appropriately with a tulip tree; which Father Brown was disposed, if partly by some confused memory, to identify with what is commonly called the Judas tree. What assisted the association was the fact that there was hanging from one of the branches, like a dried fruit, the dry, thin body of an old man, with a long beard that wagged grotesquely in the wind.

There lay on it something more than the horror of darkness, the horror of sunlight; for the fitful sun painted tree and man in gay colours like a stage property; the tree was in flower and the corpse was hung with a faded peacock-green dressing-gown, and wore on its wagging head a scarlet smoking-cap. Also it had red bedroom-slippers, one of which had fallen off and lay on the grass like a blot of blood.

But neither Flambeau nor Father Brown was looking at these things as yet. They were both staring at a strange object that seemed to stick out of the middle of the dead man's shrunken figure; and which they gradually perceived to be the black but rather rusty iron hilt of a seventeenth-century sword, which had completely transfixed the body. They both remained almost motionless as they gazed at it; until the restless Dr. Flood seemed to grow quite impatient with their stolidity.

"What puzzles *me* most," he said, nervously snapping his fingers, "is the actual state of the body. And yet it has given me an idea already."

Flambeau had stepped up to the tree and was studying the sword-hilt through an eye-glass. But for some odd reason, it was at that very instant that the priest in sheer perversity spun round like a teetotum, turned his back on the corpse, and looked peeringly in the very opposite direction. He was just in time to see the red head of Mrs. Flood at the remote end of the garden, turned towards a dark young man, too dim with distance to be identified, who was at that moment mounting a motor-bicycle; who vanished, leaving behind him only the dying din of that vehicle. Then the woman turned and began to walk towards them across the garden, just as Father Brown turned also and began a careful inspection of the sword-hilt and the hanging corpse.

"I understand you only found him about half an hour ago," said Flambeau. "Was there anybody about here just before that? I mean anybody in his bedroom, or that part of the house, or this part of the garden—say for an hour before-hand?"

"No," said the doctor with precision. "That is the very tragic accident. My sister-in-law was in the pantry, which is a sort of out-house on the other side; this man Dunn was in the kitchen-garden, which is also in that direction; and I myself was poking about among the books, in a room just behind the one you found me in. There are two female servants, but one had gone to the post and the other was in the attic."

"And were any of these people," asked Flambeau, very quietly, "I say *any* of these people, at all on bad terms with the poor old gentleman?"

"He was the object of almost universal affection," replied the doctor solemnly. "If there were any misunderstandings, they were mild and of a sort common in modern times. The old man was attached to the old religious habits; and perhaps his daughter and son-in-law had rather wider views.[2] All that can have had nothing to do with a ghastly and fantastic assassination like this."

"It depends on how wide the modern views were," said Father Brown, "or how narrow."

At this moment they heard Mrs. Flood hallooing across the garden as she came, and calling her brother-in-law to her with a certain impatience. He hurried towards her and was soon out of earshot; but as he went he waved his hand apologetically and then pointed with a long finger to the ground.

"You will find the footprints very intriguing," he said; with the same strange air, as of a funeral showman.

The two amateur detectives looked across at each other. "I find several other things intriguing," said Flambeau.

"Oh, yes," said the priest, staring rather foolishly at the grass.

"I was wondering," said Flambeau, "why they should hang a man by the neck till he was dead, and then take the trouble to stick him with a sword."

"And I was wondering," said Father Brown, "why they should kill a man with a sword thrust through his heart, and then take the trouble to hang him by the neck."

"Oh, you are simply being contrary," protested his friend. "I can see at a glance that they didn't stab him alive. The body would have bled more and the wound wouldn't have closed like that."

"And I could see at a glance," said Father Brown, peering up very awkwardly, with his short stature and short sight,

---

[2] Although here Dr. Flood refers to his sister-in-law as the old man's daughter, earlier he had twice referred to her as the old man's granddaughter. Chesterton's inconsistency appears to have been unintentional.

"that they didn't hang him alive. If you'll look at the knot in the noose, you will see it's tied so clumsily that a twist of rope holds it away from the neck, so that it couldn't throttle the man at all. He was dead before they put the rope on him; and he was dead before they put the sword in him. And how was he really killed?"

"I think," remarked the other, "that we'd better go back to the house and have a look at his bedroom—and other things."

"So we will," said Father Brown. "But among other things, perhaps we had better have a look at these footprints. Better begin at the other end, I think, by his window. Well, there are no footprints on the paved path, as there might be; but then again there mightn't be. Well, here is the lawn just under his bedroom window. And here are his footprints plain enough."

He blinked ominously at the footprints; and then began carefully retracing his path towards the tree, every now and then ducking in an undignified manner to look at something on the ground. Eventually he returned to Flambeau and said in a chatty manner:

"Well, do you know the story that is written there very plainly? Though it's not exactly a plain story."

"I wouldn't be content to call it plain," said Flambeau. "I should call it quite ugly."

"Well," said Father Brown, "the story that is stamped quite plainly on the earth, with exact moulds of the old man's slippers, is this. The aged paralytic leapt from the window and ran down the beds parallel to the path, quite eager for all the fun of being strangled and stabbed; so eager that he hopped on one leg out of sheer lightheartedness; and even occasionally turned cart-wheels—"

"Stop!" cried Flambeau, angrily. "What the hell is all this hellish pantomime?"

Father Brown merely raised his eyebrows and gestured mildly towards the hieroglyphs in the dust. "About half the way there's only the mark of one slipper; and in some places the mark of a hand planted all by itself."

"Couldn't he have limped and then fallen?" asked Flambeau.

Father Brown shook his head. "At least he'd have tried to use his hands and feet, or knees and elbows, in getting up. There are no other marks there of any kind. Of course the flagged path is quite near, and there are no marks on that; though there might be on the soil between the cracks: it's a crazy pavement."

"By God, it's a crazy pavement; and a crazy garden; and a crazy story!" And Flambeau looked gloomily across the gloomy and storm-stricken garden, across which the crooked patchwork paths did indeed give a queer aptness to the quaint old English adjective.

"And now," said Father Brown, "let us go up and look at his room." They went in by a door not far from the bedroom window; and the priest paused a moment to look at an ordinary garden broomstick, for sweeping up leaves, that was leaning against the wall. "Do you see that?"

"It's a broomstick," said Flambeau, with solid irony.

"It's a blunder," said Father Brown; "the first blunder that I've seen in this curious plot."

They mounted the stairs and entered the old man's bedroom; and a glance at it made fairly clear the main facts, both about the foundation and disunion of the family. Father Brown had felt from the first that he was in what was, or had been, a Catholic household; but was, at least partly, inhabited by lapsed or very loose Catholics. The pictures and images in the grandfather's room made it clear that what positive piety remained had been practically confined to him; and that his kindred had, for some reason or other, gone Pagan. But he agreed that this was a hopelessly inadequate explanation even of an ordinary murder; let alone such a very extraordinary murder as this. "Hang it all," he muttered, "the murder is really the least extraordinary part of it." And even as he used the chance phrase, a slow light began to dawn upon his face.

Flambeau had seated himself on a chair by the little table which stood beside the dead man's bed. He was frowning thoughtfully at three or four white pills or pellets that lay in a small tray beside a bottle of water.

"The murderer or murderess," said Flambeau, "has some incomprehensible reason or other for wanting us to think the dead man was strangled or stabbed or both. He was not strangled or stabbed or anything of the kind. Why did they want to suggest it? The most logical explanation is that he died in some particular way which would, in itself, suggest a connection with some particular person. Suppose, for instance, he was poisoned. And suppose somebody is involved who would naturally look more like a poisoner than anybody else."

"After all," said Father Brown softly, "our friend in the blue spectacles is a doctor."

"I'm going to examine these pills pretty carefully," went on Flambeau. "I don't want to lose them, though. They look as if they were soluble in water."

"It may take you some time to do anything scientific with them," said the priest, "and the police doctor may be here before that. So I should certainly advise you not to lose them. That is, if you are going to wait for the police doctor."

"I am going to stay here till I have solved this problem," said Flambeau.

"Then you will stay here for ever," said Father Brown, looking calmly out of the window. "I don't think I shall stay in this room, anyhow."

"Do you mean that I shan't solve the problem?" asked his friend. "Why shouldn't I solve the problem?"

"Because it isn't soluble in water. No, nor in blood," said the priest; and he went down the dark stairs into the darkening garden. There he saw again what he had already seen from the window.

The heat and weight and obscurity of the thunderous sky seemed to be pressing yet more closely on the landscape; the clouds had conquered the sun which, above, in a narrowing clearance, stood up paler than the moon. There was a thrill of thunder in the air, but now no more stirring of wind or breeze; and even the colours of the garden seemed only like richer shades of darkness. But one colour still glowed with a certain dusky vividness; and that was the red hair of the woman of that house, who was standing with a sort of rigidity, staring, with her hands thrust up into her hair. That scene of eclipse, with something deeper in his own doubts about its significance, brought to the surface the memory of haunting and mystical lines; and he found himself murmuring: "A secret spot, as savage and enchanted as e'er beneath a waning moon was haunted by woman wailing for her demon lover." His muttering became more agitated. "Holy Mary, Mother of God, pray for us sinners . . . that's what it is; that's terribly like what it is; *woman wailing for her demon lover.*"[3]

He was hesitant and almost shaky as he approached the woman; but he spoke with his common composure. He was gazing at her very steadily, as he told her earnestly that she must not be morbid because of the mere accidental accesso-

---

[3] Father Brown is muttering lines from the English poet Samuel Taylor Coleridge's "Kubla Khan" (1816),

> A savage place! as holy and enchanted
> As e'er beneath a waning moon was haunted
> By woman wailing for her demon-lover!

ries of the tragedy, with all their mad ugliness. "The pictures in your grandfather's room were truer to him than that ugly picture that we saw," he said gravely. "Something tells me he was a good man; and it does not matter what his murderers did with his body."

"Oh, I am sick of his holy pictures and statues!" she said, turning her head away. "Why don't they defend themselves, if they are what you say they are? But rioters can knock off the Blessed Virgin's head and nothing happens to them. Oh, what's the good? You can't blame us, you daren't blame us, if we've found out that Man is stronger than God."

"Surely," said Father Brown very gently, "it is not generous to make even God's patience with us a point against Him."

"God may be patient and Man impatient," she answered, "and suppose we like the impatience better. You call it sacrilege; but you can't stop it."

Father Brown gave a curious little jump. "Sacrilege!" he said; and suddenly turned back to the doorway with a new brisk air of decision. At the same moment Flambeau appeared in the doorway, pale with excitement, with a screw of paper in his hands. Father Brown had already opened his mouth to speak, but his impetuous friend spoke before him.

"I'm on the track at last!" cried Flambeau. "These pills look the same, but they're really different. And do you know that, at the very moment I spotted them, that one-eyed brute of a gardener thrust his white face into the room; and he was carrying a horse-pistol. I knocked it out of his hand and threw him down the stairs, but I begin to understand everything. If I stay here another hour or two, I shall finish my job."

"Then you will not finish it," said the priest, with a ring in his voice very rare in him indeed. "We shall not stay here another hour. We shall not stay here another minute. We must leave this place at once."

"What!" cried the astounded Flambeau. "Just when we are getting near the truth! Why, you can tell that we're getting near the truth because they are afraid of us."

Father Brown looked at him with a stony and inscrutable face, and said:

"They are not afraid of us when we are here. They will only be afraid of us when we are not here."

They had both become conscious that the rather fidgety figure of Dr. Flood was hovering in the lurid haze; now it precipitated itself forward with the wildest gestures.

"Stop! Listen!" cried the agitated doctor. "I have discovered the truth!"

"Then you can explain it to your own police," said Father Brown, briefly. "They ought to be coming soon. But we must be going."

The doctor seemed thrown into a whirlpool of emotions, eventually rising to the surface again with a despairing cry. He spread out his arms like a cross, barring their way.

"Be it so!" he cried. "I will not deceive you now, by saying I have discovered the truth. I will only confess the truth."

"Then you can confess it to your own priest," said Father Brown, and strode towards the garden gate, followed by his staring friend. Before he reached the gate, another figure had rushed athwart him like the wind; and Dunn the gardener was shouting at him some unintelligible derision at detectives who were running away from their job. Then the priest ducked just in time to dodge a blow from the horse-pistol, wielded like a club. But Dunn was just not in time to dodge a blow from the fist of Flambeau, which was like the club of Hercules.[4] The two left Mr. Dunn spread flat behind them on the path, and, passing out of the gate, went out and got into

[4] A reference to the namesake of Hercule Flambeau, the Hercules of Greek mythology, a club-wielding hero of superhuman strength.

their car in silence. Flambeau only asked one brief question and Father Brown only answered, "Casterbury."

At last, after a long silence, the priest observed: "I could almost believe the storm belonged only to that garden, and came out of a storm in the soul."

"My friend," said Flambeau, "I have known you a long time, and when you show certain signs of certainty, I follow your lead. But I hope you are not going to tell me that you took me away from that fascinating job, because you did not like the atmosphere."

"Well, it was certainly a terrible atmosphere," replied Father Brown, calmly. "Dreadful and passionate and oppressive. And the most dreadful thing about it was this—that there was no hate in it at all."

"Somebody," suggested Flambeau, "seems to have had a slight dislike of grandpapa."

"Nobody had any dislike of anybody," said Father Brown with a groan. "That was the dreadful thing in that darkness. It was love."

"Curious way of expressing love—to strangle somebody and stick him with a sword," observed the other.

"It was love," repeated the priest, "and it filled the house with terror."

"Don't tell me," protested Flambeau, "that that beautiful woman is in love with that spider in spectacles."

"No," said Father Brown and groaned again. "She is in love with her husband. It is ghastly."

"It is a state of things that I have often heard you recommend," replied Flambeau. "You cannot call that lawless love."

"Not lawless in that sense," answered Father Brown; then he turned sharply on his elbow and spoke with a new warmth: "Do you think I don't know that the love of a man and a woman was the first command of God and is glorious for ever? Are you one of those idiots who think we don't admire love and marriage? Do I need to be told of the Garden of Eden or the wine of Cana? It is just because the strength in the thing was the strength of God, that it rages with that awful energy even when it breaks loose from God. When the Garden becomes a jungle, but still a glorious jungle; when the second fermentation turns the wine of Cana into the vinegar of Calvary. Do you think I don't know all that?"

"I'm sure you do," said Flambeau, "but I don't yet know much about my problem of the murder."

"The murder cannot be solved," said Father Brown.

"And why not?" demanded his friend.

"Because there is no murder to solve," said Father Brown.

Flambeau was silent with sheer surprise; and it was his friend who resumed in a quiet tone:

"I'll tell you a curious thing. I talked with that woman when she was wild with grief; but she never said anything about the murder. She never mentioned murder, or even alluded to murder. What she did mention repeatedly was sacrilege."

Then, with another jerk of verbal disconnection, he added: "Have you ever heard of Tiger Tyrone?"

"Haven't I!" cried Flambeau. "Why, that's the very man who's supposed to be after the reliquary, and whom I've been commissioned specially to circumvent. He's the most violent and daring gangster who ever visited this country; Irish, of course, but the sort that goes quite crazily anti-clerical. Perhaps he's dabbled in a little diabolism in these secret societies; anyhow, he has a macabre taste for playing all sorts of wild tricks that look wickeder than they are. Otherwise he's not the wickedest; he seldom kills, and never for cruelty; but he loves doing anything to shock people, especially his own people; robbing churches or digging up skeletons or what not."

"Yes," said Father Brown, "it all fits in. I ought to have seen it all long before."

"I don't see how we could have seen anything, after only an hour's investigation," said the detective defensively.

"I ought to have seen it before there was anything to investigate," said the priest. "I ought to have known it before you arrived this morning."

"What on earth do you mean?"

"It only shows how wrong voices sound on the telephone," said Father Brown reflectively. "I heard all three stages of the thing this morning; and I thought they were trifles. First, a woman rang me up and asked me to go to that inn as soon as possible. What did that mean? Of course it meant that the old grandfather was dying. Then she rang up to say that I needn't go, after all. What did that mean? Of course it meant that the old grandfather was dead. He had died quite peaceably in his bed; probably heart failure from sheer old age. And then she rang up a third time and said I was to go, after all. What did that mean? Ah, that is rather more interesting!"

He went on after a moment's pause: "Tiger Tyrone, whose wife worships him, took hold of one of his mad ideas, and yet it was a crafty idea, too. He had just heard that you were tracking him down, that you knew him and his methods and were coming to save the reliquary; he may have heard that I have sometimes been of some assistance. He wanted to stop us on the road; and his trick for doing it was to stage a murder. It was a pretty horrible thing to do; but it wasn't a murder. Probably he bullied his wife with an air of brutal common sense, saying he could only escape penal servitude by using a dead body that couldn't suffer anything from such use. Anyhow, his wife would do anything for him; but she felt all the unnatural hideousness of that hanging masquerade; and that's why she talked about sacrilege. She was thinking of the desecration of the relic; but also of the desecration of the deathbed. The brother's one of those shoddy 'scientific' rebels who tinker with dud bombs; an idealist run to seed. But he's devoted to Tiger; and so is the gardener. Perhaps it's a point in his favour that so many people seem devoted to him.

"There was one little point that set me guessing very early. Among the old books the doctor was turning over, was a bundle of seventeenth-century pamphlets; and I caught one title: 'True Declaration of the Trial and Execution of My Lord Stafford.' Now Stafford was executed in the Popish Plot business, which began with one of history's detective stories; the death of Sir Edmund Berry Godfrey. Godfrey was found dead in a ditch, and part of the mystery was that he had marks of strangulation, but was also transfixed with his own sword.[5] I thought at once that somebody in the house might have got the idea from here. But he couldn't have wanted it as a way of committing a murder. He can only have wanted it as a way of creating a mystery. Then I saw that this applied to all the other outrageous details. They were devilish enough; but it wasn't mere devilry; there was a rag of excuse; because they had to make the mystery as contradictory and complicated as possible, to make sure that we should be a long time solving it—or rather seeing through it. So they dragged the poor old man off his death-bed and made the corpse hop and turn cartwheels and do everything that it couldn't have done. They

[5] Father Brown is referring to the fraudulent "Popish Plot" of 1678, in which Stafford and others were wrongly executed for treason. The puzzling evidence in the murder of Godfrey, the magistrate who first heard the false testimony, has never been satisfactorily explained. For Chesterton's views on these events, see his *Illustrated London News* essay for January 23, 1926, "The Titus Oates Case" (*Collected Works*, vol. XXXIV, pp. 29–32).

had to give us an Insoluble Problem. They swept their own tracks off the path, leaving the broom. Fortunately we did see through it in time."

"You saw through it in time," said Flambeau. "I might have lingered a little longer over the second trail they left, sprinkled with assorted pills."

"Well, anyhow, we got away," said Father Brown, comfortably.

"And that, I presume," said Flambeau, "is the reason I am driving at this rate along the road to Casterbury."

That night in the monastery and church at Casterbury there were events calculated to stagger monastic seclusion. The reliquary of St. Dorothy, in a casket gorgeous with gold and rubies, was temporarily placed in a side room near the chapel of the monastery, to be brought in with a procession for a special service at the end of Benediction. It was guarded for the moment by one monk, who watched it in a tense and vigilant manner; for he and his brethren knew all about the shadow of peril from the prowling of Tiger Tyrone. Thus it was that the monk was on his feet in a flash, when he saw one of the low-latticed windows beginning to open and a dark object crawling like a black serpent through the crack. Rushing across, he gripped it and found it was the arm and sleeve of a man, terminating with a handsome cuff and a smart dark-grey glove. Laying hold of it, he shouted for help, and even as he did so, a man darted into the room through the door behind his back and snatched the casket he had left behind him on the table. Almost at the same instant, the arm wedged in the window came away in his hand, and he stood holding the stuffed limb of a dummy.

Tiger Tyrone had played that trick before, but to the monk it was a novelty. Fortunately, there was at least one person to whom the Tiger's tricks were not a novelty; and that person appeared with militant moustaches, gigantically framed in the doorway, at the very moment when the Tiger turned to escape by it. Flambeau and Tiger Tyrone looked at each other with steady eyes and exchanged something that was almost like a military salute.

Meanwhile Father Brown had slipped into the chapel, to say a prayer for several persons involved in these unseemly events. But he was rather smiling than otherwise, and, to tell the truth, he was not by any means hopeless about Mr. Tyrone and his deplorable family; but rather more hopeful than he was for many more respectable people. Then his thoughts widened with the grander perspectives of the place and the occasion. Against black and green marbles at the end of the rather rococo chapel, the dark-red vestments of the festival of a martyr were in their turn a background for a fierier red; a red like red-hot coals: the rubies of the reliquary; the roses of St. Dorothy.[6] And he had again a thought to throw back to the strange events of that day, and the woman who had shuddered at the sacrilege she had helped. After all, he thought, St. Dorothy also had a Pagan lover; but he had not dominated her or destroyed her faith. She had died free and for the truth; and then had sent him roses from Paradise. . . .

He raised his eyes and saw through the veil of incense smoke and of twinkling lights that Benediction was drawing to its end while the procession waited. The sense of accumulated riches of time and tradition pressed past him like a

---

[6] Father Brown reflects on the legend of St. Dorothy, at whose martyrdom (c. 303 A.D.) angels brought roses as a rebuke to Theophilus, a young pagan who had taunted her. Chesterton seems to have in mind Philip Massinger's play *The Virgin Martir* (1622), in which Theophilus and the beautiful Dorothea are in love.

crowd moving in rank after rank, through unending centuries; and high above them all, like a garland of unfading flames, like the sun of our mortal midnight, the great monstrance blazed against the darkness of the vaulted shadows, as it blazes against the black enigma of the universe. For some are convinced that this enigma also is an Insoluble Problem. And others have equal certitude that it has but one solution.[7]

[7] Father Brown's certitude is undoubtedly meant by Chesterton to challenge the perplexity of Sherlock Holmes as expressed in his remarkable outburst at the end of "The Cardboard Box" (1917): "What is the meaning of it, Watson? What object is served by this circle of misery, violence, and fear? It must tend to some end, or else our universe is ruled by chance, which is unthinkable. But what end? There is the great standing perennial problem to which human reason is as far from an answer as ever."

A NOTE ON THE TEXTS

The great majority of Father Brown stories originally appeared in the popular British and American magazines of Chesterton's day. Five volumes of collected stories plus an "omnibus" volume also appeared in both British and American editions during Chesterton's lifetime. Following his death in 1936, new editions of these books as well as newly assembled volumes of selected stories have appeared at frequent intervals, and the stories have never been out of print.

Many printing errors have crept into the texts of the later Father Brown editions. The garbled words and omissions in some of these editions are numerous and often serious enough to interfere with reader appreciation and enjoyment. Hence the texts of the stories collected in this edition are based on a comparison of the original collections, the first British edition[1] and first American edition[2] of the Father Brown books.

Except for conventional differences, especially in matters of punctuation, the texts of the first editions are, with some

[1] *The Innocence of Father Brown*, London: Cassell and Co., Ltd., 1911. *The Incredulity of Father Brown*, London: Cassell and Co., Ltd., 1926. *The Secret of Father Brown*, London: Cassell and Co., Ltd., 1927. *The Scandal of Father Brown*, London: Cassell and Co., Ltd., 1935.

[2] *The Innocence of Father Brown*, New York: John Lane, 1911. *The Incredulity of Father Brown*, New York: Dodd, Mead and Co., 1926. *The Secret of Father Brown*, Harper and Brothers, 1927. *The Scandal of Father Brown*, New York: Dodd, Mead and Co., 1935.

exceptions, substantially the same. This edition follows the British texts except where the American version is unarguably preferable. In a number of exceptional cases in which one edition contains a word or phrase absent in the other, the fuller version is given here.

The comparisons of the early Father Brown editions were made at the Marion E. Wade Center, on the Campus of Wheaton College in Wheaton, Illinois. The curator and staff there have my sincere thanks for their help and encouragement.

A NOTE ON THE NOTES

The footnotes that accompany this collection of the Father Brown stories need a word of explanation. The stories are liberally sprinkled with literary and historical allusions and foreign phrases, many of which may be unfamiliar to today's readers.

Chesterton's allusions are not merely decorative, but add much to the atmosphere and meaning of the stories. From time to time an allusion will even provide a clue to the mystery at hand. Our references and citations, therefore, have been provided specifically to help readers enjoy the stories more. The information in the notes is limited to that purpose.

We hope that the readers who do not need or want footnotes will find these notes unobtrusive and easy to ignore.